ADVANCE PRAISE FOR
DEATH ON DARBY'S ISLAND

"I didn't see it coming. In *Death on Darby's Island*, Alice Walsh provides a surprise perpetrator and deftly ties a string of disparate events into a shocking but satisfying resolution. But the book is more than a mystery. Walsh takes readers to Newfoundland in the 1960s and '70s and tells a tale rooted deep in that culture and time, a grim story of an outport island with bloody murders, past and present, at its core."

–Hilary MacLeod, author of the Shores mystery series

"*Death on Darby Island* is a masterclass in East Coast mystery writing. More Tempest than teapot, Alice Walsh's novel brings secrets and murder to small-town Newfoundland in rich, authentic detail. With immense skill that includes a dash of humour, Walsh lures us into a storm-tossed land where we feel we could live and reveals it as a place where anyone could die. Darby's Island is a place you won't want to leave, but you probably should."

–Gerard Collins, author of *The Hush Sisters*

DEATH ON DARBY'S ISLAND

ALICE WALSH

Vagrant
PRESS

Vagrant Press is an imprint of
Nimbus Publishing Limited
3660 Strawberry Hill Street, Halifax, NS, B3K 5A9
(902) 455-4286 nimbus.ca

This story is a work of fiction. Names, characters, incidents, and places, including organizations and institutions, are used fictitiously.

Printed and bound in Canada
NB1472

Editor: Kate Kennedy
Editor for the press: Whitney Moran
Cover design: Jenn Embree
Interior design: Rudi Tusek

Library and Archives Canada Cataloguing in Publication

Title: Death on Darby's Island / Alice Walsh.
Names: Walsh, Alice (E. Alice), author.
Identifiers: Canadiana (print) 20210216093 |
    Canadiana (ebook) 20210216115 | ISBN 9781771089753 (softcover)
    | ISBN 9781771089821 (EPUB)
Classification: LCC PS8595.A5847 D43 2021 | DDC C813/.54—dc23

Canada   Canada Council   Conseil des arts   NOVA SCOTIA
          for the Arts   du Canada

Nimbus Publishing acknowledges the financial support for its publishing activities from the Government of Canada, the Canada Council for the Arts, and from the Province of Nova Scotia. We are pleased to work in partnership with the Province of Nova Scotia to develop and promote our creative industries for the benefit of all Nova Scotians.

In memory of Jackie MacQueen. 1940–2005.
Mentor and friend.

CHAPTER 1

⤡⟋❧⟍⤢

Blanche Ste Croix was sitting in her police cruiser in the parking lot of Mae's Fish 'n' Chips trying to convince herself she didn't need cigarettes. Although she'd given up smoking weeks ago, the cravings were as strong as ever. She got out of the cruiser and was making her way toward Mae's when a Chevy towing a trailer drove onto the lot. *The Great Prospero: Hypnotist & Magician* was written in large red letters across the side of the trailer. Blanche had seen the Chevy drive off the ferry earlier in the day when she crossed over from Crow's Nest. Like most people, she'd already heard about Prospero. For weeks, he'd been travelling around performing in various towns and outports.

Still, Blanche was surprised to see the hypnotist on Darby's Island where the population was less than eight hundred. Even at its peak, the ferry only crossed twice daily. Folks must have been expecting him though, because there was a sign in Mae's window: *The Great Prospero, Hypnotist and Magician. Performing at the Hall, Friday, July 18, at 7:00 P.M. Admission $2.00.*

People came out of the store to get a look at the strange vehicle that had pulled up next to Caleb Banes's pickup truck. After some time, a tall man with longish grey hair and a neatly trimmed beard got out. He looked out of place in his white tuxedo and red bow tie. Blanche watched as he opened the passenger door for a woman who looked to be in her early thirties. She wore white go-go boots,

I

a white frilly blouse, and a red mini skirt. Her dark hair, which Blanche realized was a wig, hid part of her face.

The hypnotist looked around the lot at the knot of people who had gathered. "Good afternoon," he said in a distinct British accent. "I'm Prospero." He gestured to the woman beside him. "And this is my assistant, Miranda."

By this time, more people had come to see what was going on.

"Don't he talk some grand," whispered a woman standing next to Blanche.

Prospero scanned the excited faces, his eyes settling on Blanche clad in her RCMP uniform and round-topped hat. "We are looking for a hotel," he said, "or a bed and breakfast, perhaps."

Blanche held out her hand. "I'm pleased to meet you," she said. "I'm Constable Ste Croix. There are no accommodations on the island, but if you like, you can park your trailer on the beach near Gull's Head. Turn left," she instructed, "drive until you come to a lighthouse. It's just past that. You can't miss it."

"Very well," Prospero said, looking pleased.

"If you needs anything, my love, let us know," said a woman. "We're the Pikes. We lives in that white building. Next to the lighthouse. Me husband's the lighthouse keeper."

Prospero smiled. "That's very gracious of you, Mrs. Pike. Well, then," he said, looking around. "I hope I shall see you all this evening at the community hall."

There were nods and murmurs of agreement. All eyes were on the hypnotist and his assistant as they got back into the Chevy and drove out of the parking lot.

Blanche was walking toward the police cruiser when she saw Gert, her mother-in-law—soon-to-be ex-mother-in-law—come barrelling into the parking lot with her twin sister, Nellie, in tow. *Oh no.* Although she'd planned to visit her in-laws before she left the island, she didn't feel like facing Gert right now. She kept her head down, hoping they wouldn't notice her. She had just reached the cruiser when Nellie shouted: "Oh, look, there's Blanche!"

"Blanche?" Gert said, rushing toward her. "I didn't know you was here."

"Got in this afternoon."

Gert looked around. "Where's Reba to?"

"She's home with the babysitter."

"You didn't bring Reba?"

"I'm here on police business, Gert."

"What kind of business?"

Damn the nosy woman. This was a police matter. It was none of Gert's business.

Gert squinted at her. "What kind of business?" she demanded.

"It's private," Blanche said. "I'll bring Reba to see you and Jake soon," she added before Gert had a chance to say anything else.

"Sure, since yeh took that job in Corner Brook we hardly gets to see little Reba anymore."

Blanche knew Gert blamed her for the breakup of her marriage to Gert's son, Coop. She had expressed her disapproval about Blanche's career choice often enough. For years, Blanche had held a civilian job in the police crime lab. After Reba was born, Gert insisted that Blanche stop working and stay home with her baby. She was mortified when the force started accepting women, and Blanche was one of the first to sign on. In Gert's eyes, Blanche had failed both her husband and her child miserably.

"I s'pose you'll be stayin' with your brother," Nellie said.

"Gabe's away, but yes, I'll be staying at his cottage."

"Well, since you're alone, why don't you come for supper this evening?" Nellie said. "Sure, me and Herb would love to have yeh."

"Well...yes," Blanche said, "that would be lovely. Thanks, Nellie. What time?"

"Come around five. I plans to have supper on the table early. We're going to see the hypnotist. Jake and Nellie is eating with us."

Damn, Blanche thought. She could have kicked herself for her stupidity. Jake, she could handle, but the last thing she wanted was to spend the evening with Gert and her constant criticism. Gert would probably hound her about why she was here. There was no way Blanche was going to tell her about the allegations of fraud at the Golden Age Nursing Home.

Unable to come up with an excuse to get out of the situation gracefully, Blanche forced a smile. "I'll see you around five then." She gestured toward the cruiser. "Need a lift?"

"No, maid. We can walk," Nellie said.

"Sure, we only lives down the road," Gert said. "Besides, I needs to stop at Ryan's to pick up a new tablecloth. Archbishop Malloy's arriving tomorrow for the blessing of the fleet on Sunday morning."

"He'll be staying with you and Jake, I assume."

"The bishop always stays with us when he comes to the island," Gert said proudly.

"Of course." Blanche smiled tightly. "Thanks for the invite, Nellie."

Nellie nodded. "See you around five, maid."

"Five," Blanche agreed. It was going to be one hell of an evening.

CHAPTER 2

"Well," Gert said, her voice edged with contempt as she watched Blanche drive away. "Imagine that one, now—joined the Mounties, she did. Never met nobody so selfish in all me life. And 'tis poor little Reba who suffers. I've been after Coop to file for custody."

"Things is different now," Nellie said. "A lot of women is going out to work. Sure, Ben Parsons's daughter is in St. John's learning to be a dentist."

"If they wants to be dentists and Mounties then they shouldn't marry and have youngsters." Gert folded her arms. "Poor Coop, having to chase that one around the province whenever she took it in her head to start a new job. It's not natural for a woman."

"Coop's a carpenter," Nellie reasoned. "He can pick up his hammer and find work anywheres in Newfoundland—anywheres in Canada for that matter. Where's he to now?"

"On a job in Deer Lake." Gert frowned. "But that's not the point. Blanche thinks she's so high and mighty. Do you hear the proud way she talks? Right stuck up, like. Kept her maiden name after she got married. I never heard tell of the likes. S'pose she thought the Pickford name wasn't good enough for her." Gert sniffed indignantly. "Imagine now, a Ste Croix from Benoit's Cove. Sure, everybody knows the kind of hard tickets that crowd is. Nothing but drunks and troublemakers."

"None of that is Blanche's fault," Nellie said.

"I warned Coop when he took up with that one. Sure, every-body remembers what happened when they lived in that shack down in the Cove. And look how her lunatic of a mother ended up."

"The culprit in that family was Blanche's father, not her mother," Nellie said. "I thinks Blanche went and done good for herself. I envies her, I do. All that freedom."

"Freedom?" Gert eyed her sister warily. Was Nellie getting her notions from all those novels she read? Whenever the bookmobile came, she stocked up on paperbacks. Gert borrowed recipe books, books on quilting and gardening. Last week she'd found a good book on how to get stains out of clothes. None of that made-up foolishness for her.

"Blanche deserves to be happy after all she's been through," Nellie said.

Gert glared at her twin. Wasn't it just like Nellie to take Blanche's side. But then, weren't Nellie and Blanche two of a kind? The two of them as wild as March hares. Sure, didn't Nellie her own self run off when she was just sixteen? Stowed away on a coastal boat headed for St. John's. Came home a year later in the family way. Gert sighed. She was sure it was what had driven poor Pop to an early grave. Heartbroken, he was. Him and Mom both. So ashamed they couldn't hold up their heads in public. Good thing Herb Eastman offered to marry Nellie. Couldn't find a better man than Herb. Good to Nellie, and treated her youngster like she was his own.

"I'm looking forward to the show this evening," Nellie said, breaking into Gert's musings.

"Me too, girl. I s'pose though I should stay home and bake. You knows now how much the bishop loves me banana muffins."

"G'wan, maid. All that fuss."

"I don't mind," Gert said. Everyone said she had one of the nicest houses on the island. They were the first to have a flush toilet, the first to have electricity hooked up. After the bishop's visit, the diocese always sent a letter thanking Gert and Jake for their hospitality. Gert had saved them all.

"You frets too much," Nellie told her. "What do the Catholic Church care about the people here on Darby's Island? Sure, the priest hardly comes to visit. If they cared they'd have a church built here.

We wouldn't have to attend mass in the hall." She tightened her lips. "And that Bishop Malloy…I wouldn't give *that* man a cup of me own piss."

Gert narrowed her eyes. How could she even be related to this person?

At that moment, a large van roared by with young people shouting through the open window. "Hippies," Gert said, pursing her lips. "God knows what they're up to. Their van's been parked on the Head since Tuesday morning. You never knows what kind of hoodlums'll show up here now the ferry's started bringing cars and trucks across." She shook her head. "'Tis a wonder we're not all murdered in our sleep. I keeps me door barred when I goes to bed now."

They walked a few minutes in silence until they came to a string of grey, weather-beaten buildings with long planked wharves stretching across the water. Nellie waved at the two men mending lobster pots on the landwash. One of them was her husband, Herb, the other her brother-in-law, Jake. Both men wore plaid shirts. Herb's was green, Jake's red. Herb was nearly twenty years older than Jake, but whereas Jake had a receding hairline, Herb had a full head of steel-grey hair. He was a big man in contrast to Jake, who was slightly built.

"Now, don't work too hard," Nellie sang out.

"And make sure to get home early," Gert said. "We're eating at Nellie's this evening."

"Still a lot left to do here," Jake said.

"We're going to see Prospero," Nellie reminded him. "I plans to have supper early."

"Blanche is eating with us," Gert said. "She came across on the afternoon ferry."

"Blanche bring Reba?" Jake asked.

Gert tightened her lips. "Left the poor little youngster home with the babysitter again."

"We'll be finished in time for supper," Herb said.

"Make sure you are," Gert said. "I wants to get to the hall early, get a good seat. Sure, 'tis not every day a hypnotist comes to the island."

JAKE FROWNED AS HE WATCHED GERT AND NELLIE WALK AWAY. Hard to believe they were sisters, let alone twins. Nellie was quiet, almost shy, whereas Gert was loud and obnoxious. They didn't even look alike: Gert tinted her hair, and used a home permanent, giving her a cap of dark curls. Her face was full, her cheeks rosy. In contrast, Nellie's grey hair fell in uneven strands around her shoulders. Her pale face was as lined as a crumpled paper bag. Gert was short and dumpy, whereas Nellie was tall and as thin as a Tom cod.

"I forgot all about the hypnotist," Herb said.

Jake shook his head. "Christ, if it's not one thing, 'tis another. What kind of racket is we in for now?"

"I'm looking forward to seeing people get hypnotized," Herb said.

"All we needs." Jake picked up his hammer and nailed a lath to a broken trap.

Herb chuckled. "Bad enough the bishop's coming, eh, Jake b'y?"

"Oh Jesus, Herb my son, don't remind me. Gert got me drove right mental. She's nagging me night and day." He shook his head. "Afraid I'll swear or smoke around the bishop."

"Nellie never had much use for Bishop Malloy," Herb said. "She knew him when she lived in St. John's, years before he got to be bishop."

"Herb, I hates to say it, but you ended up with the sensible one."

"Nellie's got a level head on her shoulders," Herb agreed.

"Gert's keepin' on from daylight to dark." Jake put down the mended trap and picked up another. "After me now to paper the bathroom. Ryan's got in a new shipment of wallpaper with pictures of robins and blue jays. Costs a fortune, but Gert don't care; got us in debt up to our eyeballs." He heaved a sigh. "S'pose she thinks it'll amuse the archbishop to watch birds flying around while he takes a crap."

Herb chuckled. "Yeh didn't tell me Blanche was coming."

"I didn't know meself, b'y."

"Too bad Blanche and Coop broke up," Herb said. "Good woman, Blanche."

Jake removed a lath with the claws of his hammer. "Sometimes I wonders if 'twas Gert who drove them apart with her constant criticism."

"Sometimes Gert can be a tough nut to crack."

"Yes," Jake agreed. He'd always thought Blanche was good for Coop. She was smart and educated, a wife a man could be proud of. Jake never understood why Gert was so down on Blanche joining the force. She was making almost eleven thousand dollars a year to start with. Probably as much, or more, than what Coop earned with his business. They'd had a nice home. Jake banged the hammer with more force than was necessary. Damn Coop, anyway. Didn't he know what a good thing he had?

CHAPTER 3

⟨∽≈✦≈∽⟩

DEB ROLLED DOWN THE CAR WINDOW AND BREATHED IN THE SALTY ocean air. "I'm glad we came here, darling," she told David. "It doesn't get much better than this."

"It's a beautiful island," David agreed, taking in the wooden frame houses that dotted the rugged landscape. Colourful longliners and dories bobbed at their moorings. Fish stages cut across the still water. Cows, sheep, and goats roamed freely on the side of the road. Horses grazed in fields, heads bent, long tails twitching to keep away the swarming flies.

After a while they came to a red-and-white lighthouse with a small cottage beside it. Expertly, Deb manoeuvred the car and trailer down a narrow path to the beach. She parked in a sheltered inlet, and they got out and looked around. Small waves lapped at the shore. The plaintive cries of seagulls filled the air as they wheeled and circled in a clear sky.

Deb got two folding chairs from the trailer, and set them up on the beach. She dragged out a heavy cooler and placed it on a flat rock. Farther down the beach, she could see a green van. Not far from it was grey station wagon with a small tent set up beside it.

David sat in one of the chairs and gazed at the black-and-white birds standing near the water. "Are those puffins?"

Deb shielded her eyes with her hands to get a better look. "Looks like," she said. She reached inside the cooler and brought out a quart of vodka. "Drink, darling?"

"You know I never drink before a performance."

Shrugging, Deb poured a sizeable amount of the vodka into a plastic tumbler.

"Do you need that now, babe?" David frowned. "Maybe you should wait until *after* the performance."

"Are you scared I'll get drunk and fall off the stage?" Deb teased.

"You'll perform better if you're not drinking."

"One little drink is not going to hurt."

"Just one," David agreed reluctantly.

At that moment, he noticed a tall, lanky young man making his way toward them. He was wearing a red hooded jacket and tie-dyed jeans. As he got closer, David realized he was just a lad, probably no more than sixteen or seventeen. He looked like he had been camping out for weeks. His hair came down past his shoulders, and his clothes were dirty and ragged.

David got up from his chair. "Ah, our first visitor," he said. Smiling, he held out his hand. "I'm Prospero, and this is Miranda."

The boy took the proffered hand. "I'm Ward," he said. "Ward Thompson."

"Where are you from, Ward Thompson?" Deb asked.

"Oh, here and there," the boy said vaguely. "Right now I'm staying here on the beach." He pointed toward the station wagon and tent.

"Would you like a drink?" Deb gestured to the bottle on the picnic table.

David was about to protest that the lad was underage when Ward shook his head. "Don't drink," he said. He looked at Prospero. "Got any pop bottles?"

"Pop bottles?"

"To sell," Ward explained. "The store gives me three cents apiece."

Deb disappeared inside the trailer and appeared with a plastic bag. "This is all we have at the moment."

"Thanks," Ward said, taking the bag. He smiled as he turned to leave. "Enjoy your stay on the island."

David watched him leave, taking note of the black peace sign on the back of Ward's hooded sweater.

"I should have offered him something to eat," Deb said. "He's probably hungry." She had already gulped down her drink and was pouring another.

"You said one drink," David reminded her. "Please, darling. I really don't think you should have more until after the show."

She gave him an exaggerated pout. "Oh, you're such a square." She poured the drink back into the bottle and folded her arms across her chest. "Are you afraid I'll do something to disgrace you?"

The thought *had* crossed his mind. Deb became unpredictable, often volatile, when she drank. Despite everything, David felt a wave of pity. It couldn't have been easy losing her mother and father just months apart. Their deaths had been a devastating blow. Still, Deb's drinking was hard to take. She could fly into a rage at the drop of a hat. She picked fights for little or no reason.

Deb gave him a bright smile. "You know how much I love you."

David's heart flipped over. When he'd placed an ad for an assistant eighteen months ago, he'd been looking for someone with acting skills—or at least someone with stage experience. Deb had neither. Still, when she showed up for the interview in faded bell bottoms, her blond hair spilling over her shoulders, he hired her on the spot. He'd had no idea if she could even handle the job requirements. Luckily, she turned out to be a natural with an audience.

"Darling, you worry too much." Deb got up from her chair and began rubbing his shoulders. "Loosen up."

"I've worked hard to start over." Prospero gave her a sad smile. "I've forged a new identity. I have a chance to put the past behind me."

CHAPTER 4

BLANCHE WISHED NOW THAT SHE HAD PICKED UP CIGARETTES. She could only imagine what this evening was going to be like. Her separation from Coop had caused a lot of emotional turmoil for all of them. Coop had reached out to her since the breakup, hoping they could give their marriage a second chance. Blanche had agreed and was cautiously optimistic. They had been meeting for dinner dates. Blanche had only told her closest friends, in case it fell through. She already felt like a failure knowing Reba might have to grow up in a broken home. The last thing she needed was Gert harping on about it.

Blanche came to the last stretch of paved road and a large battered green sign. *We'll Finish the Drive in '65. Thanks to Mr. Pearson.* The sign had been there since 1964—when they first started paving. It was now 1975; the Trans-Canada had been finished, but the roads on the island were no better than dusty cow paths. *The people here deserve better,* Blanche thought. It had been only five years since electricity became available to everyone. Only a couple of years since telephones were installed. It was as if they had been living in the nineteenth century.

Blanche drove through little communities with names like Poverty Cove, Lobster Inlet, and William's Tickle. It was nearly three when she pulled in front of the cottage. A simple A-frame, it tilted precariously on the side of a cliff overlooking the bay. She found the key in its usual place under a flowerpot, and opened the door.

She put her suitcase on a battered sofa and looked around. The kitchen, dining room, and living room were one open space. A rocking chair stood next to an oil stove, and in one corner was a small black-and-white television with rabbit ears. The cottage had two bedrooms, one off the kitchen and the other upstairs. The plain wooden table had three mismatched chairs. Oddly, there was a plate of biscuits left on the table. She bit into one and was surprised to find it wasn't stale.

She opened one of her bags, retrieved a small typewriter, and placed it on the table. She took out a package of unlined paper, along with a number of coil-bound notebooks. Blanche was hoping that during her stay she would get some work done on her memoirs. She smiled, thinking of how pretentious that sounded. She had been keeping a journal since she was in her teens. The notebooks were in random order, and Blanche had sorted them by year. There was enough material to fill a book. In fact, she'd already started arranging material and had written a number of chapters.

The only other person who knew about her project was Coop. She'd mentioned it to him the year before they broke up. She thought he would scoff at the idea and was surprised at how supportive he was. "You got a story that's worth telling," he had assured her.

"It's just for me," Blanche had told him. "Not for the world to see."

"Well, I think it's worth trying to get published."

Whenever they spoke now—which was often—Coop asked how her book was coming. Being a single mother, Blanche didn't have much time for writing. She scribbled down notes and recollections during her breaks and lunch hours, and after Reba was tucked into bed at night.

Blanche picked up a water bucket and went outside to the pump. She got a plate from the cupboard and filled it with grapes, cheese, and crackers—food she'd picked up on the way. She filled the kettle, and while she waited for the water to boil, she called home. Four-year-old Reba was taking a nap, the sitter told her. They'd been at Margaret Bowater Park all afternoon and had come home all tuckered out.

Blanche glanced into the downstairs room. The bed was unmade, and there was a knapsack with clothes spilling out. A pair of socks was left on the floor. It wasn't like Gabe to be untidy. *He must have left in a hurry*, she thought. She lugged her suitcase to the upstairs bedroom, where she usually slept. The room, with its steep sloped ceilings, had barely enough space for a double bed and narrow chest of drawers. She changed out of her uniform into a pair of jeans and a blue sweatshirt. After making herself a cup of tea, she switched on the television. On the single channel, she watched a Santa Claus parade making its way down a wide avenue. Adults and children waved excitedly as snowmen, elves, and reindeer passed by. Television on the island was brought in by satellite, and programs were typically five or six months behind schedule.

Switching off the set, Blanche turned to her notes. She sighed as she reread what she'd written. Chapter Ten was giving her the most trouble. She was finding it difficult to recall the events of what had happened that night. Even now, just thinking about it made her uneasy.

Blanche blew out her breath. Could she be completely honest about what had happened back then? She crumpled up the paper and put a fresh sheet in the typewriter. After staring at the paper for nearly twenty minutes, she got up from the table. *I need to unwind*, she told herself. *I'm too keyed up to concentrate.* Glancing at her watch, she saw it was nearly two. Her great-aunt was a resident at the Golden Age Nursing Home. Blanche had planned to visit her tomorrow after her interview with the administrator. *It's still early*, she told herself. No reason she couldn't jog over to visit Aunt Hattie this afternoon. The half-mile trek might help her unwind.

Blanche was panting and out of breath by the time she reached the nursing home, a low brick building. Attached to it was a cottage hospital, run by British nurses. A doctor came to visit every couple of months. Some of the residents sat outside the building in wheelchairs. Others walked around the grounds with relatives, or sat at folding tables that had been set up outside.

"Blanche?" a voice called.

Blanche whirled around to see Martin Bursey approaching. "Ah, my partner in crime," she said. "I haven't seen *you* in a while."

Blanche gave him a quick hug. "How's Emily?"

A look of sorrow clouded Martin's face. "Some days she's fine. Other times she doesn't know me from Adam."

Emily was still a young woman. "Sometimes life really throws a curve ball," Blanche said, sensing Martin's helplessness.

"I sure as hell didn't see this one coming," Martin said grimly.

Blanche touched his arm. He had taken a leave from the force to be with his wife. Although there were good nursing homes in the Corner Brook area, Martin felt she would be happier on the island where they both grew up.

"We miss you at work, Martin."

"I miss being there," he admitted. He peered at Blanche. "Are things getting any better?"

"I'm coping," she said. "I'm trying not to let the ridicule get to me."

Martin shook his head. "I heard Sue and Lisa both quit."

"You heard correctly. They couldn't take the mistreatment."

"Hang in there, Blanche," Martin said. "Things can only get better." He touched her elbow. "I would hate to lose a great officer like you."

"Thank you, Martin." Unlike many of the other male officers, Martin was supportive. He often reminded Blanche that the force was lucky to have her.

"How are your children and grandchildren?" she asked.

"Linda's here with her kids," Martin said. "Why don't you come visit before you leave? I don't think you've met my daughter."

"I'll try to drop by before I go home," Blanche promised.

"Come anytime," Martin told her. "You know where the cottage is. Linda plans to stay all summer. Her husband will be joining us in a couple of weeks."

Aunt Hattie was sitting in a chair beside her bed when Blanche walked into the room. Her grey hair, usually worn in a tidy bun, hung loose around her shoulders. Her face lit up at the sight of her grandniece. "Oh, my darling," she exclaimed. "I didn't know you was handy." She motioned to a chair across from her. "Come in, my love, and have a seat."

Blanche kissed her aunt's wrinkled cheek. "Good to see you, Aunt Hattie. How are you?"

"Can't complain, my love."

Blanche smiled. Aunt Hattie was nearly eighty, small and frail. Everything about her bore the signs of aging. Only her sharp blue eyes looked young, and they sparkled now as Blanche took a seat across from her.

"I ran into Martin Bursey in the parking lot."

"Martin comes every day to visit Emily. I never met a man so dedicated."

"He's a good guy," Blanche agreed. "A great cop. I've learned a lot from him since I joined the force."

"Too bad about poor Emily," Aunt Hattie said, "especially after everything she's gone through." She shook her head. "The poor woman's had a troubled life."

"Yes," Blanche agreed. She knew about some of it.

Aunt Hattie touched Blanche's arm. "How you been, my love? 'Tis been a while since I seen you, sure."

Blanche told her about her conflict with Gert. "She blames me for the breakup of our marriage."

"I'm sorry, my love," Aunt Hattie said. "'Tis never good when people separates."

"No," Blanche agreed, "but I never dreamed it would be so difficult." She folded her hands. "I miss Coop. He was—well, still is—a great father to Reba. We're attempting to work things out. There's a chance we might get back together." She bit her lip. "I don't know."

"I've always liked Coop. Reba needs her father in her life." Aunt Hattie peered at Blanche. "And you need your husband."

"Coop was always supportive of my work."

Aunt Hattie frowned. "The men still giving you a hard time on the job, my love?"

"It hasn't gotten any better," Blanche said. "I don't know why men feel so threatened. We're all trying to do our jobs as best as we can."

"How do the chief of police feel about it?"

Blanche snorted. "Bill Legge? He's a bigger jerk than the rest of them." She pursed her lips, thinking of how patronizing her boss could be.

"I'm sorry you're having such difficulties, my love."

"Enough about me," Blanche said. "How are *you* doing? In your last letter, you told me you had a pen pal from Halifax."

Aunt Hattie reached into the drawer of her bedside table and pulled out a photograph. "Here's a snap of Anne and Fur Ball," she said. "Anne refused to go into a nursing home when she found out Fur Ball wasn't allowed."

Blanche studied the black and white photo of a frail-looking white-haired lady holding an overweight fluffy grey cat on her lap.

Aunt Hattie opened another drawer and pulled out a manila envelope. She opened it, and photos spilled onto her lap. "I was going to send you these," she said. "Your cousin Rob rescued them from the house after…after you moved out. All those years they were in poor Louise's house. I don't know why she didn't send them to you. Her daughter brought them to me last week." Aunt Hattie picked up the picture of a man in a military uniform and showed it to Blanche. "Your father," she said, "taken during the war."

Blanche stared at the photograph, too surprised to say anything. "That's Old AC?" she whispered. "Doesn't look anything like him."

Aunt Hattie knitted her brow. "Old AC?"

"Sorry…It's what the boys…well, me too, used to call Da."

"Abraham Cornelius," Aunt Hattie guessed.

Blanche lowered her eyes. "Anti-Christ," she said. "Terrible, I know."

Aunt Hattie chuckled. "Who came up with that?"

"I'm not sure. Gabe, I imagine."

Aunt Hattie shook her head. "Abe and his sons never got along. A sad situation, I always thought. Understandable, though, with the way Abe was."

"Was Da always that way?" Blanche asked. "Ma used to say it was on account of the war. She said he came back with the shell shock, and that was why he drank."

Aunt Hattie paused, as if choosing her words carefully. "Abe was always a bully," she said. "Always angry. Felt the world owed him."

Blanche smiled at her aunt's bluntness. Aunt Hattie had a way of getting to the heart of the matter.

"Still, I can't help feeling sorry for him," Aunt Hattie continued. "Abe was the product of a poverty-stricken childhood. Felix—your grandfather—took him in when he was seven to help him fish. I recall Abe coming in from the boat, hands full of blisters. Felix would get him up at four-thirty to go fishing." She shook her head. "Nearly worked the poor youngster to death. Of course, getting wounded in the war didn't help the situation none."

Blanche took the picture from Aunt Hattie and studied it. "He looks so…so different."

"Well, he was much younger then. And as you can see, he wasn't bad looking."

Blanche could see why her mother would be attracted to him.

"Your poor mother thought she could save him," Aunt Hattie said.

Blanche put down the picture and picked up another. Two little girls were sitting on a daybed, their shadows large on the wall from the flashbulb. Both had jet-black hair cut in a blunt style with fringed bangs. "Kate and Ivy," Blanche said. "I've never seen this picture before."

"They've always looked like twins," Aunt Hattie said. "I never could tell them apart. Wasn't Ivy the eldest?"

"Ivy was eleven months older than Kate," Blanche said. "But they were the same size. Kate might have even been a bit taller back then."

"Been in touch with Ivy?"

"She came to see me a few weeks ago."

"How is she?"

"Well, you know Ivy." Blanche sighed. "Things haven't gotten any better. She's really made a mess of her life."

"Still with that brute who put her in the hospital?"

"She got rid of him, but took up with a new one." Blanche laid down the photograph. "She's been going from one abusive man to another. And she's pregnant again."

"Oh, the poor dear girl," Aunt Hattie shook her head. "Is her youngsters still with children's aid?"

"Lisa and Tommy, the two youngest, are. I doubt she'll get them back."

Aunt Hattie tightened her lips. "'Tis the poor little youngsters I feels sorry for the most."

"It's a bad situation," Blanche agreed. Ivy had five kids with three different fathers. Just a couple of weeks before, she'd shown up at Blanche's door with three of her kids, her face a mass of bruises. She'd asked if Blanche could put her up until she got on her feet. She had stayed three weeks before her boyfriend—Craig, or Greg—showed up at the door saying he was sorry, and promising never to hit her again. Blanche had begged Ivy not to go back to him.

"Let's hope she comes to her senses," Aunt Hattie said, as if reading Blanche's thoughts.

Blanche picked up a black-and-white photograph from the pile. "This must be Ma," she said, taking in the dark-haired woman standing on the doorstep holding a baby.

"I've been wondering who the baby is," Aunt Hattie said.

Blanche looked closely at the photo. "Must be Hazel," she said. "I don't think there were ever any pictures of Zakia. She was so young when…" She felt the prickle of tears behind her eyes, and blinked rapidly.

Aunt Hattie began putting the photos back inside the envelope. "Take them home, my love," she said, handing her the envelope. "You'll have lots of time to look at them while you're at the cottage."

"Thanks, Aunt Hattie." Blanche glanced at her watch. "I should be going," she said. "Nellie's invited me for supper."

"That was nice of her."

"Yes. They're eating early so they can go see the Great Prospero this evening."

"I heard about him," Aunt Hattie said. "Someone said he was on the island."

Blanche nodded. "As a matter of fact, I met him this afternoon."

Aunt Hattie frowned, her keen eyes troubled. "I heard about people getting mesmerized," she said. "No good'll come of it. Mark my words."

Blanche wondered as she walked out of the nursing home. As the eldest girl, she had tried to protect her siblings. Why had everything turned out so badly? Instead of going back to the cottage, she found herself jogging in the opposite direction. After running for nearly half a mile, she came to the cemetery. She opened the iron gate and went inside. His grave was marked by a weathered wooden cross that had a faded plastic rose attached to it. Blanche stared at the grave for a long time. After a while, she opened the envelope and took out the photographs.

Tears pricked her eyes as she looked at a picture of her mother when she was a young girl. Her black hair hung almost to her waist, her eyes round and expressive. In one photograph, she was holding baby Gabe. Blanche and Jimmy were sitting beside her, looking adoringly at their new brother. Blanche smiled now as she took in her crooked bangs. Jimmy had got hold of the scissors and given Blanche her first haircut. Where had all the years gone, she wondered as she stared at her picture. She was a skinny little kid back then, small for her age and always hungry.

There were a couple of pictures of Kate and Ivy together, another of Kate alone. She had her arms crossed, her dark eyes looking too large in her pale face. By age thirteen, Kate had the hardness of an adult—an adult that life had treated badly.

On her way out of the cemetery, Blanche stopped at another grave. This one was marked with a headstone in the shape of an angel. *Anne Foster, 1932–1973*. Blanche knelt down beside the grave. "Thank God for you, Miss Foster," she whispered.

CHAPTER 5

⤞❦⤝

October 26, 1962

"BLANCHE, CAN I HAVE A WORD WITH YOU?" MISS FOSTER ASKED AS I was filing out of our one-room schoolhouse with the other students.

I hesitated. "I should be getting home," I told her. "My mother hasn't been feeling well."

"This will only take a minute." Miss Foster gestured to a desk in the front row. "Please have a seat."

I obeyed warily. What was this all about?

"Don't forget your math book, Billy," she called after Billy Vokey. "And Margaret, try to remember to bring your homework, okay, dear?" After the last student left the classroom, Miss Foster pulled up a desk and sat facing me. "How have you been, Blanche?"

"Fine," I said, automatically.

"I've been meaning to speak to you about your absenteeism," Miss Foster said. "It's been less than a couple of months since school started and already you've missed eighteen days." She gave me a concerned look. "Is everything okay?"

"It's Ma. She hasn't been feeling well." Some days, my mother was so sick, I didn't feel like leaving my little brother with her.

"Blanche, I can't emphasize enough how important an education is." She peered at me. "You're very bright; you could go far. Have you thought of what you might do when you finish school?"

I shrugged. I had no idea. I would like to work in an office, perhaps. Or, a job in a library would be nice. I could imagine myself checking out books, stamping the dates on the back of a little card with a small rubber stamp. I'd seen a lady do this whenever the bookmobile visited the island. "I don't want to go into service," I said. "Cleaning someone else's house and taking care of their youngsters is not something I want to do."

Miss Foster gave me a sad smile. "There's no need for you to be stuck at a job like that. With your intelligence, you could do almost anything. You could even go to university, if you put your mind to it. Have you given that any thought?"

"University?" The word sounded foreign to my ears.

"It will take a lot of hard work, of course. But I'm confident you could do it."

I stared at her, trying to grasp what she was saying. "It's hard to pass the grade nine exam," I reminded her. "Hardly anybody does."

Miss Foster nodded. "Those provincial exams are a curse," she said. "They've been the bane of many of my students, and it's so unfair."

I thought of my eldest brother, Jimmy, who passed every grade until it came time to take the provincial exam. One look at it, and he knew he was doomed to fail. That was not part of his lesson plan. He was asked to write a paragraph on each of the four characters in Louisa May Alcott's *Little Women*, a book he'd never read. There were math and science concepts he had never heard of.

"It's difficult when the exam is made up by some bureaucrat in St. John's," Miss Foster continued. "I read an article in the newspaper about the disadvantages outport kids have in getting an education. It's very discouraging, and there's really no need for it."

I recalled Jimmy coming home in tears after the exam. He threw all his textbooks over the wharf and never went back to school again.

Miss Foster got up from her seat and went to her desk drawer. She pulled out a stack of papers. "I've saved a number of the exams from previous years," she said. "They vary each year, but some of the questions are the same. I've been preparing my two grade nine students by having them learn questions from past exams."

She put the exams back in her desk. "I've helped Coop Pickford and Jenny Foley prepare for their finals. Both of them managed to graduate. When the time comes, I can tutor you, if you like." She turned to look at me. "But Blanche, you have to spend more time in the classroom."

"I know that," I said as I stood up to leave. "I'll try my best to get to school more often."

As I walked home that day, Miss Foster's words played in my mind as soothing as a lullaby. *You're very bright; you could go far in life.* Was it possible? Could I go to university? Work in a library? Could I be a teacher like Miss Foster? Most of the students on the island dropped out of school before they reached grade nine. There were no grade ten or eleven students this year. Wanda Drover and Mitch Greene were the only grade nine students.

Our house was at the end of a narrow, rutted road. Grey and weathered, it stood apart from the other houses like a sad, neglected orphan. Sheets of plastic nailed over the windows billowed in the fall breeze. Like many people on the island, we covered our windows to keep out the winter snow and cold. Other people removed the plastic sheets when warm weather came, but ours stayed on year-round. A chopping block with an axe stood near the door. A big galvanized tub, used for washing clothes and for our weekly bath, hung from a large rusty nail on the side of the house.

I opened the door, unsure of what I'd find inside. The fire in the wood stove had gone out, and the house was icy cold. The only heat came from the stove in the kitchen. Our bedrooms were freezing cold in winter.

My sister Ivy was sitting on the daybed in the kitchen with my three-year-old brother, Eddie. They had blankets wrapped around their shoulders. Ma was nowhere in sight.

Grey blinds, ragged with age, hung from the window. Very little light could penetrate the plastic sheets, and it was always dark inside. The furniture was sparse: A plain wooden table with a chair at each end. Wooden benches ran along the sides. There was a pine shelf where dishes were kept. A daybed stood against one wall. Next to the stove was a wooden rocker. Our house didn't have a front room like other houses on the island. Off the kitchen was a small pantry where food and pots and pans were kept. Our house had three small bedrooms, not nearly enough space for seven people.

"You're late," Ivy said accusingly. "The fire's gone out and we're cold."

"Cold," Eddie said, lifting up a small foot that was starting to turn blue.

"Where's your socks, Eddie?" I asked. "It's freezing."

"Gone," Eddie said. "Socks gone."

I turned to Ivy. "Miss Foster kept me after school," I said. "Where's Ma and Kate?"

"Ma's not feeling well. She's in bed. Kate's in the bedroom." Ivy rolled her eyes. "Probably drawing them silly pictures again." She gestured to the far wall where two of Kate's drawings hung. "Sure, 'tis all she does."

I went to the woodbox and pulled out a couple of birch junks. "Miss Foster says our Kate's got quite an imagination." I lifted the damper off the stove. "She hung two of her paintings in the classroom."

"Mr. Keating didn't think so," Ivy said, referring to a teacher we'd had before Miss Foster came. "He said Kate shouldn't waste time on such nonsense."

"Mr. Keating is no longer the teacher," I said, taking in Kate's drawings. She had drawn an angel with monarch butterfly wings. The angel was holding a baby who resembled Hazel, our baby sister who had died. The other picture depicted an angel at the table with the family. Kate often painted angels, sometimes with the wings of butterflies, ladybugs, or other insects.

I pulled another junk of wood from the woodbox. The wood was getting low, I noticed. Would Da remember to buy more? I took some kerosene from the lamp on the shelf, poured it on top of the wood, and lit a match. There was a ppfff as the flame leapt up, causing me to jump backward. "There," I said. "Won't be long now before the house heats up."

Eddie got down from the daybed and came to stand beside me, his thumb plugging his mouth. "Let's go see Ma," I said, picking him up. I blew on his strawberry-blond bangs, making him laugh. Beneath his long lashes, Eddie had the strangest eyes. One of his irises was slightly bigger than the other. His left eye was hazel while his right eye was a darker green. Many people commented on the strangeness of his eyes. "You should have been a girl with those long lashes," I told him.

"Nooo." Eddie laughed.

I carried him down the short hallway to our parents' bedroom. Ma was curled in a tight ball beneath the threadbare blankets. There were no sheets or pillowcases on the bed. The mattress was lumpy, dirty, and stained. One of the bed's legs was missing, and was propped up by blocks of wood.

Not wanting to wake her, I closed the door softly. I went across the hall to the bedroom I shared with Ivy, Kate, and Eddie. There was barely enough space for the double iron bed where we all slept. Our clothes—what little we had—were kept in cardboard boxes under the bed. My brothers, Jimmy and Gabe, shared a third cramped bedroom.

Kate was sitting on the bed with her coat on, flipping through the pages of the Eaton's catalogue. The bed was covered with a few blankets and some old overcoats. There were never enough blankets. In winter we slept with our clothes on, covering ourselves with coats and any other clothing we could find. We were always cold.

On the bedroom wall were more of Kate's paintings. She was fascinated with her geography book, *Visitors in Other Lands*, and loved reading about the characters in it. She often spoke of Bunga from the jungle, and Netsook and Klaya from the far north. In one painting, she had drawn Bunga spearing a fish from beneath the ice. In another, Netsook and Klaya were walking in the jungle, wrapped in furs and carrying harpoons. Only our Kate would imagine Eskimos in the jungle.

Kate looked up from the catalogue. I noticed one side of her face was red and puffy. "I wish I could have a dress like that." She pointed to a page filled with dresses, some with lace trimming the collar and sleeves.

"Maybe someday, Katie," I told her. But even as I spoke, I knew it wasn't likely. There was never enough money for food, let alone fancy dresses.

"Juney Pickford got a dress just like this one." Kate pointed to a picture of a green velvet dress with a black bow and a lace collar. "Her mother got it for her for Easter."

"Is your tooth bothering you again, Kate?" I asked.

She put her hand to her jaw. "It ached all day at school. Couldn't keep me mind on me lessons, sure."

"When Gabe gets home, I'll have them run over to Aunt Hattie's for cloves."

"That always makes it feel better," Kate said.

I went back to the kitchen, which was already starting to heat up. After pulling a pair of woolen vamps on Eddie's feet, I put him on the floor to play. He pulled a chair over to the window and peeked through the large rip in the plastic. Eddie liked to watch for birds. He got really excited when a crow or partridge came into the yard.

After putting a pot of water on the stove to boil, I got some potatoes from the pantry. I opened a bottle of moose meat that Nellie Eastman had given us. As I scooped it out of the bottle, I wondered how I was going to divvy it up among seven people.

"Ohhh!" Eddie exclaimed from the window.

"What is it, Eddie?" I asked. "See any birds out there?"

"Old AC come," Eddie said, mimicking my brothers.

"Shhh." I crossed the room and took his small pale face between my hands. "Eddie, you mustn't ever call Da that," I told him. "It'll make him mad." I lifted him down from the chair. "Go see what Kate is doing."

As Eddie headed for the bedroom, I braced myself. *Please, let him be in a good mood,* I prayed silently. Da often got drunk, but his moods were darkest when he was sober. It was as if he needed alcohol to feel human.

Moments later, he lumbered into the kitchen. Without a word, he removed his jacket. His white gut spilled out over his trousers like bread dough left too long to rise. His head was bald except for a small grey patch that looked like dandelion fluff. Most of his teeth were missing. His bulbous nose was red and full of small blue veins. He glared at me with bloodshot eyes, but didn't say anything.

"Where's that lazy old bitch?" he said to no one in particular.

I gritted my teeth, hating the contempt Old AC showed toward Ma. He was always calling her terrible names.

"Ma's sleeping," I told him. "She's not feeling well."

"Christ Jesus," he bellowed. "Is that how it's gonna be for the next six or seven months? Is she gonna sleep until the youngster gets here?"

I looked at him in confusion. Youngster? Then it dawned on me.

My breath caught in my throat. It all made sense now: The exhaustion and morning sickness, all the trips to the outhouse.

CHAPTER 6

THE COTTAGE DOOR WAS SLIGHTLY AJAR. BLANCHE WAS SURE SHE'D closed it when she left. She entered cautiously. No one bothered to lock their doors on the island. "Anyone here?" she called. Nothing seemed to be out of place. If Coop was here, he'd say it was her city paranoia kicking in. Then she noticed the plate on the table. The biscuits were gone; all that was left were a few crumbs. The few leftover crackers and grapes were also gone. Someone *had* been here. *Probably kids*, she thought. They'd wandered in, seen the food, and decided to help themselves. But there was something else: The paper she had put in the typewriter had been removed. It lay on the table with the other pages. *Why would kids do that?*

Blanche made herself a cup of tea and sat down in front of the television. A rerun of *The Mary Tyler Moore Show* was playing. Blanche had already seen the episode twice before. She switched off the set and went to a shelf near the stairwell that held knick-knacks as well as a dozen or so books. On the top shelf was a framed picture taken at her and Coop's wedding. Blanche picked it up and studied it. Coop had his arm draped around her shoulder, looking handsome in a black tuxedo. Blanche wore a simple white dress with a short veil. Coop was looking at her, adoration in his eyes. Even Gert had admitted she'd never seen Coop look happier.

Still holding the photograph, Blanche sat down on the sofa. They were so happy back then, and full of hope for the future. She recalled Coop holding a newborn Reba. Coop at her swearing-in ceremony. How had things gone so wrong? Relatives and friends blamed Gert for the breakup of their marriage. Yes, her mother-in-law interfered more than she should have. At times she drove Blanche crazy with her constant nagging. Blanche knew, though, that it wasn't Gert who had broken them up. She could still recall the pain in her husband's eyes when she told him the secret she had been harbouring. "I thought we were partners," he'd said. "I thought we were in this together." They'd drifted until the distance between them felt like a chasm.

Blanche put the photograph back on the shelf. Could things ever be the same between them? Could they get back the happiness they'd once had? Blanche turned her attention to the small collection of books. Westerns mostly, but there were a couple of mysteries mixed in. She reached for an Agatha Christie, *Witness for the Prosecution*. As she was lifting it from the shelf, she knocked a card to the floor. She picked it up and saw it was an invitation to an art exhibition—one of Kate's showings, at the Art Gallery of Ontario. Sadness squeezed Blanche's heart. *Dear Kate*, she thought as she tucked the card back inside the novel.

It was nearing four-thirty when Blanche pulled up in front of Nellie and Herb's white clapboard bungalow. The two-storey house next to it belonged to her in-laws. It was much bigger than the other houses in the area. Gert kept the place immaculate. She was forever ordering expensive furniture that came in on the coastal boats. Back in the spring, she had ordered a piano even though no one in her family knew how to play.

The door was open, and Blanche walked in without knocking. Patsy, Nellie and Herb's granddaughter, was setting the table. The girl's mother had left for the mainland years ago, leaving her with her grandparents. "Oh, hello, Blanche," Patsy said, brightly.

"Patsy, you're all grown up," Blanche said, giving her a hug. "Look at you. You must be what…fifteen?"

"I'll be sixteen next month."

"Well, you've certainly grown up since I last saw you," Blanche said, taking in Patsy's slim figure and shoulder-length red hair.

Nellie stood by the stove testing a roast with a fork. The aroma of corned beef and cabbage permeated the small kitchen. "Glad you could make it, Blanche," she said. She took the lid off a pot and a cloud of steam rose into the air. "We hardly gets to see you anymore, sure."

"I know," Blanche said. "Life can get really busy."

"I was some glad when Nan told me you were coming for supper," Patsy said.

Blanche smiled and reached for Patsy's hand. "What's this?" she asked, staring at the ring on her finger. It was square and clunky with a gaudy red stone the size of a grape.

"You can buy them at Ryan's for ninety-nine cents." Patsy looked down at her finger. "Comes with five different stones."

The ring was the ugliest thing Blanche had ever seen, but she kept her opinions to herself. Turning to Nellie she said, "Would you like some help?"

"No, my love, I'm almost done here." Nellie gestured toward a bottle of wine and a flask of whiskey that stood on the counter. "Like something to drink before supper?"

"A little wine would be nice, Nellie."

Nellie got a glass from the cupboard and poured wine from the bottle. "Jake and Gert is in the front room with Herb," she said. "I'll join you as soon as I gets a chance."

As Blanche walked down the hallway to the front room, she heard voices and laughter. She stood in the doorway for a brief moment. Jake and Gert were sitting on the sofa. Gert's pale green dress matched her clip-on earrings. Jake wore jeans; he had changed into a blue flannel shirt. Herb sat in a rocker across from them wearing tan pants and a blue sweater.

Jake noticed Blanche first, and got up to embrace her. "Good to see yeh, my love."

"Come on in and have a seat, maid," Herb said. In his seventies, he was nearly twenty years older than Nellie. His thick hair had gone completely white, and deep lines had set in around his mouth.

Blanche took a seat across from Gert and Jake.

"I was just telling Herb how busy I've been, getting ready for the archbishop's visit," Gert said. "Spent all day scrubbing the house top to bottom."

Jake shook his head. "You'd think God His own self was coming, the way Gert goes on."

"I tries me best to make everyt'ing nice for the bishop," Gert said. "Sure, he only comes a couple times a year."

Blanche sipped her wine without comment.

"S'pose to blow," Herb said. "Big nor'easter coming. We gets that, there'll be no blessing the fleet or anyt'ing else."

"Herb, my son, don't talk like that," Gert groaned. "Not after all me hard work. If there's a storm the ferry won't run."

Herb shrugged. "Can't do nothing about the weather."

After some time Nellie and Patsy came into the room, each carrying a wine glass.

"You're not letting that youngster drink alcohol," Gert said, appalled.

"Raspberry syrup," Patsy said, holding up her glass. "Sometimes Nan lets me have wine with supper." She took a seat on the sofa next to Jake and Gert. Nellie took the only other chair.

Gert kept up a running commentary about the archbishop's past visits. Bishop Malloy loved her cooking, and always had seconds. He especially liked her homemade buns. Said they were even better than the ones his beloved mother used to make. How she put little sachets of lavender in his bed to make the sheets smell nice. Whenever someone managed to change the subject, Gert found a way to bring it back.

"Been to see Aunt Hattie, Blanche?" Jake asked when he could get a word in edgewise.

"I just came from the nursing home, actually," Blanche replied.

"How is she?" asked Nellie. "I must go visit. I haven't seen her in a while, sure."

"Aunt Hattie's doing well," Blanche said. "I don't think she likes being in the home, but she's not one to complain." She looked around the room. "I also ran into Martin Bursey, who was there to see Emily. His daughter is visiting with her children."

"Linda got here a couple of days ago," Nellie said. "Her young-sters must be getting big. My, where do the time go? Seems like only yesterday Linda and Judy was little girls playing in the backyard." She shook her head. "They grows up some fast."

"They were close, Linda and Judy," Herb said. "It was like they were joined at the hip. We used to call them the Siamese twins, sure. Never seen one without the other."

"Linda's my godmother," Patsy said. "She wants me to go back with her to St. John's for a few days before school starts."

"Do yeh a world of good, sure," Gert said.

From the kitchen a timer went off.

"The rolls I put in the oven," Nellie said. "Supper's ready."

Herb rose to his feet, followed by Jake.

"Goin' to see the hypnotist, Patsy my love?" Jake asked.

"Don't think so, Uncle Jake. I'd rather stay home."

"G'wan, Patsy," Gert said. "Might be the last time a hypnotist comes to the island. Sure, all the young ones is going. Annie Foley, Shirley Tully, the Battens, and all Ben Butler's crowd."

"I hear he can cast a spell just by snapping his fingers," Herb said.

"I don't believe none of it," Jake scoffed. "Nothing but a racket is all it is."

"No, my son," Herb said. "He's hypnotized people over in Round Harbour. Had them running around the stage barking like dogs. I heard he glued Jim Barnes to a chair." He chuckled. "Jim couldn't move 'til Prospero undone the spell."

"What fun!" Gert said gleefully. "I can't wait for this evening."

"Nothing but a bunch of foolishness," said Jake.

"Well, we'll see," Herb said.

"That we will."

"Bet he can hypnotize *you*, Jake," Herb challenged.

Jake shrugged.

"Bet yeh ten dollars he can."

Jake reached for Herb's hand. "Okay, Herb, my son, we got a deal."

CHAPTER 7

⟨⟩

BLANCHE HADN'T PLANNED TO GO TO PROSPERO'S PERFORMANCE, BUT at six-thirty she found herself standing outside the hall with Herb and Nellie and her in-laws. Half the people on the island were there, clutching two-dollar bills. Gert left her place in line to talk with an elderly couple. From where she stood, Blanche could hear her discussing the bishop's visit.

Nellie leaned toward Blanche. "That Gert gets right on me nerves," she whispered. "All she talks about is Bishop Malloy."

"So I noticed," Blanche said with a smile. Not that she'd minded. During supper, Gert was so wrapped up in the bishop's visit she barely mentioned Coop or drilled Blanche about Reba's babysitters.

"His Grace is not as *holy* as he likes everyone to believe," Nellie continued.

Blanche blinked in surprise.

"By Jesus, I knows a thing or two that could knock the archbishop off that pedestal he got hisself up on."

Blanche raised an eyebrow. "Sounds personal."

"I'd say 'tis personal." Nellie's mouth hardened into a grim line. "Son of a bitch."

Blanche was taken aback by the force of Nellie's words. Before she could respond, the hall door opened and people began pushing forward. Gert resumed her place in line and they walked inside together. They were lucky enough to find seats near the front. In no time, the hall was packed; people stood at the back, and against the walls. Children and teenagers sat on the floor in front of the stage.

At one minute past seven, Prospero and Miranda appeared on the small wooden stage, where a row of chairs had been set out. Prospero looked striking in a white satin tuxedo. Miranda wore a pink wig, and a short skirt and vest. Prospero held up his hand until the room grew quiet. "Good evening," he said. "It's a pleasure to visit your charming little island. I'm Prospero and this is my lovely assistant, Miranda."

Miranda curtsied, and the audience clapped.

"Before we get started, I will need a volunteer," Prospero said, looking around the room. When no one came forward, he made his way down into the audience. "There must be a willing subject," he said scanning the rows of people. He stopped in the aisle where Blanche and the others were seated. "How about the lovely lady in the green dress?"

Nellie poked Gert in the ribs. "I thinks he means you, maid."

Gert stood up. "Is it me you means, sir?"

"Well, you *are* a lovely lady, and I need a lovely lady."

Jake chuckled. "What you needs, my son, is your eyes checked."

Blanche shook her head. She loved Jake, but at times she felt he crossed a line when it came to Gert. She knew he didn't mean any harm; it was just his way.

"Don't mind him, b'y," Gert said, glaring at her husband.

Prospero took Gert's hand and led her to the stage. "I want you to fold your hands," he told her after she was seated.

"Me hands?"

"Like this." Prospero folded his own hands to demonstrate.

Gert did as she was instructed.

"On the count of three, I will stick this lovely lady's hands together," Prospero said. "One, two, three—"

"Oh, my Gawd!" Gert struggled to free her locked hands. "Me hands is stuck. Look, Nellie," she called. "Mr. Prospero went and stuck me hands together."

Laughter ripped through the audience.

Jake leaned toward Blanche. "Too bad he won't stick her mouth together."

There was a collective gasp as Prospero freed Gert's hands with a snap of his fingers. He looked around the hall. "I need more volunteers," he said. "Would anyone care to join me?"

A handful of people left their seats and began walking toward the stage.

Herb reached for Jake's arm. "C'mon Jake, my son. We got a bet, remember?"

Jake got out of his seat and reluctantly followed Herb down the aisle.

"Are there more volunteers?" Miranda asked.

When no one came forward, she went down into the audience. After some persuasion, a few more people got up from their chairs. Prospero smiled and nodded as they joined him on stage. "Just close your eyes and relax," he told them after they had settled into their seats. "Listen only to the sound of my voice."

Prospero paced the stage, his big voice filling the room. "You are becoming deeper and deeper relaxed," he repeated. "Deeper and deeper, calmer and calmer…Let your mind drift. More and more relaxed…"

Blanche watched as the subjects began to nod off, heads dropping onto their chests.

"Let go now…Let go and listen only to the sound of my voice," the hypnotist continued. "Only my voice matters now. And what my voice is telling you is true."

After a while, Prospero picked up Jake's arm and let it drop. It flopped at his side like a dead fish. The audience watched in awe, the room deadly quiet. "When you awake," Prospero told his subjects, "you will believe you are the greatest singer in the world. You will want to show off your beautiful voice." He snapped his fingers, and the volunteers opened their eyes.

For the next while, Blanche listened as the men and women on stage sang Newfoundland songs and ballads: "The Squid Jiggin' Ground," "Star of Logy Bay," and "The Dark Rolling Waters of Harbour Le Cou." When Jane Coombs sang the Newfoundland anthem, the audience stood. Everyone, right down to the youngest child, crossed their hands over their hearts and sang along. Blanche doubted if any of them even knew the words to "O Canada."

When it was Jake's turn to sing, he walked to the edge of the stage and gazed out at the audience. "I would love to go back home again to Ireland," he belted out. "If only that old hen would pass away. Her mouth is bigger than Galway Bay."

"Good thing Gert's under a spell and can't hear him," Nellie whispered to Blanche.

"When I count to three," Prospero said, "you will be seagulls flying along the beach searching for food. One. Two. Three." He snapped his fingers and the volunteers jumped up, arms flapping as they ran around the stage. Some of them came swooping down into the audience, squawking and flapping.

Gert's loud squawking could be heard all over the building. She fought with the other "gulls," trying to take away their food. She knocked Jake to the floor and was pecking at his face when Prospero grabbed her shoulders. He snapped his fingers and Gert, looking dazed and confused, returned to her seat.

"At the count of three, the seagulls will return to the stage," Prospero said in his deep, authoritative voice: "One. Two. Three."

"I don't see Jake nowheres," Nellie whispered as the subjects joined Prospero back on stage.

Craning her neck, Gert looked around the hall. "Now where's that fool gone to?"

Blanche followed her gaze, but Jake was nowhere to be seen.

"You are now fully awake," Prospero told the volunteers. "Thank you for participating. You may return to your seats." Despite the empty chair, he seemed unaware that Jake had not returned with the others.

Gert turned to Blanche. "Jake didn't get un-hypnotized," she said, sounding worried. "We got to let Mr. Prospero know."

CHAPTER 8

꧁ ❦ ꧂

PATSY WAS STRETCHED OUT ON THE SOFA READING *TRUE CONFESSION*.
She enjoyed those rare moments when she had the house to herself.
Donna Penny, a woman whose kids she babysat, had a subscrip-
tion. A new magazine came in the mail every month. After Donna
finished reading them, she passed them on to Patsy. Nan called
the magazines trash and threatened to burn them. Patsy had to
be careful not to leave them lying around where her grandmother
could find them.

She was absorbed in a story about a girl who was trying to
decide whether to go all the way with her boyfriend when a knock
came at the door. People on the island never knocked. She got up
from the sofa and looked through the window.

A fancy orange car with shiny hubcaps was parked on the road
in front of the house. Its thick wheels were so low on the ground
that Patsy wondered how the driver managed to get in and out.
Since the ferry started bringing cars and trucks across, strangers
were coming and going all the time. Some people on Darby's Island
had cars of their own now. Aunt Gert was after Uncle Jake to buy
one. The knock came at the door again. *Probably a tourist*, Patsy
thought as she went to answer it. They came from all over the place.
Just last week she'd met a family from New York City.

Patsy opened the door, and stepped back startled. "Bishop
Malloy," she gasped.

The bishop smiled.

Patsy stared at him, taking in the large crucifix hanging from his neck, the purple robes billowing around him. He was tall with silver hair, and looked almost as old as her grandfather.

"May I come in?"

Patsy took another step backward. "But Aunt Gert's not expecting you 'til tomorrow," she blurted.

"I came over on the afternoon ferry. I've been visiting at the nursing home all afternoon."

"Oh." Patsy stood awkwardly in the doorway. "Want to come in, Your Grace?"

"Thank you, Miss…?"

"I'm Patsy." She held open the door, feeling a wave of panic as the bishop stepped inside. Should she offer him something to eat or drink? "Perhaps you'd rather sit in the front room," she said. Patsy led him down the hallway, already wishing she'd taken him next door to Aunt Gert's house.

Bishop Malloy took a seat on the sofa, his long robe settling around him. He looked around the room, his gaze falling on the stack of magazines on the coffee table. The one on top had a picture on the cover of a man and woman kissing. The man's chest was bare and the woman wore a flimsy negligee that exposed most of her breasts.

Patsy had forgotten about the magazines, and now she felt a rush of panic. "Aunt Gert and Uncle Jake have gone to see the hypnotist," she said, hoping to distract the bishop.

"I see." Bishop Malloy folded his hands in his lap and smiled at her.

"But they always leaves the door unlocked," Patsy said, hoping he'd take the hint. "Aunt Gert's gonna be some disappointed when she finds out you came while she was out."

"No harm done." The bishop picked up a magazine from the coffee table. "What do we have here, now?"

Patsy watched in horror as he flipped through February's issue. It was the special Valentine's Day edition, twice as thick as the other issues. The featured story was titled "My Husband Had a Heart Transplant and Now He Loves the Donor's Wife."

It got really racy in some places. Patsy had underlined some of the steamier parts. She felt her heart speed up. *Please, dear God, no,* she prayed. *Please don't let him read that stuff.*

"What's this then?" the bishop said, eyebrows knitted together.

Mortified, Patsy wanted to run from the room.

The bishop read aloud one of the passages she'd underlined. "'He kissed my neck, my throat, and my entire body trembled as he reached for my breast.'" He turned to Patsy, his eyes narrowing.

With her face flaming, Patsy lowered her head to avoid looking at him. *Wait 'til Nan finds out about this,* she thought. All hell would break loose. And if Aunt Gert ever got wind of it, Patsy knew she'd never hear the end of it.

Bishop Malloy studied Patsy with interest. She looked away, unable to meet his stare. A sheen of sweat broke out on her forehead, and her legs felt like cooked noodles.

This couldn't be happening. Even in her worse nightmares, Patsy couldn't have imagined anything this awful. It felt as if all the air in the room was being sucked up and she couldn't breathe.

⌒⌒⌒

WHAT COULD POSSIBLY HAVE HAPPENED TO JAKE, BLANCHE WONDERED as she followed Gert, Nellie, and Herb to the kitchen at the back of the hall. It was used for potluck suppers, weddings, garden parties, and other gatherings.

Prospero and Miranda, who were sitting at the table sipping sodas, looked up in surprise when the foursome burst into the room.

"Jake didn't get un-hypnotized," Gert blurted.

"Jake?" Prospero's forehead furrowed, but Blanche could see amusement in his eyes.

"Jake Pickford. The feller in the blue flannel shirt," Gert explained. "After he got hypnotized, he went flying out the door and never come back."

"I'm sure he'll be fine," Prospero said.

"But where's he gone to?" Gert demanded.

"I don't know." Prospero shrugged, dismissively.

"Funny he should disappear so soon after you cast that spell on him," said Nellie.

"My son, Jake lacks good sense on any given day," Gert said. "There's no telling what he'll do now that he thinks he's a gull. He could fly off the government wharf, hop off a cliff." She wrung her hands. "Sure, he could be somewheres right now with his arms and legs broke."

"He'll be flyin' around for the rest of his life," said Herb.

Although Blanche understood their concerns, she didn't think Jake was in any real danger.

"Mr. Prospero," Gert said, taking a step toward him. "My son, yeh got to find Jake. Yeh got to get him un-hypnotized."

"No one stays under the spell of hypnosis forever," Prospero said. "A subject cannot get stuck in a hypnotic state. Mr. Pickford will come out of it with or *without* my intervention."

"C'mon, Nellie," Gert said, sounding disgusted. "Alls we're gonna get from that feller is big fancy words." She headed toward the door and the others followed.

"Maybe we can split up and look for him," Blanche suggested when they were outside. "Jake couldn't have gone too far."

"Good idea," Herb agreed. "Nellie, you and Gert search along the beach while me and Blanche checks his fish store."

"Fine mess that Prospero got us in," Gert grumbled as they walked down a worn path to the beach. "If anything happens to Jake, it'll be his fault."

Once they reached the landwash, Nellie and Gert turned toward Gull's Head. Blanche and Herb walked in the opposite direction. They strolled in silence for a couple of minutes. After a while, Herb said, "I hear you've come to the island to investigate Olive."

Blanche glanced up at him in surprise. She hadn't told any-one why she was here. Olive was the administrator at the nursing home. She was also Herb's daughter from a previous marriage. "I can't discuss the case with you, Herb. It's confidential."

Herb nodded. "I hope Olive's not in trouble again." He shook his head. "It's been one thing after another with that girl."

Olive was in her fifties, hardly a girl. Still, Blanche understood Herb's concern. It wasn't the first time his daughter had been in trouble. After her mother died, Olive had been raised by Herb's aunt. Around that time, Herb had started drinking heavily. It was no secret that Olive and her father didn't have a good relationship. After Herb married Nellie, they'd invited Olive to live with them. But she wanted nothing to do with her father.

Blanche and Herb continued walking along the shore until they came to a sprawl of unpainted, weathered stores.

"That's Jake's store over there." Herb pointed to a building poised on wooden pilings. It had a long wharf that extended over the water. "He's probably in there right now."

The door creaked on its hinges when Herb pulled it open. He walked into the building, Blanche at his heel.

"Jake?" Herb called. "Jake?"

It was dark inside, the air heavy with the sharp odour of salt, tar, rope, and fish. Herb struck a match. He found a lantern on a low shelf and lit it. From the shadowy amber light, Blanche saw that the walls had been papered with pages from Simpsons-Sears and Eaton's catalogues. An old rocker stood near the window, a pot-bellied stove in one corner. A crude wooden stand held mugs, tea, and sugar. Jake had even hung red gingham curtains at the small square window.

"Jake spends most of his time here," Herb said. "Some days he only goes home to sleep."

"Why?"

"'Tis Gert, maid. Always naggin' and keepin' on. Got the poor man drove right mental."

Blanche said nothing.

"Sometimes, he sits for hours brooding," Herb continued. "One day he says to me, 'Herb, my son, I wishes I was thirty years younger and knows what I knows now.'"

There was a faded calendar from Ryan's Variety Store with a picture of Jesus surrounded by children. A small shelf held glass jars filled with fishhooks, nuts, bolts, and screws. Blanche peered at a single sheet of paper tacked to the wall. "What's this?"

Herb brought the lantern closer. Blanche saw it was a poem written out in pencil: "The Lake Isle of Innisfree." When had her father-in-law become interested in poetry?

"Jake copied that from a book." Herb scoffed. "Thought the words sounded nice. Not much of a poem. I likes limericks, or at least poems that rhymes." He chuckled. "That Jake's a queer one."

Where could he have gone? Blanche wondered. She was tired from her trip, eager to get back to the cottage. She needed her rest if she was going to carry out interviews at the nursing home tomorrow.

Herb blew out the lantern and set it back on the shelf. "Jake could be anywheres," he said as if reading Blanche's mind.

Walking back to the hall, Blanche felt a spit of rain against her cheek. Dark, threatening clouds had moved in over the ocean. The storm that had been forecasted was on its way.

Prospero and Miranda were just leaving the building when they arrived.

"Any luck?" Prospero asked.

"No, my son," Herb said. "Jake's not in his store. Yeh sure he'll be okay?"

"Of course," Prospero assured him.

Herb turned to Blanche. "Go home, my love," he said. "I'll keep searching for Jake."

"Are you sure?"

Herb waved her away. "Jake's probably gone home by now."

"There was a phone call from someone name Patsy," Miranda said. "She was looking for her grandmother. She sounded upset."

CHAPTER 9

⚬❈⚬

AS THEY WALKED ALONG THE BEACH, JIGGER MCGHEE COULD HEAR the waves crashing against the rocks. He and Skid Snooks had been drinking all evening at Skid's house. When they ran out of booze, they decided to go to Jigger's brother's fish store. Delbert always hid bottles of homebrew in his store. The wind was strong, blowing rain in their faces. Skid carried a small flashlight that gave off a pale beam of light. The only other illumination came from the lighthouse that carved an arc of light around the bay. In the darkness, they tripped over rocks, driftwood, and other debris that had washed up on shore.

Skid, the more inebriated of the two, suddenly burst into song: "We'll rant and we'll roar like true Newfoundlanders. We'll rant and we'll roar on deck and below. Until we sees bottom inside of the sucker…"

Christ, Jigger thought. Skid couldn't carry a tune to save his life. If he had to sing for his supper, he'd probably starve. Jigger was about to say as much when Skid tripped and fell. He cursed as the flashlight went flying, the light snuffing out. "Help me find the goddamn light, Jigger," he shouted.

Groping in the darkness, Jigger grasped at sticks and seaweed. "Where'd the damn thing go to?" His hand touched something claw-like. He tugged on Skid's jacket.

"Christ, Jigger, my son," Skid said, pulling away from him. "What is it?"

Jigger tugged harder. "Just feel this," he said, guiding Skid's hand to the claw.

"A flipper," Skid said, excitedly. "I went and tripped over a goddamn seal."

It was too late in the season for seals, Jigger thought, but he decided to humour Skid. "You really think 'tis a seal?"

"What else could it be?"

Jigger stood up. He kicked at the object with his boot. It was soft, like a mattress. Could it really be a seal?

"We needs a net so we can drag him home," Skid said. "If we leaves him here, he'll be washed away by morning."

"Delbert's got all kinds of nets in his store," Jigger said.

"Well, let's go, b'y."

The two of them were staggering along the beach when they saw a faint yellow light bobbing in the darkness. "That you, Delbert?" Skid sung out.

"No, Skid b'y, 'tis me, Herb."

"Herb," Jigger called, "bring that light down here."

"Me and Jigger found a seal," Skid said.

"A seal…this time of year?" Herb sounded dubious.

"Yes, b'y," Skid said. "I went and tripped over him."

"Seen Jake anywheres?" Herb asked as he approached with the lantern. "Been looking for him for hours now."

"No, b'y, we never seen nobody," Skid said.

"Jake got hypnotized, and now he thinks he's a gull," Herb said. "Took off, he did. We can't find him nowheres."

"Hypnotized?" Jigger couldn't believe what he was hearing. "Jesus."

"Where's the seal to?" Herb asked.

"Back there," Skid pointed vaguely. "Come on, I'll show yeh."

They searched up and down the beach, Skid swearing as he tripped in the darkness. "He's got to be around here somewheres," he said, "unless he got up and walked away." He chuckled at his own lame joke.

"Sure 'twas a seal?" Herb asked.

"'Twas a seal," Skid said. "I had a hold of his flipper, sure."

This could take all night, Jigger thought as he helped Skid and Herb search the beach.

After a while, Skid called: "Over here. I nearly tripped over the bastard a second time."

Herb came toward him, the lantern casting wild shadows on the beach rocks.

"Right here," Skid said.

Jigger watched as a sphere of light fell on a pair of black shoes.

"First time I seen a seal wearing shoes," Herb said dryly.

Jigger gasped. "Christ Jesus. A dead man. The poor bastard must've drowned. Probably off one of them foreign vessels."

Herb swung the light over the body. A gust of wind blew in from the sea, making the flame in the lantern flutter. "Will yeh look at that," he exclaimed, fixing the light on the corpse's face. The mouth gaped open, the cloudy eyes wide and staring.

Both Skid and Jigger jumped back.

"Holy mother of Christ!"

CHAPTER 10

❦

November 1962

ON THE WAY HOME FROM SCHOOL, I SPOTTED MY BROTHER JIMMY huddled in the alcove of the post office smoking a cigarette. He waved when he saw me, his black hair tumbling into his eyes. "Tell Ma I won't be home for supper," he said as I got closer. He shivered inside his thin windbreaker that didn't look warm enough to keep out the autumn chill.

"Ma worries about yeh, Jimmy," I said. "Especially when you don't come home nights."

"No need for Ma to worry, maid." He took a drag from his cigarette and blew out the smoke. "Sure, I can take care of me own self. Right now, I'm waiting for the *Northern Ranger* to come in. A chance for me to make a few bucks helping unload the freight."

"The boat won't be here for hours," I said. "Won't you at least come home for supper, Jimmy? Sure, you hardly spends time at home anymore. The little ones all miss you."

Jimmy took a final drag from his cigarette and threw the butt on the ground. "Yeh knows I can't stand being around Old AC." He ground out the butt with the heel of his shoe.

Nodding, I took in the white scar that ran across Jimmy's chin. A couple of months ago, Da had hit him with a belt buckle.

One side of his face was mottled yellow and green—bruises from another beating that were only now fading.

"Well, I better go," I said. "I promised Ma I'd come straight home from school." I reached up to give him a hug, and he pulled me tightly against him.

At home, I found Ma sitting at the kitchen table with a cup of tea. Her black hair hung limp around her gaunt face, and there were dark circles around her eyes. Although the baby was due in five months, she looked as if she'd lost weight instead of gaining. Still, it was good to see her up and about. She even had a little colour in her cheeks. "How are yeh, Ma?" I crossed the room and enfolded her in a hug.

Kate and Ivy had draped a quilt over the two benches to make a tent for Eddie. A smile lit up his small face as he crawled in and out of it. He seldom smiled, and it was a welcome sight to see him happy and playing.

"Would you like me to start supper, Ma?"

"No, my love. I made some soup and there's potatoes baking in the oven. There's tea steeped on the stove. Pour yourself a cup, and come sit down."

I poured myself a cup of tea from the dented aluminum teapot, and took it to the table. I pulled the only other chair up beside Ma. "I saw our Jimmy on the way home," I told her.

"Is he okay?" she asked anxiously.

"Jimmy's fine," I assured her. "He's waiting for the *Northern Ranger* to come in. It's a chance for him to make a few dollars. They're always looking for men to help unload." I touched her arm. "Jimmy's okay, Ma. No need to worry."

Before Ma had a chance to say anything, Gabe came out of the bedroom. Although he was eighteen months younger than me, and three years younger than Jimmy, he was taller than both of us. Gabe was as blond as the rest of us were dark. He and Eddie were the only two in the family who didn't have jet-black hair.

"Gabe, come have a cup of tea with us," Ma said. "Pull the rocking chair up to the table."

"That's okay, Ma." Gabe got a mug from the shelf, poured a cup of tea, and placed it on the table. He disappeared into the bedroom and came back carrying a wooden apple crate Jimmy had found on the beach. He turned it upright to use as a seat.

"Matt Foley told me that Joey Smallwood wants to move all the people off the island," Gabe said. "Says his father heard it on the radio."

"Where would we go?" I asked.

Gabe shrugged. "St. John's or Corner Brook, I s'pose. Or maybe some other big place like Deer Lake or Gander. Matt's father says Joey's cracked if he thinks he'll get his family to move."

"Joey's a good man," Ma said. "I thinks he wants what's best for Newfoundlanders." She tasted her tea and added more sugar. "The problem is that he don't understand outport people. He thinks they hates to fish, and we all know that's not true."

"What kind of jobs do he expect people to find on the mainland?" Gabe asked.

"Factory work, I guess." I took a sip of tea. "I can't see many people around here working in factories."

As we sipped our tea, the younger children took pleasure in their play. I actually heard Eddie laugh out loud as Ivy crawled under the blanket with him.

It was just starting to get dark when we heard the heavy approach of footsteps on the stoop. Ivy looked up, startled. Without a word, Kate folded the quilt and took it into the bedroom. Gabe helped Ivy put the benches back in place. Eddie climbed onto Ma's lap, leaned his head against her chest, and began sucking his fingers.

Da was obviously in a dark mood. He looked around the room. "No supper on the table yet?"

Kate and Ivy took a seat on the daybed looking uneasy. Ma got up from the table. She went to the shelf and began taking down cups and plates. "Supper's almost ready, Abe."

During supper, the children were quiet, as if afraid to breathe. We were all on edge, knowing the smallest thing could set our father into a rage. I watched nervously as he stabbed a fork in his potato. "Them spuds ain't cooked," he complained. "Hard as goddamn rocks."

"Nothing wrong with the spuds," Gabe said. He cut off a piece with his fork and put it in his mouth as if to demonstrate.

Da gave him a dirty look. "Don't you argue with me."

Please don't fight, I prayed silently.

Gabe opened his mouth to say something, but Ma gently placed a hand on his arm.

"The spuds ain't cooked and the soup's like water," Da continued. He gave Ma a disparaging look. "Yeh tryin' to poison me, bitch?"

Ma lowered her eyes to her plate. She seemed to shrink inside herself.

Gabe put down his fork. "Her name's Grace," he said evenly. "And there's nothin' wrong with the spuds or the soup."

"You shut the hell up," Da roared. "No one asked for your two cents' worth. 'Tis none of yer goddamn business."

The younger children stared, their eyes wide with fear. Eddie's face crumpled like he was going to cry.

"Can I get yeh some tea, Da?" Ivy offered.

I shot my sister a grateful look. Ivy was always the peacekeeper.

Da either didn't hear her, or chose not to answer. Turning to Gabe, he said, "Why don't yeh make yerself useful and run up to Ryan's? Get some lassy, some yeast cake, and a pack of tobacco."

"Abe, let Gabe eat his meal in peace," Ma said. "He can run up to Ryan's after supper."

Gabe stared hard at Da. "Got money?"

"No need. Tell Leo to put it on tick. I'll pay up when me cheque comes."

"Leo says we can't have nothin' else on tick 'til we pays what we owes," Gabe said.

There was a long silence.

Da glared at Gabe like it was his fault. The room was so thick with tension, it felt like a stick of dynamite was about to go off.

Ivy concentrated on taking the skin off her potato.

Kate stared silently at her plate.

My throat was so tight, I could barely swallow.

"Gert Pickford dropped by today," Ma said, breaking the silence.

Da looked up from his plate. "What did that old bag want?"

Ma let her gaze stray from Da to me. "She wants Blanche to go work for her. She'll pay ten dollars a week, plus vegetables and preserves from her cellar."

Da belched. "Sounds like a good deal to me."

I stared at him in disbelief. "What about school?" I said. "Miss Foster's going to help me prepare for the grade nine exams. She says I can go to university. She—"

"Well now, will you listen to Lady Alderdice," Da scoffed.

The potato suddenly felt too thick to go down my throat. "I'd like to stay in school," I said, hating the way my voice quivered. I looked at Ma. *Don't let Old AC take this away from me,* I pleaded silently.

Ma gave me a pitying look, but said nothing.

Da pointed his fork at me. A piece of potato was stuck to his greying whiskers. "No more school for you," he said. He looked at Ma. "When do Gert want her to start?"

I bit the inside of my cheek.

Shaking her head, Ma looked at me from across the table. "Blanche should stay in school for a couple more years, Abe," she said. "Her teacher says she's very bright. Sure Mr.—"

Da banged his fist on the table, making the cups jump in their saucers. Eddie stared at him, his lower lip quivering. "Christ almighty, woman. When do Gert want Blanche to start?"

Ma swallowed. "As soon as possible. She's got three boarders now."

Tears pricked my eyes, and I blinked rapidly. Going to work for Gert Pickford was the worst thing that could happen to anyone. I'd heard stories from servant girls who had worked for her. Gert had a sharp tongue and was impossible to please. Her kids were mean and nasty. Well, not all; Dave was nice enough, and everyone liked Coop. But I couldn't imagine being in the same house with Juney Pickford, who made fun of my clothes.

I got up from the table, went into the pantry, and picked up the water bucket. I couldn't stay in the house a minute longer.

Gabe followed after me, taking the bucket from my hand. We walked to the well in silence. By now, the night was so dark we had trouble finding our way. The only sounds were the roar of the ocean, the hoot of an owl, and the distant bark of a dog.

"Maybe he'll change his mind," Gabe said as he lowered the bucket into the well.

"Old AC? Not likely," I said, feeling a wave of resentment. "What I don't understand is why Ma told him in the first place. She could've told Gert no. Da didn't have to know anything about it."

"Don't be mad at Ma," Gabe said. "I don't think she meant for any of this to happen." He pulled up the bucket from the well. "I'm sure she was just trying to keep Old AC from going off his rocker. Probably said the first thing that popped into her head."

Even though I knew Gabe was right, I couldn't help feeling angry with her.

As we walked back to the house, rage for Old AC build up inside me. He received a pension from the government because he'd been wounded in the war. It was supposed to be for all of us, to buy food and clothing. Instead he drank it away. Little Eddie was so thin his ribs showed. And now Old AC wanted to take away my only chance of getting an education. The only chance I had to get away from the dirty, stinking hovel we lived in.

CHAPTER 11

❧

THE SHRILL RING OF THE TELEPHONE JOLTED MARTIN AWAKE.
He had been dreaming. He and Emily were young again, dancing
in a park surrounded by children. Emily wore a long white dress
and had roses in her hair. Martin's hand shot out automatically.
"Hello," he murmured sleepily, impatient to get back to the dream.

"Martin? It's Blanche. Sorry to call so early."

"Blanche?" Martin looked at the clock on his night table, and
saw it was quarter of six. Why was she calling so early? By now, the
storm was in full force. Rain lashed against the windows and wind
slammed into the side of the cottage.

"I just spoke with the chief, and he thought I should call you."

Martin felt his heart speed up. He thought immediately of his
son, who lived in Corner Brook with his wife and their two little
girls. "Has something happened to Marty?" he asked anxiously.

"No, no," Blanche assured him. "Your family's fine. Well, as far
as I know." Through the telephone wires, Martin heard Blanche
exhale noisily. "Martin, there's been a murder."

Martin sat up in bed, fully awake now. Had he heard right?
"A murder," he repeated. "Here on the island?"

"Yes," Blanche confirmed.

"But who…?"

"Bishop Malloy. His body was discovered on the beach around
two this morning."

Martin gripped the receiver. "The *archbishop?* Christ, Blanche, you can't mean that."

"He was stabbed to death."

"Someone stabbed the archbishop?"

"Weather's too bad to get forensics over here," Blanche continued. "Don't know when the storm will pass. Still, it's crucial to get statements from the locals."

Martin agreed. He knew better than anyone how critical the first twenty-four hours of an investigation were.

"I'm at the hall," Blanche continued. "I thought we could make it into temporary headquarters. I told the chief I'd carry out interviews. But it's a big job, and well…I don't have your experience or expertise, Martin. I know you're on leave, but I'll need your assistance. With this storm, it's going to be a while before help comes."

"Of course, I'll do whatever I can."

"I appreciate that, Martin. I'll fill you in on the details when you arrive."

Martin hung up. A cold dampness had seeped into the room and he shivered as he pulled on his clothes. He shook his head in disbelief. The archbishop was dead. Murdered. Martin scribbled a note to Linda, telling her he wouldn't be home for lunch. That if she needed him, she could reach him at the hall.

At this early hour there was no one on the road. During the night the wind had risen, and it was gusting about a hundred knots. The force of the storm scattered fallen leaves and hurled debris against the windshield of the truck. Rain was pelting down so hard Martin could barely see the road. Twice he had to pull off to the side and wait for the rain to let up.

Martin pulled his truck up behind Blanche's cruiser, which he found parked on the road outside the hall. He got out and started toward the building, struggling against the wind that sliced though his jacket, blowing him backward.

Blanche, wearing jeans and a sweatshirt, sat on the edge of the stage smoking a cigarette. Her black hair was pulled into a high ponytail, stray wisps falling carelessly around her face. "Martin," she called, getting to her feet, "thanks for coming."

"What the hell's going on, Blanche?" Martin asked as he approached.

Blanche snuffed out her cigarette in a nearby ashtray. "Let's go into the kitchen."

Martin followed her across the stage and down the four steps to the kitchen. There was a plate of store-bought biscuits on the table and he could smell coffee brewing. He removed his rain jacket and hung it on a peg before taking a seat at the table.

Blanche poured a coffee for Martin and one for herself before taking a seat across from him. "Right now the number one suspect is Jake," she said.

"Jake Pickford?" Martin asked incredulously.

Blanche nodded. "Jake was found with the murder weapon, a hunting knife that belongs to Herb. Herb claims he lost the knife on the beach yesterday morning."

"How do you know the knife belongs to Herb? All those knives look the same."

"Herb's had red paint spilled on the handle."

"But…why would Jake do a thing like that?" Martin couldn't wrap his head around it.

"I'm not saying he *did* it, Martin. But for now, he's definitely a suspect."

Martin rubbed his eyes. *Could Jake have snapped? Gone over the edge?* Everyone on the island knew Gert was making his life miserable. "Who found the body?"

"Jigger and Skid were walking along the beach late last night— drunk as usual—when one of them tripped over it. Herb got there shortly afterwards."

"What was the time of death?"

Blanche consulted her clipboard. "Nurse Duncan examined the body just after two. She thinks the death occurred somewhere between nine-thirty and eleven o'clock last night."

"Someone must have seen *something*," Martin said. "Usually, there are people on the beach night and day."

"The body was found out near Devil's Rock," Blanche said, naming an isolated stretch of beach not far from Gull's Head. "I've made a list of people to interview, starting with those who were in contact with Bishop Malloy. We need to find out who had opportunity, but most of all who had a motive."

Martin nodded his approval. Blanche was handling things. "You've really taken charge here," he told her.

"Well, the case just happened to fall in my lap."

Martin looked at her with admiration. Many of his colleagues were uneasy about having women on the force. He wished they could see Blanche now. A pro.

"Where's the body now?" Martin asked.

"They lugged it to Delbert's fish store."

Martin winced. "That doesn't help the crime scene."

"Herb suggested they take it there," Blanche said. "Of course at that point, no one realized the archbishop had been murdered." She took a sip of coffee and put down the cup. "In any case, the body couldn't be left out in this weather. I've locked the doors, and Peter Foley and Earle Greene are taking turns guarding the place."

Martin nodded. "What was the archbishop doing on the beach? I thought he wasn't supposed to arrive until today."

"Apparently, he crossed over yesterday afternoon and went straight to the nursing home. He always visits the residents during his stay. Gert and Jake were here at the hall when he arrived." Blanche took a bite from her biscuit, chewed, and swallowed. "Finding no one home, he went next door to Herb and Nellie's. Patsy said he stayed about twenty minutes."

"And Jake was found with the murder weapon?"

"Yes. Herb found Jake in Delbert's store, huddled in a corner with the bloodied knife. Problem is, Jake can't remember anything. Judging by the size of the lump on his head, he must have taken a bad fall."

"Well, that would explain his memory loss."

"There's something else you should know," Blanche said.

Martin glanced up at her.

"Jake got hypnotized last night."

"Hypnotized? At that show?" Martin had seen the posters.

Blanche nodded. "While he had them under hypnosis, Prospero told his subjects they were seagulls," she said. "When he called everyone back to the stage, Jake wasn't with them."

"Where'd he go?"

Blanche shrugged. "No one knows."

"We need to have a chat with this Prospero character," Martin said.

"I have him at the top of the list of people to interview. He and his partner are staying in a trailer on Gull's Head."

"Have you spoken with Jake?"

"I spoke with him briefly at the hospital while he was having his wound treated. But I thought we should interview him again. See if his memory's returned."

"It seems you've thought of everything, Blanche." Martin was thoughtful. "You don't suppose being under the influence of hypnosis had anything to do with Jake stabbing the bishop?"

"We don't know for certain if it *was* Jake who stabbed him," Blanche said. "The evidence is circumstantial."

"True," Martin agreed. He couldn't imagine Jake Pickford harming anyone. He was a good, decent man with no prior arrests or convictions. Martin had never known Jake to lose his temper or say a bad word about anyone. But if Jake didn't do it, who did? Martin knew all the people on the island. They were his friends and neighbours. Ninety percent of them were devoted Catholics, for heaven's sake.

Blanche drained her cup. "I'll need to call the glebe in Corner Brook," she said. "Let them know about their archbishop. They shouldn't have to hear about his murder on the news. Afterwards, we can get statements from Jigger and Skid." She studied her notes. "I called Jigger earlier. His mother told me he was still in bed. There was no answer at Skid's house."

"Before you call Corner Brook, I'd like to see the body," Martin said.

⚭

WIND TORE AT THEIR CLOTHES AND DROVE RAIN INTO THEIR FACES AS Blanche and Martin walked to the cruiser. They drove in silence until they came to a small cove with a number of stores and fish stages. Gigantic waves crashed onto the beach, and water came up to the top of the pilings. Boats tied to their moorings tossed and pitched wildly.

Despite the early hour and bad weather, a cluster of people stood outside Delbert's store. Blanche felt a swell of sympathy as she scanned the confused and bewildered faces. Ida Mae Bennett clutched her rosary, her eyes red-rimmed. Harold Tobin had an arm around his wife, Betty, who was crying softly into a handkerchief. Mary Penny and her mother, Elaine, clung to each other, distress clear on their faces.

"Is it true?" Ida Mae asked tearfully. "I heard His Grace was murdered, that Jake Pickford went and stabbed him to death."

"We don't know who did it," Blanche said. "The case is still under investigation."

She looked from one anxious face to another. These were people who had known tragedy and sorrow. Death was no stranger, but murder of their archbishop was not something they thought they'd be faced with.

"Go home," Martin told them as he headed toward the fish store. "There's nothing you can do. We will take care of things."

It was dark inside the store, and Peter Foley, the man guarding the body, had lit a second lantern. The bishop's remains were covered with a blue tarp that smelled of fish. His feet stuck out at one end, and one of his shoes was unlaced. Blanche pulled back the tarp, taking in the open eyes, the frozen shock on his face. His hands were slender, fingernails neatly manicured. His violet robe was speckled black in places where his blood had spattered. *Why am I not surprised he's wearing his chasuble?* Blanche thought. She knew the archbishop had an ego; he didn't leave the glebe unless he was in full regalia. Bishop Tully, his predecessor, only wore his bishop attire during mass or when performing sacred functions. Bishop Malloy, however, had enjoyed all the pomp that went with his title.

"What's this?" Martin picked up a red object lodged just beneath the bishop's collar.

Blanche leaned forward to get a better look.

Martin frowned. "Looks like a stone from a cheap ring."

CHAPTER 12

⚜

"I'm not sure if Father Donovan is available," said the pleasant-sounding woman who answered the phone. "He may have already left for the cathedral to get ready for the eight o'clock mass. I'll see if he's still here."

A minute later the priest came on the line. "Father Donovan here," he said briskly.

"Good morning, Father. This is Constable Blanche Ste Croix with the RCMP."

"Good morning, Constable. How can I help you?"

Blanche's tone changed. "I'm afraid I have bad news, Father."

"Don't tell me there's been another accident involving young people."

Blanche guessed the priest was referring to an accident that had happened a couple of weeks ago when a car carrying a load of teenagers had lost control and gone careening down Humber Heights, crashing into a tree. Luckily, no one had been killed. "No, Father. It's about your bishop, I'm afraid."

"Phil…er…Archbishop Malloy?"

"Yes, I'm sorry to say he was found dead this morning."

"Dead? Phillip's dead? Was it his heart?"

"No, Father. He…he was murdered."

"Merciful Saviour!"

"His body was found on a beach on Darby's Island early this morning," Blanche continued. "He was stabbed to death."

59

There was a silence that lasted so long Blanche was afraid they had been disconnected. "Are you still there, Father?"

"Someone murdered the archbishop?" His voice was barely a whisper.

"Yes, I'm afraid so, Father."

"But who? Who would do such a thing?"

"We're still investigating," Blanche said. "Do you know of anyone who might have wanted to harm the bishop? Someone who had a grudge against him?"

Again there was silence.

"Father?"

"Yes, sorry, Constable. It's all such a shock, you see."

"I understand, and I'm sorry. But do you know of anyone who might have wanted to harm the archbishop?" Blanche asked again.

"No…no, I have no idea. The archbishop was a good man. A godly man. I don't understand why *anyone* would want to harm him."

Something in his voice, however, told Blanche that Father Donavan wasn't entirely convinced.

Not more than fifteen minutes later, Martin and Blanche were sitting across the table from Jigger, a cigarette burning in an ashtray beside him. Blanche studied him quietly, taking in his unbuttoned shirt, porcelain skin, and hairless chest. To say he was hungover was an understatement. His eyes—to use her brother Jimmy's expression—were like two piss holes in the snow.

Martin glanced at Blanche and gave a curt nod.

Blanche knew he was waiting for her to begin the interview. This was an opportunity to prove her competence. How she handled this could have a significant impact on her career. For a moment, she felt panicked, her father's voice playing in her head: "You'll never amount to nothing." Blanche shook her head as if to clear away the hateful words.

"Go ahead, Blanche," Martin said, encouragingly.

Blanche recalled her telephone call with the chief earlier. "Well, at least we have an officer over there, even if…" Although his voice had trailed off, Blanche knew what he was thinking:

Even if the officer is a woman with no experience. "Martin will be there to help," he had added. "I'll be perfectly fine," she'd told him with much more confidence than she felt.

Opening her notebook now, she turned to Jigger. "Do you mind going over the events of last night?"

Jigger ran a hand through his tousled dark hair. "Me and Skid was on our way to Delbert's store," he said. "He hides bottles of brew in a barrel by the door." Jigger glanced from Blanche to Martin. "We always puts them back," he said. "'Tis not like we're stealing."

Blanche nodded, suppressing a smile. "I understand you tripped over the bishop's body."

"Skid tripped over the body. Couldn't see nothing in the dark. Not 'til Herb come by with his lantern." Jigger took a drag from his cigarette and blew out the smoke. "I thought he drowned. Thought the body washed ashore—like that Russian sailor they found over in Round Harbour a few months back. Nearly pissed meself when I seen 'twas the archbishop."

"What happened after that?" Blanche prompted. "After you found the body."

"Skid stayed with the bishop while me and Herb went to find something to lug his body back to Delbert's store. We found an old screen door and used it for a stretcher. After we lugged the body back and had a chance to look at it, Herb says, 'Jesus Christ, looks like the bishop's been stabbed.'"

Blanche wrote in her notebook.

Jigger blew a perfect smoke ring across the table, his eyes locking with Blanche's. "Herb said we should call you."

Nodding, Blanche watched the ring of smoke collide with a bottle of catsup.

"Before he got a chance to call," Jigger continued, "we seen Jake huddled in the corner of the store. Holding a knife, he was."

"Was Jake there when you went to pick up the bishop's body?"

"Could've been. Like I said, 'twas too dark to see much." Jigger shuddered. "I couldn't believe me eyes. The friggin' bishop laid out in front of us with a hole in him, and Jake Pickford not three feet away holding a goddamn big knife. Felt like I was in a horror movie."

"Must have shaken you," Blanche said.

Jigger nodded. "Sobered me up pretty fast."

"How did Herb react when he saw Jake with the knife?"

"He was right shocked." Jigger butted out his cigarette and lit another. "He goes over and kneels beside him. 'Oh, my Jesus, Jake, my son,' he said. 'Don't tell me you went and stabbed the bishop?'"

"And what did Jake have to say?" Blanche asked.

"Never said nothing. Just sat there right stunned like. Herb shook him, but he didn't even blink. 'What's wrong with him?' I asked Herb."

Blanche and Martin both looked at Jigger expectantly.

Jigger heaved a sigh. "But then I remembered something Herb told us." He fixed a stare briefly on Martin before shifting his gaze to Blanche. "Jake went and got hypnotized."

After their interview with Jigger, Martin and Blanche got back into the cruiser and drove to Jake and Gert's house. Blanche had left her package of Export A at the hall, and was craving a cigarette badly.

They drove in silence, the wind whistling around the cruiser. Blanche's mind kept drifting to the stone Martin had found on the bishop's body. *Dear God, did it come from Patsy's ring?* Half the kids on the island probably had rings like it, Blanche reasoned. Patsy said they sold them at Ryan's. It didn't mean anything. Still, she would have to let Martin know about that connection at some point. She would speak with Patsy first, she decided.

"You did a good job with the interview," Martin said after a while. "You'll make a fine detective, Constable Ste Croix."

"Thank you," Blanche said, brightening.

"If you like, I'll interview Jake," Martin said, "but feel free to jump in at any time."

"Thank you."

When they pulled in front of Jake and Gert's house, they saw an orange Camaro parked on the side of the road. "That must be the bishop's car," Martin said.

Blanched parked the cruiser behind it. "It's kind of flashy," she said. "I expected His Grace to be driving something more conservative."

They got out of the cruiser, and Blanche opened the car door. "Nice," she said, running her hand over the sleek leather upholstery. A pine air freshener dangled from the rear-view mirror. On the front seat was a copy of the *Humber Log*. There was also a copy of *The Exorcist* by William Peter Blatty. She checked the glove compartment and found the bishop's driver's licence. "Phillip Patrick Malloy," she read aloud. "Date of birth, August 2, 1907."

"He would've had a birthday soon," Martin said. "His sixty-eighth."

The bishop's crozier and mitre were in the back seat along with a small suitcase. A garment bag blocked one of the windows. Pushing the front seat forward, Blanche reached for the suitcase. She handed it to Martin, who put it in the cruiser. It was a long shot, but the items in the luggage might hold some clue to the bishop's murder.

Gert answered the door, a scowl on her face. "No need to knock," she said. "You're not in the big city now."

"This isn't a social visit," Blanche said. "We're here to interview Jake."

Gert folded her arms, eyeing them warily. "He can't remember nothing more than he did earlier this morning."

"We'll need to question you too, Gert," Martin said.

Gert glared at him. "I don't know nothing." She held open the door. "Youse gonna come in or what?"

Martin and Blanche stepped inside and followed Gert to the kitchen. Jake, looking pale and shaken, sat at the table staring into a cup of tea.

"We need to have a word with you, Jake," Martin began.

Jake looked up at them, his eyes red. "Have a seat."

Martin pulled out a chair from around the table for Blanche, and then another for himself.

Gert took a seat across from Jake and folded her hands on the table.

"We'd like to interview Jake in private," Blanche said.

"Shouldn't he have someone with him? He's not hisself—not after what happened last night. God knows what that Prospero went and done to his mind."

"I'll be fine, Gert maid," Jake said. "Go wait in the front room."

Gert stood up, muttering under her breath.

Martin took a pen and notebook from his pocket. "Do you recall anything about last evening, Jake? Anything at all?"

"No, my son, that's the problem. I don't remember nothing."

Blanche saw that Jake's hands were trembling. "Could I have done this terrible thing?" he asked quietly.

"We'll get to the bottom of it," Martin promised. "Do you remember leaving the hall?"

"The last thing I remembers is being on stage. Me and Herb had a bet." Jake shook his head. "Such foolishness. I wish now I'd had the good sense to stay home."

"What do you recall after coming out of hypnosis?" Martin asked.

"I remembers being in Delbert's store. Herb was there, along with Jigger and Skid. Herb took me to the clinic." Jake sighed. "It all seems like a dream now."

"Don't suppose you recall how you got that bump on the head?"

"I probably fell. The nurse thinks I got a concussion."

Martin scribbled in his notebook. "How did you and Bishop Malloy get on?"

"I felt uneasy around him," Jake admitted. "Mostly because of Gert…always nagging me to act proper…and all that foolishness."

Martin smiled. "It's difficult always having to be on our best behaviour."

Jake's shoulders sagged. "When the police gets in from Corner Brook, will they arrest me? Haul me off to jail?"

Blanche felt a stab of pity. She wanted to reassure Jake that everything was going to be fine. But he was in serious trouble, and there was no way to sugarcoat it.

"It looks bad, Jake," Martin said.

Blanche nodded. Right now, Jake was their number one suspect.

"Try not to worry," Martin said. "We're doing our best to get to the truth."

"If you got no more questions, I think I'll go lie down," Jake said.

"A rest might do you good," Blanche agreed.

In the front room, Gert was watching *The Edge of Night* on a small black-and-white television. The room had a sofa and a number of easy chairs. The wallpaper had a floral design of violets. Framed pictures of Gert's family lined the walls and stood on end tables.

Gert gestured to the television. "Brandy's at it again," she said. "Got poor Nicole drove right mental."

"We need to ask you a few questions, Gert," Martin said.

Gert glared at them. "I told you, I don't know nothing."

Martin motioned to a wing chair across from her. "Mind if I sit?" Without waiting for an answer, he plopped himself down. Blanche took a seat next to him.

"Where did you go after you left the hall?" Martin continued.

"Me and Nellie started toward Gull's Head. Nellie didn't get far before her legs started aching. She's got varicose veins." Gert kept an eye on the television as she talked. "I keeps telling her she should have an operation. Worked wonders for Mary Skinner over in Duck Cove. Sure, Mary—"

"After Nellie's legs started bothering her, did you turn back?" Martin cut in.

"Nellie did, but I kept walking."

Martin wrote in his notebook. "Did you meet anyone along the way?"

Gert made a face. "The hippies that got their van parked out on the Head."

"Anyone else?"

"Only some teenagers. I forgets who they all were. I knows Murray Parnell's young fellow was among them. And Shawn Mercer." Gert turned away from the television and looked at Martin. "Shawn sung out to me. 'Gert,' he said, 'I seen the bishop walking along the beach. I thinks he's out looking for you.'" Gert chuckled at the memory. "I thought the young devil was stringing me along. Likes to tease, Shawny do."

Blanche made a mental note to talk with Shawn and the other boys.

"Anyone else?" Martin asked.

"Skid Snooks."

"Was he sober?"

Gert shrugged. "How would I know?"

"What time was this?" Martin asked.

Gert was shaking her head, her eyes riveted to the television. "Well, well, yeh talk about the devil. Looks like Brandy's up to her old tricks again."

"What time did you see Skid and the others?" Martin tried again.

"Around nine o'clock, I s'pose."

Blanche nodded. If the performance got over at eight-thirty, the timeline fit.

Gert furrowed her brow. "Dear God, what will people think? I won't be able to hold up me head when I goes out in public." She cast a reproachful glance at Blanche. "Bad enough that me Catholic son is getting a divorce."

"This isn't about you, Gert," Martin said.

"I'm heartsick about what happened to the bishop," Gert continued. "I was looking forward to him staying with us. Don't know who got the time mixed up." She tightened her lips. "And that young Patsy...stunned as me arse, that one. Never even had the good sense to offer the archbishop a cup of tea. She should've come to the hall and got me."

"What time did you get home, Gert?" Martin asked.

She shrugged. "It was just starting to get dark out. I thought Jake might've come back to the house. I was worried sick about him out there hypnotized." She locked eyes with Martin. "That damn Prospero. Yeh talked to him yet?"

"All in due course, Gert."

"'Tis all his fault." Gert's lips tightened. "Like I told that reporter who called here this morning—"

"Reporter?" Blanche stared at her.

"Feller from the *Humber Log* in Corner Brook." Gert folded her arms. "And didn't I give him an earful. I told him about Prospero casting a spell over poor Jake. He thinks we should get a lawyer. He says that it wasn't...oh...what was the word he used? *Wilful*... it wasn't a wilful act that Jake committed. He went and done it because he was hypnotized."

Sweet Jesus, Blanche thought.

At that moment, the outside door opened and closed. "Anyone home? Gert?"

"We're here in the front room," Gert called.

Moments later, Nellie appeared in the doorway, her grey hair tangled from the wind. "Oh," she said, taking in Martin and Blanche with their pens and notebooks. "I'm sorry. I didn't mean to interrupt. I seen Blanche's car outside, but I thought she'd just come for a visit."

"It's okay, Nellie." Martin closed his notebook. "We were just wrapping up here."

"Have a seat, maid," Gert said. "I was just watching *The Edge of Night.*"

"Nellie," Blanche said. "We'll need to question you, Herb, and Patsy at some point."

"Whenever you're ready," Nellie said. "We're not goin' nowheres on a day like this."

"How's Patsy?" Martin asked. "We've been meaning to have her over for supper some evening. Linda mentioned it yesterday, as a matter of fact."

"That might do Patsy good," Nellie said. "Get her out of the house, sure. She's been in her room the whole blessed morning. Wouldn't even come out for breakfast." She frowned. "I heard her crying earlier. Won't tell me what's wrong."

"Is she not feeling well?" Blanche asked.

Nellie shrugged. "I don't know. I imagine she's upset over what happened. Thinks the world of her uncle Jake, Patsy does. Probably worried sick about him."

"When she gets up, tell her we'd like to have a word with her."

CHAPTER 13

❦

December 23, 1962

On the morning of Tibbs Eve, it was snowing and blowing so hard the glass in the windows rattled. The younger children were huddled around the wood stove with blankets wrapped around their shoulders, teeth chattering from the cold. During the night, the drinking water in the bucket had frozen over. Da hadn't even bothered to come home. Ma was still in bed, too exhausted to get up. Jimmy and Gabe were outside shovelling snow from the door. All night long, I had tossed restlessly, waking up in the freezing cold. We had put heated rocks in our beds during the night, but by morning they were ice cold. The wind whistled through the cracks in the walls, and despite the sheets of plastic, there was a layer of snow on the windowsill. A small pile had drifted into the corners of our bedroom. Eddie had a cough and sounded congested. The younger children often caught colds and constantly had runny noses.

I scraped molasses on dried scraps of bread for the children's breakfast. I gave Ivy and Kate cups of weak tea. There was a small amount of Carnation milk left in the can, and I poured it into a glass of warm water for Eddie.

"Why can't we have a Christmas tree?" Ivy asked. "Everyone else got one."

"Yeah," Kate said. "Some people even got Christmas lights on theirs."

"Only those with electricity," I reminded her.

"You're lucky," Ivy said. "You gets to go to the Pickfords' all day where 'tis warm."

"And they got electricity," Kate said.

I felt my chest tighten. *I'm sorry*, I wanted to tell them. Instead, I forced a smile. "Yeah, but I got to put up with Gert all day long," I said. "That's no picnic, believe me."

Ivy pulled the tattered blanket tighter around her thin shoulders. "Better than staying around here, freezing."

"Tomorrow when Gert pays me, I'll buy some good food for Christmas," I promised.

"Can we get a turkey?" Kate asked.

"That's the plan," I said, trying to make my voice cheerful. "And I'm going to make mincemeat pies for dessert." I turned to Ivy. "Don't let the fire go out. If it does, go wake Ma. Don't try to light it on your own."

I felt uneasy leaving the younger children while Ma was in such a state. I knew Jimmy and Gabe would be gone most of the day. On days like this, they tried to make a buck shovelling people's walkways. Ma was spending more and more time in bed. This pregnancy was very hard on her. Some days, she was so tired she could barely keep her eyes open. But not only that, she seemed low in spirit. It was as if she'd given up on life. *Things will get better after the baby comes*, I tried to reassure myself.

As soon as I opened the door, an icy wind blew in my face. Snow had drifted up the sides of our small house, almost to the eaves. On the walk to Gert's, the visibility was so bad I could barely see my way. In some places, I had to wade in snow up to my waist. The soles of my boots were worn thin, and there was a large hole near the toe. I was tempted to take a shortcut across the harbour. I knew, though, there was the chance the ice might not be frozen in places. Last winter a local man had drowned attempting to cross.

It took me nearly twice as long to get to Gert's as it normally would. My face was stiff with cold. There was snow in my boots, and my feet felt like blocks of ice. Gert glared at me as I walked in the door. "You're late," she said.

"I'm sorry," I told her. "The weather's been so bad."

Jake was sitting at the kitchen table in his stocking feet. "Silent Night" was playing on the radio. A strong aroma of pine emanated from the front room where a Christmas tree, decorated with glass ornaments and colourful electric lights, stood. Ropes of garland crisscrossed the ceiling with a paper bell hanging in the middle.

Gert folded her arms across her chest. "There's lots to be done this morning."

"Ah, let her catch her breath, maid," Herb said. "Come sit down, Blanche my love, and have a cup of tea."

Gert pursed her lips. "The beds is not going to make themselves," she said. "The hens needs to be fed, and the eggs gathered."

I was torn between pleasing Gert and sitting at the table with Jake. "My feet's wet," I said, taking off my socks.

"Juney?" Jake called, and his daughter appeared in the kitchen. With her dark hair and round face, she was starting to look more and more like her mother. "Juney, go find Blanche some dry socks," he said, "before she catches her death of cold."

Juney scowled, but headed toward the stairs. She came back a minute later with a pair of wool socks. "These belongs to Coop," she said.

Jake poured me a cup of steaming hot tea. There was milk and sugar on the table. I didn't know how long it had been since I'd had both milk and sugar to put in my tea. On the radio Elvis Presley was singing. *I'll have a blue Christmas without you.* "Amazing," Jake said, shaking his head in wonder. "People singing hundreds of miles away can be heard here on the island."

"Sure, in Corner Brook they got televisions," Juney said. "I can't wait to go visit Aunt Doreen in April."

The hot cup felt good as I wrapped my cold hands around it. The tea seemed to revive me. I could feel Gert's eyes on me and I gulped it down. I knew she was impatient to have me get started on the housework.

"We'll begin with the bedrooms," Gert said, starting for the stairs.

What I hated most about working for Gert was the constant criticism. She eyed me like a hawk. The first time I made a bed, she tore it apart. "No," she said, "that's not how we does it. The corners needs to be tucked in. Like this," she demonstrated. She had me do it over and over again until I got it right. All the while tsk-tsking and muttering how young people these days don't know nothing.

"S'pose to get a new boarder this evening," Gert said when we reached the top of the stairs. "I'll put him in John's room."

John Dennison was a writer and photographer from Ontario. He worked for a magazine that sent him to Darby's Island to take pictures. "I thought Mr. Dennison was going to stay until after Christmas," I said.

Gert shrugged. "I wasn't sad to see that feller go. Him and that strong Canadian twang I hates so much. Nosy bugger, too, he was." Gert shook her head. "I can't believe some of the questions he asked. Wanted to know why we calls our noon meal our tea. On the mainland they calls it lunch."

Work that morning was even heavier than usual. I worked non-stop, scrubbing, dusting, sweeping, and doing laundry. At least Gert had a washing machine. No scrubbing laundry on the board here.

Once the clothes were rinsed and put through the wringer, I loaded them in a basket and took it upstairs to the pipe room—where the stovepipe went through the ceiling. In summer, Gert rented the room out. Now it had clotheslines strung from one end to the other. As I hung up towels, sheets, and other articles of clothing, I couldn't help wishing we had a pipe room. In winter, we hung our laundry over chairs, on the back of doors, and on the small clothesline that ran behind the kitchen stove.

When I went downstairs to get tea ready, Juney was sitting at the kitchen table. She had a pen and notebook in her hand. "How do you spell orange?" she asked.

"What is yeh going on with now, Juney?" Jake asked.

"I'm writing a letter to Mr. Eaton," she said. Juney read what she'd written: "Dear Mr. Eaton, could you please send me a dress just like the one you sent Doris Foley. Any other colour except orange."

"Orange would look good on you, Juney," came a voice from the doorway. "You could go out trick-or-treating as a pumpkin."

I looked to see Coop standing in the doorway. He took off his boots and winter jacket before coming into the kitchen. Coop was tall and lanky with hair so blond it was almost white. Today he was wearing jeans with a green pullover that matched his hazel eyes. He smiled when he saw me. "Hello, Blanche. Is Ma running you off your feet?"

I returned his smile. "I'm doing okay, Coop."

Juney and Coop were the only two of Gert's kids still living at home. Coop was waiting to get into the carpentry program at the vocational school. He had to be out of school a year before he could apply. He'd just received word he'd been accepted. Juney, being the youngest, was spoiled rotten. Gert gave her everything she wanted.

Coop sniffed the air. "Something smells good."

Gert had made rice and tomato soup, thick with beef and vegetables. I'd not had anything to eat or drink since the tea that morning. My stomach grumbled as I ladled the soup into bowls and served it with thick slices of homemade bread.

After I'd finished serving everyone, I took a place at the table. It felt wonderful to be off my feet. I tried not to gulp the hot, delicious soup. I wondered how the children at home were faring. For their tea, there was only the watery cabbage soup leftover from yesterday. I especially worried about Eddie, wondering if his cough had gotten worse.

After the dishes were put away, Coop brought out flour and other ingredients. Although Gert complained that he was always making a mess in the kitchen, she often bragged that he could bake cookies, buns, pies, and cakes as good as any woman.

Today he was making molasses buns and tea biscuits. While he waited for them to bake, he played his guitar and sang.

In the afternoon, Gert had me wash down the walls in Juney's bedroom. From downstairs I could hear Coop strumming his guitar and singing, "It came upon a midnight clear, that glorious song of old."

By four o'clock I was so tired I was swaying on my feet. Coop must have noticed, because he said, "Ma, I'm taking Blanche home now. It's been a long day." To me, he said, "No need for you to walk home in this weather. I'll hitch up Riley."

I half expected Gert to protest. I still had half an hour to go and I'd arrived late. I prayed she wouldn't dock my pay for the time I'd missed. I needed every cent for Christmas. I planned to buy peppermint knobs for the children's stockings. Seldom did they get sweets. A shipment of oranges had arrived at Ryan's last week. I decided I would buy one for each of them. Aunt Hattie always dropped by with a Christmas box. She usually put in apples, along with the mitts, scarves, and vamps she knitted.

Coop got my coat from the closet in the porch and helped me into it. "It'll only take me a minute to hitch up the horse," he said.

I was so grateful I wanted to hug him. I hadn't been looking forward to walking home in the dark and cold. Outside, it was still snowing. Gert had turned on the Christmas-tree lights, and they shone through the window like coloured glass eggs. I knew Eddie would love it.

The ride home was pleasant. I leaned against the back of the sleigh. Coop had thrown in a pillow and blankets. In places it was rough going, and the horse strained as he pulled the sleigh through the deep snow. A couple of times, Coop had to stop and shovel snow from the path.

When we pulled into the road that led to our house, the feeble light from the kerosene lamp was barely visible. As we got closer, I saw a small figure. At first, I didn't know if it was human or animal. As we neared, I realized it was Ivy shovelling snow from the door.

"Whoa!" Coop pulled the reins and the horse came to a stop. He got down from the driver's seat and helped me out of the sleigh.

Ivy stopped shovelling and came toward us.

"Give me that shovel, Ivy my love," Coop said. "You shouldn't be out in the cold."

Ivy handed over the shovel and went to the horse. "What's his name?" she asked as she rubbed his nose.

"That's Riley," Coop said.

"Must be nice to have a horse."

"Sure is," Coop told her. "Would you like a sleigh ride sometime?"

"Can I?" I could hear the excitement in Ivy's voice.

"How about tomorrow afternoon? I'll come by and take you and your brother and sister for a ride."

"Wow! Really?" Ivy wrapped her arms around Coop. "I can't wait to tell Kate," she said. "And I knows Eddie will love it."

"Yeh best run inside now," Coop said. He handed me a paper bag. "I thought you might like to sample some of my baking."

"Santa's come early," I told Ivy. "Thanks, Coop."

"No problem." Coop picked up the shovel and began clearing away the snow. "I'll see you tomorrow around eleven," he told Ivy.

I waited until I was inside before I opened the bag. There must have been a dozen or more tea biscuits and molasses buns. Considering our bare cupboard, it was a gift every bit as welcome as a Sunday feast.

CHAPTER 14

⁓

"THIS MIGHT BE A GOOD TIME TO INTERVIEW PROSPERO," MARTIN said. "While it's quiet."

Blanche nodded. She had an appointment with Olive later in the afternoon, but there was plenty of time. It had been a hectic morning. A number of reporters had called from various newspapers and television stations. Blanche and Martin had put out a statement giving sketchy details about the archbishop's death, stating that the case was under investigation.

Despite all the intrusions, they'd managed to interview a number of people, including Herb and Nellie. Except for a few minor details here and there, Herb's statement was the same. It was consistent with what Jigger had told them. Nellie had seen nothing on her walk back from Gull's Head. She was asleep when Herb got home, and hadn't learned about the bishop's death until this morning. They had yet to interview Skid Snooks, Shawn Mercer, and the other boys Gert had reported seeing on the beach. Patsy was asleep when they interviewed Herb and Nellie. Nellie had offered to wake her, but Martin thought it could wait.

Blanche was putting on her coat when the telephone rang. "Not another reporter," Martin groaned as he reached for it. "Martin Bursey here," he said curtly. "Linda?…What's wrong?…I see." Martin frowned. "No, I wasn't able to make it. We have a, umm… situation here. How long has she been that way? Oh. Okay, my love, thanks for calling…Yes, I'll try to get out there as soon as I can."

Martin put the receiver back in its cradle and closed his eyes momentarily.

"Is everything okay?" Blanche asked.

"It's Emily," Martin said. "Linda says they can't calm her down. She ran out of the nursing home last night and tried to do the same again this morning." He rubbed the back of his neck with one hand. "Look, Blanche, I hate to do this, but I'm afraid I'm going to have to postpone our interview. Emily needs me."

"Of course," Blanche said. "Go take care of your wife, Martin. I'll go to Gull's Head and get a statement from Prospero."

"I appreciate that, Blanche."

They left the hall together. The rain had not let up, and the wind was every bit as chilly as it had been that morning. Martin got into his pickup and drove off. Blanche climbed aboard the cruiser and started the engine. The heavy rain made it difficult to drive, and in some places the road was nearly washed out.

Afraid the cruiser might get stuck, Blanche parked on the side of the road and took a narrow footpath to the landwash. The wind whipped her hair from beneath the hood of her jacket as she picked her way along an outcrop of rocks. Far off, she could hear the muffled bleat of a foghorn. The sea exploded against the rocks, hurling salt spray in her face.

Prospero's trailer was parked in a sheltered inlet, the Chevy beside it. Visitors often used the area to park their trailers and tents. The island was becoming a popular spot for tourists, and some people had bought land here to build summer homes.

Blanche stepped up onto a small ramp and knocked on the trailer door. No one answered, but she could hear voices within. With the wind howling around her, she strained to listen. "Stuck here…God knows how long." The voice was male, deep and husky, a voice Blanche didn't recognize. Did Prospero and Miranda have company? Blanche couldn't imagine who'd be visiting on a day like today.

She pressed her ear against the door. "Thought the island… exotic…And now…stuck here," she heard Miranda say.

"How…know there was…to be a storm?" came the male voice again.

"Not blaming…"

It sounded like they were arguing. Blanche knocked again, louder this time.

A few moments passed before Prospero opened the door and peered out. He was wearing a red silk dressing gown and fuzzy red slippers. Miranda stood behind him in cotton pyjamas, a surprised look on her face.

"Well, well, if it isn't Constable Ste Croix." Giving Blanche a broad smile, Prospero stepped aside to let her enter. "To what do we owe the honour of your visit?"

Blanche pulled the door shut behind her. "I need to have a word with you."

"Of course." Prospero removed some books from a chair and motioned her to sit.

Blanche lowered herself into the chair and studied the contents of the trailer. It was small and cramped with barely enough space to move around. No wonder they'd been arguing, she thought, cooped up in this place for hours. Prospero's white tuxedo lay on the back of a chair. There were posters and photographs of him taped to the walls. Blanche took in the quart of vodka on the tiny counter.

"What can we do for you?" Prospero asked. He and Miranda had remained standing, Miranda eyeing Blanche guardedly.

"For starters, you can drop the phoney accent," Blanche said. "Wherever you came from, it wasn't jolly old England."

Prospero grinned sheepishly. "Ah, you're onto me," he said, his accent evaporating.

Blanche stared at him. "Who are you, really?"

"David Stevens," he said. "This is Debra Brown." He gave a short laugh. "You really didn't think Miranda and Prospero were our given names? Although being on this exotic island in such a storm, it's easy to pretend we are the characters whose names we've adopted."

"David's a performer," Debra said defensively. "The accent is part of his act."

"Where are you from, David Stevens?" Blanche pulled a pen and notebook from the inside pocket of her jacket.

"Please," he said, "call me Prospero. We are, after all, in the process of changing our names legally." He glanced at Miranda who gave a quick nod. "I grew up in Toronto; Miranda's from Mississauga."

"And where did you learn hypnosis?"

"In medical school. Actually, I'm…well…I *was* a dentist. I used hypnosis in my practice. For the past five years, I've been using it for entertainment purposes." He crossed his arms. "Is there a reason for your visit, Constable?"

"There is, in fact." Blanche's eyes locked with Prospero's. "You remember Jake Pickford, the man you hypnotized last night? The man who didn't return to the stage?"

"He's still missing?"

"No, no, he's been found, but there's a little problem."

Prospero waited.

"While Mr. Pickford was under hypnosis last evening, he may have murdered a man."

Miranda reached for Prospero's arm. "Murdered?" she gasped, her eyes wide with fright.

A blast of wind hit the trailer, and for a moment Blanche was afraid it would topple over. She could imagine them being blown out to sea.

"The archbishop was stabbed to death early this morning," Blanche continued. "Jake Pickford was found with the murder weapon, a knife. Problem is, he doesn't remember anything."

Miranda let go of Prospero's arm and, like a marionette with broken strings, collapsed into a chair. Prospero stared at Blanche, a startled look on his face.

For a moment, the only sound was the rain pummelling the roof.

Prospero quickly regained composure. "What is it you want from me?"

"Well, naturally I'm curious about how Mr. Pickford was affected by hypnosis."

For a long minute, Prospero stared out the small window at the waves crashing over the rocks. "It's a myth that subjects are completely under my control during hypnosis," he said finally.

"In fact, they retain full control over their minds and bodies. A subject will never compromise his values or convictions. If Mr. Pickford killed the archbishop, it was not because he was hypnotized."

"You had Jake convinced he was a gull," Blanche reminded him.

Prospero turned away from the window and looked at her. "During hypnosis a subject goes into an altered state of consciousness," he explained. "Suggestibility is heightened. But a subject can come out of a trance any time he or she wishes."

"Maybe this Jake guy had a grudge against the bishop," Miranda said, "and now he's using the incident to make his case."

Prospero nodded. "I assume Mr. Pickford is in custody."

"We do not feel Mr. Pickford is a danger to the public," Blanche said. "And the case is still under investigation." She didn't mention that there were no jails or holding cells on the island. Until now, there had been no need. The most common crimes committed were disturbing the peace, underage drinking, and catching lobsters out of season.

Prospero frowned. "You mean there's a murderer running loose?"

"Tomorrow, if the storm lets up, the police from Corner Brook will be handling things," Blanche said vaguely. She got to her feet. "That's all for now." She reached for the door handle. "If you think of anything that might be important, I'll be at the community hall. My partner and I have set up temporary headquarters there."

"Any idea when the ferry will run again?" Prospero asked. "We are both anxious to get away. I have shows booked in Twillingate, Fogo, Tilting, and Morton's Harbour."

"The ferry will depend on the weather." Blanche looked from Miranda to Prospero. "In any case, forensics will want to interview you before you leave here."

"There are no restaurants here," Miranda complained.

"There's Mae's Fish 'n' Chips," Blanche reminded her, "and the cafeteria at the nursing home is open to the public. You can get a decent meal for a reasonable price."

"Cafeteria food," Miranda said indignantly.

Blanche shrugged. "They serve a good moose stew." She reached for her raincoat, which she'd hung over the back of her chair.

"If word gets out that a man committed murder while under hypnosis, people will be afraid to come to the stage. Everything I worked hard for could come unravelled."

Blanche detected a note of worry in Prospero's voice.

Miranda leaned her head against his chest, and Prospero wrapped his arms around her. "We should never have come here," he said. "I'm sorry I talked you into it."

"Darling, you were captivated. The guidebook described this place as an enchanted little island, remember?"

"They did paint an idyllic picture." Prospero kissed the top of Miranda's head. "I can't help it if I'm a hopeless romantic."

Miranda broke away from him. "Can we get away from here, David? Let's go for a drive." She glanced around the cramped space. "Anywhere. I need to get away from this dreary little trailer."

Blanche zippered up her rain jacket and pulled up the hood. "A walk along the beach is always nice in this weather," she said. She opened the door and a blast of wind blew into the trailer, knocking a poster from the wall.

Miranda and Prospero turned to look at her as if they'd forgotten she was still there.

"Thank you for your cooperation," Blanche said. "Enjoy the rest of your stay."

CHAPTER 15

HATTIE STARED AT THE GREEN BLOB ON HER PLATE, HER STOMACH rolling. It was the third time this week they'd been served Jell-O. And if it wasn't that, it was powdered custards or puddings that came out of an envelope. "Not fit for a dog," she muttered.

Outside, wind whipped against the window and rain pounded the roof. From down the hallway she could hear Emily Bursey howling. She'd been going on for hours about her poor father who had fallen from the roof and broken his neck.

"Dear God in Heaven," Hattie muttered. "What brought that on? That stuff happened years ago." She debated whether to go to Emily to offer comfort. *If the staff can't calm her, there's probably not much I can do,* she reasoned. Still, she found it disturbing. If the weather wasn't so bad, she'd go outside, get away from it all. She was looking forward to Blanche's visit this afternoon.

Poor lamb, Hattie thought as she heard another shout. Life hadn't been easy for Emily. Her mother had died while she was still a baby. After her father got killed, she'd gone to live with Lucille Parsons, a relative on her mother's side. She never got over watching her father die. As a young woman, she'd had a nervous breakdown.

An aide poked her head inside the door. "All finished, Aunt Hattie, my love?"

Hattie put the cover back on the tray. "Take it away, Irene, my dear. I'lows if I have to look at another bowl of Jell-O I'll throw up."

"Father fell," Emily cried out. "Father fell."

"Looks like poor Emily's having a bad day," Hattie said. "She's remembering her father's death when she was a child."

Irene nodded. "They're trying to get hold of Martin. His daughter said he left the house early this morning."

Hattie looked at the clock on her bedside table. "Martin's usually here by now."

"Yes," Irene agreed. "He probably got held up on account of the storm."

"I wonder what's upsetting the poor soul."

"Could be the weather," Irene said. "Some people here gets right upset whenever there's a storm." She picked up the tray. "Well, you take care, Aunt Hattie."

"Thanks, my love."

No sooner had the aide left than Edie Batten came in, leaning heavily on her cane. She was a short woman with hair so thin you could see her pink scalp through the white strands.

"Hello, Edie, my dear," Hattie greeted. "Terrible weather we're having. Move me slippers off that chair now, and have a seat."

Edie put the slippers on the floor and eased herself into the chair. "Blanche not here yet?"

"No. But I expects her by and by."

"I dare say she's busy with all the goings on. Her being a Mountie and all."

"Goings on, Edie?"

"Yes, my dear." Edie leaned toward her, and lowered her voice. Hattie noticed a glint in her eye. "There was a murder on the island last night."

"*What?*" Hattie didn't think she'd heard right.

"A murder," Edie repeated, nodding her head.

Hattie put her hand to her chest. "Dear God in heaven. Where to? St. John's, no doubt. That place is getting as bad as any city on the mainland."

"Oh, no," Edie said. "It happened right here on Darby's Island."

"Now, Edie, surely that can't be right."

"Yes, my dear," Edie licked her lips. "Archbishop Malloy was stabbed to death on the landwash last night."

"The Catholic bishop? God Almighty, Edie! Are you certain?"

Edie nodded, a satisfied smile on her face. "Got a call this morning from me niece, Pauline, in Corner Brook. Her husband Lenny's a caretaker at the convent. He overheard Mother Superior talking about it on the phone when he went into her office to empty the wastebasket."

Hattie stared at her in disbelief. "The archbishop was here just yesterday, sure. Who'd want to kill such a fine man?"

"They're saying Jake Pickford done it."

"Jake? No...no. For God's sake, Edie."

"He was under a spell," Edie said, her voice filled with awe. "Went to see the Great Prospero last night and got hypnotized."

Hattie fell back against her pillow. "Didn't I say this would lead to disaster? Sure, I warned Blanche that no good would come of it."

"Lenny said the bishop got stabbed out near Devil's Rock."

Hattie shook her head. "Heaven help us."

"Well," Edie said, getting up from her chair. "I must go tell the news to Agnes and Eva."

Hattie watched her leave. Could Jake really have killed that nice young man? The bishop had stopped by to visit her yesterday, even though she wasn't Catholic. Stayed a nice while too. Must've been a good fifteen minutes or more. Sure, even her own minister, Reverend Harvey, didn't give her that much time. Always rushed. Always looking at his watch or staring out the window. And it wasn't like the bishop was trying to convert her. Never mentioned religion the whole time he was there. Not like them Pentecostals that comes around badgering the residents to get saved.

Hattie glanced again at the clock. God only knew when Blanche would get here now. She must feel terrible. Jake was her father-in-law, after all. And Reba's grandfather. Hattie closed her eyes. The wind rattled the windows and shook the building. Down the hallway, she could hear Emily. "Father fell. Father fell."

⌒∾☙∾⌒

BACK AT THE HALL, BLANCHE CALLED THE BABYSITTER. "Tara, I'm going to be away longer than I expected," she explained. "Can you stay with Reba for another day or so?"

"No problem," Tara assured her. "Reba's a perfect angel."

"Thanks, Tara. Hopefully I'll be home by tomorrow evening."

"Blanche, what's happening over there? I heard Bishop Malloy got into a fight at a bar and got stabbed."

Sweet Jesus, Blanche thought. Word of the bishop's death was out, and rumours were already swirling. "A fight in a bar, Tara?"

"Everybody's talking about it."

"Tara," Blanche said, trying to suppress her impatience, "the bishop was *not* killed in a bar fight."

"Well, it's all over the news," Tara continued. Before Blanche had a chance to respond, she said, "Coop called this morning. He's dropping by this afternoon. Said he got some business in Corner Brook. He wants to take Reba out for ice cream. I…I didn't know if that was okay with you."

"That's fine, Tara. Coop can see Reba whenever he likes."

"Okay, good. I'll put Reba on now."

Blanche could hear Tara's muffled voice. "Mommy's on the phone."

"Hello?"

"Mommy?"

"How are you, baby?"

"Mommy, guess what? Daddy's taking me for ice cream."

"Wow! You're such a lucky girl."

"I think I'll have chocolate…or maybe pink…No, I think I'll have green."

"Sounds like a big decision."

"I'm watching *Romper Room,* Mommy. Miss Nancy sang a new song today. I'm going to sing it for Daddy. You want to hear it?"

"Sure, baby."

"Hop, little bunny, hop, hop, hop."

Blanche heard footsteps coming down the stairs, and moments later, Skid Snooks came to stand in the doorway. Drops of rain beaded his forehead, and his blond hair was plastered against his head. She waved him inside, and motioned for him to sit.

On the phone, Reba continued to sing. "Hop, little bunny, hop, hop, hop."

"That's a great song, Reba. Maybe you can sing it for me when I get home."

"When you coming home, Mommy?"

"Probably tomorrow, baby, but I have to go now. There's someone waiting to see me. Have a nice visit with Daddy. I'll call you again this evening. Okay?"

"Okay, Mommy. Goodbye."

Blanche hung up the phone and turned to Skid, who had taken a seat at the table. He had hung his raincoat on a peg, and it was dripping water onto the tiled floor.

"Hi, Skid," she said, taking a seat across from him. "Thank you for coming out in such wet weather. I could've picked you up, though."

"That's okay, maid. I don't mind the rain." Skid's eyes didn't quite meet hers as he spoke. Blanche had met him on a couple of occasions. He looked no more than twenty. When he was drunk—which was often—he could be obnoxious, but sober he was quiet and reserved.

"I was just going to make a cup of tea. Would you like tea or coffee? I can have it ready in a few minutes."

"Can I have some water? Me mouth is right dry."

Blanche found a tea bag and plugged in the kettle before getting a glass of tap water for Skid. She was about to sit down when the phone rang. "Constable Ste Croix here," she said in a clipped voice.

"Hello, Blanche."

"Chief Legge? Hello."

"Would Martin be around?"

"Not at the moment. He had to go out. Is there anything I can help you with?"

"When is Martin expected back?"

"I'm not sure. Would you like for me to have him call you?"

"No. No, I'll get back to him."

"Are you sure there's nothing I can do for you?"

"No, I'll wait for Martin."

Of course you'll wait for Martin. Blanche poured water on the tea bag and brought the mug to the table. She picked up her notebook and got down to business.

"Skid, I understand you found the archbishop's body."

He nodded. "Me and Jigger did."

"Tell me what happened."

Skid looked down at his hands. "I don't remember much."

"Herb and Jigger said they took the body to Herb's store."

Skid shrugged. "Yeah, I guess that's what happened. Jigger says we were walking along the beach, and I tripped over the body."

"You mean, you don't remember?"

"I was drunk," Skid said sheepishly.

Blanche nodded, recalling her father's alcoholic blackouts. "What *do* you remember?"

"I remembers walking along the beach to Jigger's house, but that was before."

"Before you started drinking?"

Skid sighed. "Yeah."

"And what time was that?"

"Around nine...I guess..."

"Did you see anyone?"

"Gert and Nellie was walking along the shore. And I seen a couple of guys from that van that's parked out on Gull's Head."

Blanche nodded. This was consistent with what the others had told her. "Anyone else?"

"The only other person I seen was Linda Bursey."

Blanche stared at him. "Martin's daughter?"

CHAPTER 16

◦~✹~◦

April 1963

BY MID-APRIL MOST OF THE ICE HAD LEFT THE HARBOUR AND THE ferry had started running again. Sun filtered in through the long, narrow windows in Gert's kitchen. My spirits lifted as I arranged biscuits on a tray and poured tea for Gert and her sister, Nellie. Even Juney, sitting at the kitchen table with her sour look, couldn't dampen my mood. Nellie had brought her granddaughter, Patsy, who she held on her lap. Patsy, a plump, rosy-cheeked little girl, was bigger than Eddie, even though she was six months younger.

"Your mother's time must be nearing," Nellie said. She took a biscuit from the plate and handed it to Patsy.

"Ma's due in another three weeks."

"I s'pose if she gets a girl, she'll name it Hazel after the baby she lost," Gert said.

"Oh, no," I said. "If it's a girl, her name's gonna be Zakia. And if it's a boy, she's calling him Abdul. Kate wanted to name him Bunga."

Gert looked stunned. "Where in the name of God did she find names like that?"

Juney rolled her eyes. "From the grade four geography book."

"Our Kate loves *Visitors in Other Lands*," I said.

"Bunga lives in a jungle in Africa," Juney said. "And Zakia..." She wrinkled her forehead. "I forgets where Zakia and Abdul lives."

"In a village on the west bank of the Nile," I said.

"Good God," Gert said. "Don't tell me she's naming the poor youngster after some heathen."

"Ma really likes the names," I said.

"I thinks Zakia is a cute name," Nellie said. "It's different, that's for sure."

Gert shook her head. "Who names their youngster after people in a book?"

"Sure, that book's been around since Judy was in school," Nellie said. "Judy was right fascinated with the Eskimos. I s'pose 'tis good for youngsters to know there's other places in the world besides the island."

"I hates that book," Juney said sullenly. "When I finishes school, I wants to be a hairdresser. Won't need to know geography or none of that stuff to cut and style hair."

Gert made a face. "Half the stuff they teaches nowadays is useless."

"We're learning about Confederation now," Juney said. "What can be more useless than that?"

I stared hard at Juney. Why did she get to go to school and not me? I missed the stories Miss Foster told of jungles and plains and people in faraway places. I missed writing essays and discussing the stories we read. I missed being with people my own age.

"'Tis good to know about Canada," Nellie said. "We're all Canadians now, sure."

"Not me," Gert said. "I'm no Canadian."

"You is, whether you likes it or not," Nellie said. "Sure, 'tis going on fourteen years since we joined."

"Miss Foster says there are advantages to being a Canadian," I said.

"I can't think of none," Gert said.

At that moment, I glimpsed Ivy through the window. She was making her way to the front door, and I could tell she was upset. I felt my stomach twist. Was something wrong with Ma? She'd been feeling poorly lately.

I went to the door, opening it just as Ivy reached the stoop. Her eyes were puffy from crying, her cheeks streaked with tears. "Blanche," she said, grabbing my arm, "you got to come home."

"What's wrong, Ivy?" I asked, pulling her into the foyer. Fear grabbed at my gut. "Is it Ma?" I asked anxiously. "It's not her time, is it?"

Kate shook her head. "'Tis Da. He knocked Gabe out cold. Ma can't get him to wake up." She tugged again on my arm. "Please, Blanche. You got to come home."

Without a word, I went to get my coat, my heart racing. "I have to go," I told Gert.

Nellie came into the foyer, looking concerned. "Is everything okay, my love?"

"Da beat up Gabe," Ivy said.

Nellie took a step toward Ivy. "Is he hurt?"

"He's knocked out," Ivy said.

"Good heavens, is they killing one annuder?" I heard Gert tsk-tsking from the kitchen.

"Take care, now," Nellie said as we were leaving. Her face was filled with concern.

"Was Da drinking?" I asked Ivy once we were outside.

Ivy shrugged. "I dunno, but he's really mad. He kicked Gabe in the ribs. When Ma tried to stop it, he hit her in the face."

My stomach went queasy. It wasn't the first time Old AC had used his fists or feet on Gabe—on all of us. I had felt the weight of his thick paw up the side of my head. Old AC terrorized all of us. Ma, however, took the brunt of his cruelty. We often heard her muffled cries at night. She would appear at the breakfast table the next morning with bruises on her face.

We walked the rest of the way in silence. Boats, stages, wharves, and lobster traps that had been covered with snow all winter were now visible. A few stubborn icicles hung dripping from the eaves of houses. Water gurgled from gutters, pouring into rain barrels. We carefully walked around the large puddles in the road to avoid getting our feet soaked.

My stomach tightened with dread as we neared the house. "Is Kate or Jimmy home?"

"Jimmy's helping Ken Foley with his lobster traps," Ivy said. "Ma told Kate to take Eddie outdoors for a walk. He was crying and right upsat."

I couldn't help wondering what all of this was doing to Eddie.

I hesitated before opening the door, not knowing what I would find inside. Gabe was sitting on a chair at the kitchen table, bent over in pain. Ma was beside him, a basin of water in front of her. She dabbed at a cut on his lip. His left eye was nearly swollen shut, his face already starting to darken into bruises. Da was nowhere in sight.

Ma handed me an enamel washbasin. "Here, Blanche, throw this away and get more water from the kettle."

I took the basin, feeling sick at the sight of the bright red water. I threw the water outside the door and poured more from the kettle.

After placing the basin on the table, I knelt beside Gabe's chair. "Looks like he beat you up pretty bad," I said. "What set him off this time?"

"He don't need nothing to set him off," Ma said. "I can't believe the brute could do that to an innocent youngster." Her voice was angry, and for a moment I remembered the kind of mother she used to be—fierce, protective.

"Where's Da now?"

"Damn coward took off." Gabe pressed his lips together. "I oughta go after him and beat him up." He shifted in his chair, and let out a moan of pain.

"Probably over at Rosie's, drinking away the last of his money," Ma said. "He don't even bother to come home most nights now."

Rosie O'Leary was the local bootlegger. She made homebrew and moonshine which she sold night and day, seven days a week. Men, and sometimes women, could be seen coming and going from her place at all hours. The RCMP had closed down her business twice. However, as soon as they left, Rosie would open up her house and it was business as usual.

"Ma, have you thought of pressing charges?" I asked.

"If I thought it would make a difference, I would," she said. "I'd like to see him locked up. Problem is, he'd get away with it, and he knows it."

Ma got up from her chair and looked around the dismal room. Her face sagged with exhaustion. It looked as if everything had been sucked out of her. "I'm sorry," she said, but it wasn't clear if she was speaking to me, Gabe, or both of us. And it wasn't clear just what she was sorry for. Sorry for bringing us into this mess? Sorry we were trapped in a dirty hovel with a drunk? Sorry there was not a thing she could do about it?

CHAPTER 17

❦

"EMILY'S SLEEPING," MARTIN REPORTED WHEN HE RETURNED TO THE hall later that afternoon. "They gave her a sedative to calm her."

"What's bothering her?" Blanche asked.

"It's her father's death." Martin removed his raincoat and hung it on one of the row of pegs. "It had a great impact on Emily. I can't imagine what the trigger was this time."

"I'm sorry," Blanche said.

"Everything's under control now." Martin poured himself a mug of coffee before taking a seat at the table. "I'll be happy when the forensic team gets here," he said. "It's difficult to do a job when we don't have the right tools."

"We can only do the best we can," Blanche said.

"Linda told me a reporter called the house this morning. I told her to tell them to direct all calls to this number."

"No reporters called while you were out," Blanche said. "There are all kinds of rumours circulating, though." She told Martin about her phone call with the sitter.

"A bar fight?" Martin shook his head in disbelief.

"She said she heard it on the news."

"No doubt she did." Martin ran a hand through his thick hair. "God knows what kind of stuff they're making up. But we have no control over that." He smiled at Blanche. "How's our sweet Reba?"

"She's great. Coop's coming by this afternoon to take her out for ice cream."

"Ah, the way to a kid's heart."

"Both Reba and Coop love ice cream." Blanche grinned. "Coop more so than Reba."

Martin peered at her. "Blanche, don't answer this if you think I'm being too personal, but why did you and Coop break up? I always thought you were good for each other. I recall Emily saying, 'Don't Blanche and Coop make a handsome young couple.'"

Although Martin was Blanche's superior, he was also her friend. "We drifted apart," she said. "We're working on getting back together, but..." She shrugged. "Who knows? In any case, we still care about each other, and we'll always remain friends for Reba's sake."

Martin nodded. "A child needs her father in her life. Sometimes when parents separate, they become bitter and it's the children who suffer. I'm glad that is not the case here."

"Coop has always been a good father," Blanche said. "I wouldn't deny him access to our daughter. I blame myself more for the breakup than Coop. His trust in me is broken. I've kept so much from him."

Martin stared at her. "You told him about...about that night?"

Blanche nodded. "I just wish I hadn't waited so long."

Martin frowned.

"Don't worry," Blanche hurried on. "Coop vowed never to mention it."

"Is that the reason you broke up?"

"No. It was because I had kept things from him. Coop was very disappointed—more disappointed about the secret I'd kept than anything else." Blanche looked down at her hands. "By that time the gap between us had grown so wide, we couldn't bridge it."

Martin looked at her with concern.

"I'm sure you must have told Emily."

"Yes, I did," Martin admitted. "It helped. I trusted Emily completely."

"The same way I trust Coop," Blanche said. "You know he's a good man. He's always put mine and Reba's welfare above all else."

"I've known Coop Pickford all his life. He *is* a good guy." Martin touched Blanche's arm. "I sometimes wonder if I made the right call back then." He blew out his breath. "You were no more than a

child, and burdened with things no child should be burdened with."
He leaned back in his chair and studied her. "Blanche, tell me
honestly, did I do the right thing?"

"I'm glad you did what you did," Blanche said without hesita-
tion. "It would've been horrible no matter what, but I'm glad you
made the decision you did." She reached for her cigarettes. "I still
have nightmares. The secret is like a dark shadow at the centre of
my life. Still, I'm glad only a few people know about it."

Martin nodded, looking relieved.

Blanche lit a cigarette. "I was able to get a statement from
Miranda and Prospero this afternoon," she said, eager to change
the subject.

"How did that go?"

Blanche gave a short laugh. "The Great Prospero is no more
British than I am. A dentist from Ontario, for Christ's sake. His
real name is David Stevens."

"Why pretend to be British?"

"He says it's part of his act." Blanche gave Martin a brief
rundown of her visit. "He claims his subjects are never completely
under his spell. He says they can come out of hypnosis at any time
they want."

"Hmm. That's not going to help Jake's case if Prospero is
called to testify."

"Testify? I hope it doesn't come to that."

"It's a possibility." Martin took a gulp of coffee and set down
his mug. "Have you had a chance to do more interviews?"

"I did, actually. Skid Snooks came in this afternoon.
Unfortunately, he was too drunk last night to remember much."

Martin shook his head. "That lad's headed for big trouble—he
and Jigger both."

"A shame," Blanche said. She couldn't put off telling him any
longer. "But Martin, Skid says he saw Linda walking on the beach.
That was *before* he started drinking."

"My Linda?"

Blanche shrugged. "Well…according to Skid."

"That's strange," Martin mused. "Linda must have gone out
while the kids and I were watching *Little House on the Prairie*."

"What time was that?"

"It's on seven-thirty to eight-thirty."

Blanche consulted her notebook. "Skid says he saw Linda around nine o'clock."

Martin shook his head. "No, that's not possible. Linda came into the living room as soon as the program ended to tell the boys it was time to get ready for bed."

"Could she have gone out *after* the children were asleep?"

"No," Martin said. "Linda was with me all evening. In fact, the only other time she left the house was yesterday morning to go visit her mother."

Blanche pondered this. Could Skid have gotten the time mixed up? Not if he'd seen Nellie and Gert walking toward Devil's Rock. They were both at the hall until eight-thirty.

"I'll speak with Linda when I get home," Martin said.

Before Blanche had a chance to say anything else, the phone rang. "That's probably Chief Legge," she said. "He called earlier wanting to speak with you."

Martin picked up the phone. "Hello?...Bill. What's happening?"

Blanche hoisted Bishop Malloy's suitcase onto the table. She'd brought it in from the cruiser earlier, but hadn't had a chance to go through it.

"Everything's fine here," she heard Martin say into the phone. "Blanche has everything under control."

Blanche tried not to show her annoyance. Of course, Martin had more experience. Still, she was in charge of the investigation. Martin was only there to help out. She undid the clasps of the suitcase and lifted the lid. Two neatly pressed mauve shirts lay on top.

"His real name is David Stevens," she heard Martin say.

Blanche laid the shirts on the table and removed a knitted cardigan, pyjamas, and slippers from the suitcase. She picked up a woollen garment, a band of white adorned with six black crosses.

Martin hung up the phone. "Bill's going to check out Prospero and Miranda."

Blanche nodded, still trying to keep her emotions in check. She showed Martin the garment. "What do we have here?"

"That's a pallium," Martin explained. "It's worn around the archbishop's neck, pinned to his chasuble." He touched her shoulder. "Are you okay?"

Blanche nodded. "I feel like a voyeur," she said, "poking through a dead man's belongings." She concentrated on the task at hand. As much as she tried to ignore Bill Legge and his chauvinistic views, she found herself wandering down memory lane. She recalled the questions Legge had asked at her interview after she applied to the force. "You have a young child. What if she gets sick? How does your husband feel about you wanting to join the force? I can't see my wife taking on something like that."

Blanche had batted the answers back just as quickly as Legge had asked the questions. "My husband is very supportive. If my child has a cold or sniffles, the sitter is perfectly capable of taking care of her. If she becomes seriously ill, I will take time off from work like you did when your son was ill." Bill's underage son, who had been hospitalized for alcohol poisoning, had been on the critical list. She recalled how Bill had looked her up and down, taking in her slim figure. "There are a lot of bad people out there," he said. "Sometimes we have to apprehend them. That takes a lot of physical strength. Think you can you handle it?"

"I'm in great shape," Blanche had told him, looking pointedly at Bill's protruding gut. "I will have no problem chasing down and apprehending criminals."

"A penny for your thoughts, Blanche," Martin said, bringing her out of her reverie.

"I was just recalling my interview, when I wanted to join the force."

"You did really well," Martin told her. "Even Bill thought so." He smiled. "Rather begrudgingly."

Blanche put down the pallium, picked up a small beige cord with tassels at both ends, and showed it to Martin.

"That's a cincture," he said. "It symbolizes chastity."

"Looks like tea or pop got spilled on it." Blanche rubbed at a small stain before placing the cincture on the table with the other items. At the bottom of the suitcase, she found a bottle of wine, a chalice, and a bag of communion hosts. She removed two pairs of drawers made from white woven linen. "I've always wondered if the archbishop wore boxers or briefs," she joked.

Martin chuckled. "Well, now you know."

"What do we have here?" Blanche pulled a flask of whiskey from the suitcase. "Can whiskey be used in the chalice instead of wine?"

"Christ, Blanche." Martin barked out a laugh. "No, I'm pretty sure whiskey wasn't passed around at the last supper."

Blanche shrugged. "I'm afraid I'm a lapsed Catholic," she said. "When Coop and I were together, we attended mass every Sunday. Coop still does, I imagine, but I drifted away."

"Most Catholics don't know a whole lot about their religion," Martin said.

Blanche held up the half-empty bottle. "Looks like His Grace already had a nip or two."

Martin narrowed his eyes. "The bishop was driving with open liquor in his car."

Blanche checked a side pocket on the inside of the suitcase. She found a roll of Tums, a package of gum, and a pack of Ex-Lax. There was also a vial of prescription drugs. "Seconal," she said, reading the label. "Take one capsule at bedtime when necessary for sleep." The prescribing physician was Dr. John Cunningham, a well-known psychiatrist in Newfoundland. The RCMP often brought him in to testify in criminal cases.

"Barbiturates and booze," Martin said grimly. "A deadly combination."

Among the paraphernalia in the suitcase, Blanche found two letters addressed to the bishop. On one envelope the sender had written *Private and confidential.* She was about to open it when she heard footsteps walking across the stage.

"Anybody home?"

Patsy.

"We're in the kitchen," Martin called.

Blanche shoved the items back inside the suitcase and closed the lid. She stuffed the letters in the pocket of her trousers.

Patsy came to stand in the doorway, wet hair plastered to her head. She was wearing a blue jacket with a pattern of Dalmatians, and it was soaked through. "Nan said you wanted to talk to me."

"You didn't have to come out in the rain, my love," Martin said. "We could've gone and picked you up."

"It's okay." Patsy heaved a sigh. "I wanted to get away from the house."

"Why don't you get out of that wet coat?" Blanche handed Patsy a tea towel.

"Patsy, you'll have to come visit us soon," Martin said. "Linda's been asking about you."

"I've been meaning to call after she gets settled." Patsy removed her coat and wiped her face with the towel. "How's Timmy and Myron?"

"Timmy's going into grade one in September," Martin said. "And Myron will be starting preschool."

"I can't wait to see them again," she said, but Blanche noticed a shadow pass over her face. Patsy took a seat at the table, and Blanche poured her a cup of steaming tea.

"Have a biscuit." Martin pushed the plate toward Patsy.

Patsy took a biscuit and slathered it with butter.

Blanche glanced at Patsy's finger, noting the turquoise stone in her ring. Had she replaced it after losing the first stone?

Martin opened his notebook. "What time did Bishop Malloy arrive at your grandmother's house, Patsy?"

"Between seven-thirty and eight, I guess."

"You must have been surprised when he showed up unannounced."

"Well, I wasn't expecting him." She looked at Martin. "What a nice car he got...had. Who'll get that now?"

Blanche stared at her. It was an odd question.

"I imagine it will go to the church," Martin said, glancing up at her. "What did the bishop say when you opened the door?"

"He...I don't remember, exactly."

"You invited him in?"

"Yeah."

"How long did he stay?"

Patsy studied her red nail polish. "I don't know. Twenty minutes, maybe."

"And what did you two talk about?"

Patsy shrugged. "Nothing much. I told him Aunt Gert and Uncle Jake was out. Told him Aunt Gert wasn't expecting him 'til tomorrow."

"Anything else?"

Patsy fidgeted with a paper napkin, twisting it in her hands. "I told him that Aunt Gert always keeps her door unlocked." She glanced up at Martin. "I wanted him to know that he could go over there if he wanted to."

Martin nodded. "And what else?"

Patsy shook her head. "Nothing."

She's nervous, Blanche thought as she studied her carefully.

"That's a very short conversation," Martin teased. "I'd say it would take about two minutes, tops." He smiled at Patsy. "What did you and His Grace do for the remaining eighteen minutes? Sit and stare at one another?"

"I can't remember *everything*," Patsy said, her eyes downcast.

"What *do* you remember?" Martin asked.

"I told you everything I can think of," Patsy said, and there was no mistaking the anxiety in her voice.

"Where did you go after you left the house?" Blanche asked.

"I went for a walk on the beach."

Blanche and Martin exchanged looks.

"Did you see anything suspicious?" Martin asked. "Did you talk to anyone?"

"Nothing suspicious," Patsy said, "but I met a boy from away. He was about my age. Maybe a bit older. He was searching the beach for pop bottles."

"What did he look like?" Blanche asked.

Patsy picked at her fingernails. "He was like right scraggly looking. He had on a red hooded sweater with a black peace sign on the back."

"Do you know his name?"

"No, he didn't say."

Martin scribbled in his notebook. "Anything else?"

"No."

Martin peered at her. "Are you sure?"

Patsy pushed her chair away from the table and stood up. "I have to go."

"Aren't you going to finish your tea?" Blanche asked.

"I have to go." Patsy reached for her coat.

"Okay, my love," Martin said. "But if you think of anything else, let us know. Want me to drive you home?"

"No, I'm okay." Patsy put on her wet coat and buttoned it up.

"Thank you for coming in," Blanche said, following her to the door.

Patsy didn't answer.

"She's keeping something from us," Blanche said when Patsy was out of earshot.

Martin nodded. "That's obvious."

"Martin," Blanche said, "about that stone you found this morning."

Martin waited.

"Patsy was wearing a ring last evening with a similar stone. They sell them at Ryan's, so a lot of young people probably have them."

"I noticed she was wearing a different ring today," Martin said.

"Actually, it's the same ring." Blanche brushed at crumbs on the table. "It comes with interchangeable stones."

Martin stared at her for a long moment. "You think Patsy might be mixed up in this?"

"She's hiding something."

"Yes," Martin agreed. "And we have to consider that Patsy was one of the last people to see the archbishop alive."

CHAPTER 18

April 1963

Gabe had been missing for two days now and Ma was nearly out of her mind with worry. The day before, Jimmy and I had gone all over the Island, knocking on doors, trying to find out if anyone had seen him. We had already searched the woods and the abandoned fish stages down by the waterfront. We showed his picture to the crew on the ferry. No one had seen him. We figured he must have stowed away on the *Northern Ranger* when she came to the island the night after Da's beating. Where else could he be?

On the third day of Gabe's disappearance, Ma woke me up in the middle of the night. "It's time," she said clutching her stomach. "I need you to run over to Rosie's and get your Da. Wake Ivy and Kate up; have them go fetch Aunt Hattie."

"Ma, you should go to the nursing station," I told her. "They'll even send someone to get you in the hospital Jeep, sure."

Ma shook her head. "Aunt Hattie borned all my babies," she said with determination. "I wants her here when this one comes. I don't feel comfortable around them British nurses."

By this time Ivy had come into the kitchen. "What's goin' on?" she asked, rubbing sleep from her eyes.

"Ivy, my love, you got to go fetch Aunt Hattie," Ma said. "Go wake up Kate. Blanche is going to look for your Da."

"Why don't I go for Aunt Hattie?" I said, thinking of the long walk my sisters would have in the darkness. "Kate and Ivy can go for Da."

A wave of pain crossed Ma's face, and I saw her clutch her stomach. "No, Ivy and Kate will go for Aunt Hattie," she said firmly.

Kate came into the kitchen, her hair tousled from sleep. She gave Ma a hug. "You okay?" she asked, sounding anxious.

"I'm fine," Ma said. "Go, my love, and fetch Aunt Hattie."

It was close to midnight when we set out. There was no moon, and the night was as dark as ink. I could hear the hoot of an owl, the cry of some animal. I turned on the flashlight that I intended to give to Ivy and Kate when we reached the end of the road. Rosie and Aunt Hattie lived in opposite directions.

"Maybe one of us should've stayed with Ma," Kate said. "What if the baby comes while we're out?"

Although that thought was not far from my mind, I tried to reassure my sisters. "Babies take their time coming," I said. "Ma's labour has just started. Besides, if we hurry, it shouldn't take us too long."

We walked in silence, the flashlight making pale, bobbing circles on the path. Surf crashed against the rocks, and the desolate bleat of the foghorn could be heard in the distance.

"I don't see why you have to go get Da," Ivy said. "What can he do?"

Nothing, I thought. *He'll only be in the way. He doesn't care about Ma or any of us.* "He'll probably want to know," I said.

Just before we reached the road, I thought I saw a figure huddled on a large rock. My first thought was that it might be a coyote. I stopped walking.

"What is it?" Ivy whispered. She sounded scared. We knew a foreign fishing boat was docked at the government wharf, and we were wary of strangers. We'd heard stories about men who came in off boats, breaking into houses and raping women. Nothing like that had ever happened on Darby's Island. I wasn't even sure if the stories were true. Still, we were cautious. We never went out at night unless it was absolutely necessary.

"Is someone there?" I called, aiming the flashlight at the figure. It was two figures, I realized—entwined in each other's arms. They broke apart quickly at the sound of my voice. A light went on in the darkness, and they began moving toward us.

"Well, now, what do we have here?" a voice rang out.

Coop Pickford?

"Who is it, Coop?" the person with him asked.

I recognized the voice as Susan Skinner's, Coop's latest girlfriend. Her father was the new manager at the fish plant. They had moved here a couple of months ago from St. John's. I'd seen Susan around the island, and she'd been at Gert's house a couple of times while I was there. She was a pretty girl with honey-coloured hair and large grey eyes. Coop often made her cookies and fudge. For Valentine's, he'd baked her a chocolate cake and decorated the icing with red candy hearts.

"Coop? You scared us," I said.

"What are you doing out this late, Blanche?" he asked. "And with the youngsters?"

"I could ask you the same thing,"

"It's Ma," Ivy said. "The baby's ready to come. We're going to get Aunt Hattie."

"She refuses to go to the nursing station," I said.

"Where's Jimmy?" Coop asked.

"He's over in Clark's Harbour helping Levi Diamond renovate his house. Left early this morning."

"Come with me," Coop said. "I'll hitch up the horse. That way, Aunt Hattie won't have to walk all the way down here in the dark. I know her legs's been bothering her."

Tears filled my eyes at Coop's kindness. I was glad it was too dark for anyone to see. "I appreciate it, Coop," I said.

"I'm happy to do it, my love."

"You two should go back to the house," I told Kate and Ivy. "Ma could use you right now. Coop will get the message to Aunt Hattie." I handed Ivy the flashlight. "Take this."

"You'll probably need it," Ivy said. "Sure, 'tis only a short ways back to the house."

"Aren't yeh coming with us?" Coop asked, sounding confused.

"I have to find Da," I said.

"He's over at Rosie's," Kate said. "Probably drunk again."

I felt my face burn, and again I was thankful for the darkness.

"Why don't we give Blanche our flashlight, Coop?" Susan said.

"Of course." Coop handed me the light. "It's not very bright, but it'll help." He touched my shoulder in the darkness. "Don't you worry about a thing, Blanche," he said. "Soon as I drops Susan off, I'll go straight to Aunt Hattie's."

As I approached Rosie's, I could hear music, shouting, and laughter. Lights blazed in all the windows. Patsy Cline was singing "So Wrong" on the gramophone. As I hurried up the narrow path to the house, I prayed that Da would be in a good mood. He was happiest when he was drinking.

I opened the door and walked into the kitchen. About half a dozen men were sitting at a large table playing cards. Stashes of change and dollar bills were in front of them. No one seemed to notice me as I walked in. I didn't know most of the people around the table. They came from all over the Island and beyond to visit Rosie's. Beer bottles lined the counters, and cases were piled up against one wall. Freddy Butler, Laverne Butler's seven-year-old son, was asleep on the daybed. His mother was nowhere in sight. Freddy lived with his father, but visited his mother on weekends. He was a hyper little boy who drove everyone crazy with his constant chatter. Even Miss Foster sometimes lost patience with him.

I walked down a narrow hallway and into the front room where couples were dancing. Others sat on sofas and chairs, drinking beer, talking, and laughing. I could have been invisible for all the attention they paid me. I didn't see Da anywhere. As I was about to leave, a man approached me. He put his arm around my waist. "Wanna dance, honey?"

"No," I said curtly, giving him a small push.

After a quick search of all the rooms on the first floor, I made my way up a set of wooden stairs that ran off the kitchen. At the top, I found myself in a narrow hallway with doors on each side. I opened the first door on my left. A naked man sat up in bed, shielding his eyes from the light that spilled in through the doorway. A woman was in bed beside him. I closed the door quickly, and hurried away.

I could hear voices and laughter coming from a room at the end of the hallway. I stopped a moment to listen. There was no mistaking Da's harsh laughter. I made my way down the hall, my heart pounding. I stood outside the open doorway for a brief moment. Da was sitting in a wing chair with Laverne Butler on his lap. She wore a tight black skirt and a white silk blouse. Her hair was teased into a beehive on top of her head. Her eyes were thick with mascara, and large hoops hung from her ears. Red lipstick kisses covered Da's face and bald head. My stomach turned queasy at the sight of them. I wanted to turn and run.

"Blanche?" Laverne said, her face registering surprise at the sight of me. "Something wrong?"

Da's head jerked up, and he stared at me in confusion.

"Ma asked me to come get you," I said. "Her time is come."

"Time?" he said, giving me a puzzled look.

"The baby's coming," I said.

"Oh, the baby," he said, as if he'd forgotten. He belched heartily. "I'll be home by and by, darling." He held up his bottle. "Soon as I finishes me beer."

Laverne smiled at me. "Would yeh like a beer, honey?"

I glared at her. "I'm too young to drink."

"How far apart is her contractions?" Laverne asked as I started toward the door.

Pretending not to hear, I kept walking.

"You never told me Grace was expecting," I heard Laverne say as I was walking away.

"Probably another split ass," Da said. "I already got three of them."

Laverne laughed. "You sounds just like my ex. He told me not to bring the baby home if it wasn't a boy. Not that he cared…"

Disgust filled me as I hurried down the wooden steps. At that moment, I hated old AC more than I hated anyone.

CHAPTER 19

◦◦◦◦◦

BLANCHE FELT HER STOMACH TIGHTEN AS SHE DROVE TO OLIVE'S office for her interview. Was Patsy keeping something from them? She'd talk to her again when she got a chance, she decided. Patsy might open up if they were alone. Something was going on with her, and Blanche intended to find out what it was.

There was no answer when she knocked on the administrator's door. *Strange*, she thought, glancing at her watch. Olive said she'd meet her between two and four. It was now twenty minutes past three.

"I think she's gone for the day," said a voice behind her.

Blanche whirled around to see Matt Stone, the caretaker. He was holding a mop. A package of tobacco stuck out of his shirt pocket. Matt was jack of all trades around the clinic and nursing home. He did janitorial work, carpentry, even drove the ambulance. He gave rides to the elderly and those too sick to walk to the clinic. He had his certificate in CPR and first aid.

"Seen Olive get in her car half an hour ago," he said.

"She went home?"

Matt shrugged. "I s'pose that's where she's gone to."

"She said she'd meet me."

Matt gave another shrug. "Never said nothing to me."

"She bought Charlie and Maud's house, right?"

Matt nodded. "That bungalow across the road from her father's house."

"Thanks, Matt. I'll drop by on my way home."

Had Olive forgotten their appointment? Blanche wondered as she walked down the hallway to Aunt Hattie's room. If something had come up, she should have called. Olive knew how important this meeting was.

Blanche was walking past the nurses' desk when Emily Bursey came shuffling along the corridor in green hospital garb. She stared straight ahead, her face blank.

"Hello, Emily," Blanche said. "Do you remember me? I'm Blanche Ste Croix. I work with Martin."

Emily gave her an empty stare, her eyes dull.

Blanche recalled what Martin had said: "Most days Emily doesn't even remember me."

Blanche felt a pang. Emily looked like a shadow of her former self. Her shoulders sagged and her mouth drooped sadly. Gone was the quiet elegance that had always impressed Blanche. Before Alzheimer's took its toll, she remembered Emily coming to staff parties with Martin, her clothes and makeup meticulous.

As she watched Emily shuffle out of sight, something niggled at the outer reaches of Blanche's consciousness. Something she couldn't quite put her finger on.

Aunt Hattie was staring out the window when Blanche walked into her room. "Blanche," she said, "I'm glad you could make it."

"Sorry it took so long."

"I heard about the archbishop." Aunt Hattie frowned. "They're saying Jake—"

"Jake's a suspect," Blanche confirmed, taking the chair reserved for visitors. "But the murder is still under investigation."

Aunt Hattie shook her head in that *I told you no good would come of this* sort of way. "Bishop Malloy came to see me on Friday. It was right after you left."

"Oh, that was nice of him."

"I thought so. He spent the afternoon here, and ate his supper in the cafeteria."

"I had an appointment with Olive this afternoon," Blanche said, "but she went home. I don't know if she forgot."

"Olive seems right...I don't know...distracted these days."

"When did you last speak with her?"

"Day before yesterday. I had a complaint about the food."

Blanche stared at her. Aunt Hattie never complained.

"The food here's not fit for a dog: Jell-O three times a week, canned beans and spaghetti, stale bread." Aunt Hattie made a face. "I hopes I never haves to stomach another hot dog."

Blanche frowned. "How long has this been going on?"

"For months now. We're all getting pretty sick of it."

"You had the right to complain," Blanche said, feeling a surge of outrage. If the allegations against the nursing home were true, someone needed to be held accountable.

"I s'pose," Aunt Hattie said. "Still, I've always had a soft spot for poor Olive. She was only eleven when her mother passed away."

Blanche nodded. "From what I hear, Herb took it hard."

"He started drinking heavily after poor Rita died. Left his two sons to fend for themselves." Aunt Hattie shook her head. "For years they lived in squalor without rules or supervision. By the time Herb married Nellie, they'd moved out of the house."

"I understand Olive and Nellie were good friends."

"They used to be playmates," Aunt Hattie said. "Sure, you'd see them together all the time. Olive was angry at her father for a long time. She'd come to the island and not even go visit him. She still has a lot of anger."

"I can only imagine," Blanche said.

Aunt Hattie looked sad. "Poor child."

"I just ran into Emily Bursey," Blanche said, taking the conversation in a new direction. "She didn't know me, of course. Martin said she was in a state this morning."

"She's not doing too well these days." Aunt Hattie frowned. "The past is coming back to haunt her. At least Emily's got a caring family. Her daughter came to visit yesterday afternoon. My, what a beautiful girl Linda turned out to be: beautiful green eyes and that long blond hair. She reminds me so much of Emily at that age."

"Linda was here yesterday afternoon?"

Aunt Hattie nodded. "Saw her in the cafeteria."

"What time was that?"

"Right after you left."

That's strange, Blanche thought. She was certain Martin had said that the only time Linda had left the house was to go visit her mother in the morning.

⚜

IT WAS NEARLY FOUR BY THE TIME BLANCHE PULLED IN FRONT OF Olive's bungalow. Tall pines surrounded the house. There were flowers beds planted on the well-tended lawn. Blanche parked the cruiser in a gravel driveway next to Olive's red Plymouth. Olive was one of the few people on the island who owned a vehicle. She took trips to St. John's, Nova Scotia, Ontario, and even to the United States for weeks at a time.

Blanche entered a long porch with storage shelves built along one wall. There was a deep-freeze next to a utility closet. Blanche knocked on the door, and waited.

"Come in," Olive called after a few moments.

Unlike most houses on the island, the front door opened into the front room, not the kitchen. Blanche heard running water and the rattle of dishes. "I'm in the kitchen," Olive said.

Blanche went to stand in an archway that divided the kitchen from the dining room. Olive was at the sink wearing a beige suit. Her hair, once dark, was now a coppery tone. It looked brittle from too many colourings. She had a rabbity overbite and spoke with a slight lisp.

"Hello, Olive," Blanche said casually.

Olive rinsed a glass bowl and put it on the drying rack. "Have a seat in the sitting room, Blanche," she said. "I'll be with you in a moment."

Blanche settled herself in a floral chair and looked around. The dark-panelled walls were bare except for a calendar with a picture of a Newfoundland dog. *Ryan's Variety* was written across the top. The furniture consisted of mismatched chairs and end tables. The television—a colour floor model—stood at one end of the room. On screen, a newscaster was interviewing President Ford.

After a while, Olive came out of the kitchen and sat across from her. "I was just washing up my breakfast dishes," she said.

She offered no explanation for leaving her office after agreeing to meet Blanche there.

"Nice house you have here."

Olive nodded without comment. She picked up a slim silver cigarette case from the end table and flicked it open with her thumb.

"Smoke?" She held the case out to Blanche.

Blanche rose from her chair and took a cigarette. Olive struck a match, lit Blanche's cigarette then her own.

"Yes, I thought it was right to pardon Richard Nixon," Ford was saying on television. "It's time we put this national nightmare to rest."

Olive got up from her chair, crossed the room, and turned off the set. "Speaking of nightmares," she said, "do you have any leads in the archbishop's murder? I heard you and Martin Bursey are in charge of the investigation."

"Just until forensics can get here." Blanche took a drag from her cigarette and blew out a plume of smoke. "Did you know Bishop Malloy, Olive?"

"Our paths have crossed over the years. When I worked for the Department of Social Services, I made placements for children at Mount Cashel and other Catholic orphanages." Olive gave Blanche a sidelong glance. "But of course you'd know that, since you were one of the children we rescued."

Suddenly it was too hot in the room. Old memories stirred to life.

For a moment, neither of them spoke.

"Aunt Hattie said Bishop Malloy came to the nursing home on Friday," Blanche said. "She was pleased he took time to visit her."

Olive smiled. "Whenever the bishop came to the island, he made a point of visiting the nursing home. I think he enjoyed the fuss the old people made over him. He had a good rapport with senior citizens. Aunt Amy always enjoyed his visits."

"How is Aunt Amy?"

"Doing well for a woman her age. A reporter from the CBC called last week wanting to interview her about being a midwife at the turn of the century."

"It would make a good story," Blanche said.

Olive agreed. "She was a midwife for over fifty years. She has stories about travelling by dog team to deliver babies."

"Aunt Hattie had the same experiences." Blanche turned to look at Olive. "I'm sure you know why I'm here."

Olive frowned, and for a few moments there was an awkward, tense silence. "Isn't it ironic?" Olive gave a short laugh.

Blanche stared at her, not sure what she was getting at.

"Honey, we thought you'd be the one on the wrong side of the law."

"We?" Blanche shot Olive a puzzled look.

"Well…the people at Child Protection Services."

Blanche glared at her.

"I certainly didn't expect you to be interrogating *me*." Olive flicked an ash from her cigarette. "You and your siblings were in a dire situation when we rescued you from that shack over in the Cove."

Please, Blanche thought, searching for a way to change the subject.

"A good thing we got there when we did," Olive continued.

"That was a long time ago," Blanche said, fighting to control her emotions.

Olive took a drag from her cigarette and squinted through a haze of smoke. "We were concerned about your family. What with your mother…"

Blanche balled her hands into fists. Who was Olive to judge—Olive with her criminal record? She'd given up two babies for adoption, and lost custody of her other two children. "Let's get back to the reason for my visit," she said firmly. "There are allegations that money is missing from the nursing home."

Olive waved a hand dismissively. "My former brother-in-law, Robert Dawe, is a lawyer in St. John's. He was supposed to be here today but got delayed because of the storm. I'd prefer to wait until he's present."

Blanche studied Olive with narrowed eyes. "I understand this is not the first time you've been investigated for fraud."

"No," Olive said stonily, "but I'm sure you know all the details."

Blanche couldn't deny that she'd been briefed before leaving Corner Brook yesterday. She had learned some disturbing information. During her tenure at Social Services, Olive had a client who was receiving disability benefits. He'd won a case against an insurance company for five thousand dollars. Olive told him he couldn't keep the money while on disability. She had him sign the cheque over to her then cashed it into her own account.

"I paid dearly for my mistakes," Olive said with a tinge of bitterness. "I lost my job, my husband, custody of our boys. It just about ruined my life." She shot Blanche a sour look. "I'm innocent until proven guilty."

"Of course," Blanche said, "but everything will come to light in the end."

Secrets have a way of destroying us, she thought, thinking of her own marriage.

CHAPTER 20

PATSY WALKED HOME IN THE RAIN, HER CONVERSATION WITH BLANCHE and Martin lingering in her mind. *I should've told the truth,* she thought. It was clear that Blanche had suspected something. *Maybe they think I killed Bishop Malloy.* She felt her face flush now, remembering her conversation with the archbishop on Friday evening. She recalled the glint in his eye as he read passages from *True Confession.* She had been so embarrassed she wanted to get up and run. And the bishop kept smiling, like he was enjoying himself. "Do you have a boyfriend, Patsy?" he asked her after he finished reading. "How far do you let the lad go?" She couldn't believe a bishop would ask such questions. She was never so glad to get a call from Joey Ryan. He wanted to know if they needed anything when he delivered their groceries on Saturday. After she'd hung up, Patsy told the bishop she had to go out. A friend needed her. She knew she was being disrespectful, but she'd had enough of his embarrassing questions.

She had roamed around the island for almost an hour before going down to the beach. The last person she expected to see again was Bishop Malloy. *And now he's dead,* Patsy thought as she walked toward the house. She shivered from the cold and from the memory. *No,* she told herself. *I can't think about that. Not now.*

"What were you doing out in weather like this?" Nan scolded when Patsy walked into the kitchen. "You're soaked to the skin, for God's sake. Where were you?"

"I was at the hall talking to Blanche and Martin. You said they wanted to see me."

"Well?" Nan looked at her, her face anxious.

"Well what?" Patsy took off her shoes and jacket. She laid the jacket across the woodbox next to the stove.

"What did you tell them?"

"I told them the bishop came and then the bishop left."

Patsy expected a reprimand for her flippant answer, but Nan seemed nervous. "They questioned me and your grandfather for half an hour," she said. "I told them everything I knows." She turned to Patsy, still anxious with worry. "Did they ask about us?"

"You mean, did they ask me if you or Grandpa killed Bishop Malloy?"

"Now, Patsy, don't you be so foolish." Nan shook her head. "Sure, the way you goes on is something ridiculous."

"They're questioning *everybody*, Nan."

"Yes, I s'pose they is." Nan was thoughtful. "They questioned the Ryans, the Foleys, the Duffys, all the Battens."

"Well, 'tis only natural that we'd be on their list."

"Yes," Nan said pensively.

Patsy glanced out the window. "Oh, no," she said, "here comes Aunt Gert. I think I'll go hide away in me room."

"Now, you be nice," Nan chided, but there was a hint of amusement in her eyes.

A few moments later, the door opened and Aunt Gert walked in. "The blessing of the fleet's been postponed 'til next Sunday," she said without preamble. "They're sending Father Schmidt from Racket Cove." She took a seat at the table and folded her hands in front of her. "I was hoping they'd send Monsignor Tobin."

"You should've told them you don't like Father Schmidt," Patsy said.

"G'wan with yeh, Patsy," Aunt Gert said. "What makes you think I don't like Father Schmidt?"

"You said so your own self. I heard you tell Uncle Jake that the Germans were all heathens."

"I said I *thought* they were heathens," Gert corrected. "What I *don't* like is Father Schmidt telling jokes and making people laugh in church."

"Sure, we could all use a good laugh once in a while," Nan said.

"Not in church," Gert said, adamantly. "Some of Father Schmidt's jokes is not fit to tell in a tavern, let alone on the altar." Her mouth tightened. "Take that joke he told on Christmas Eve during Midnight Mass."

"The Schmidt House joke," Patsy said.

"Schmidt House?" Nan looked confused.

"Father Schmidt's friend in Germany sent him a Christmas card," Patsy explained. "It had a picture of Santa's reindeer flying over an outhouse. His friend took a marker and wrote *Schmidt House* above it."

"Now, what kind of priest tells jokes like that in church?" Gert shook her head. "And right up on the altar where the Blessed Sacrament is."

"I thought it was funny," Patsy said.

Gert crossed her arms. "I'm sure *you* would."

"Aunt Gert, my dear, you needs to get a sense of humour."

"*Patsy!*" her grandmother reproached. "You knows better than to talk to Aunt Gert like that. Go get out of them wet clothes before you ends up with pneumonia."

"Youngsters nowadays." Gert pursed her lips. "No respect for nobody. One thing about my crowd is that they knows better than to talk back. Neilsy found that out the hard way, and he got that bump on his nose to remind him."

Patsy rolled her eyes as she disappeared down the hallway. Aunt Gert had the annoying habit of adding a 'y' to the names of her children: Neilsy, Lizzy, Coopy, Juney, Petey, Davy.

⤎ↁↂↃ⤏

"Patsy's not herself, maid," Nellie said when Patsy was out of earshot. "This whole business with the archbishop got her all upset."

Gert glared at her twin. "What's that got to do with anything?"

"Sure, you knows now how soft-hearted Patsy is. She's worried sick about her Uncle Jake. Stuff like that plays on her mind. Judy was the same way."

Gert tightened her lips. "You're spoiling that youngster, Nellie—spoiling her just like Pop spoiled you. Remember what poor Mom used to say about us?"

"Yes, I remembers," Nellie said fiercely. "I remembers only too well."

Their mother was forever comparing Nellie to her twin. Gert could knit, sew, and crochet, whereas Nellie was "all thumbs." She was about eight or nine when she'd heard a comment her mother made to a neighbour: "Somebody must've stole me other twin and left Nellie in her place. Never seen a youngster so clumsy. God help the man who gets that one."

"Sure, Mom always talked about how smart you was in school," Gert said, as if guessing what Nellie was thinking.

"That didn't impress Mom none," Nellie said. "As far as she was concerned, I'd never amount to anything. Then I ran away and got pregnant—"

"Well, Pop thought you was the icing on the cake. Sure, he used to brag to the men on the wharf about how good you could read, how fast you could add up sums."

Nellie nodded. There was no doubt her father had been proud of her. They'd been close when she was a child. Sometimes, it felt like he was the only one on her side. But after Nellie came home pregnant, she sensed a distance between them. Their relationship became strained, no longer easy and carefree. That had hurt Nellie more than all her mother's criticism.

A silence fell between the two sisters.

"God only knows when the ferry'll cross over again," Gert said after a while.

"I imagine Blanche is eager to get home," Nellie said. "Must be a big responsibility taking on a murder case. Her new on the force and all."

Gert sniffed. "Better she stayed home and looked after Reba."

"Blanche got a job to do," Nellie reminded her.

"Looking after Reba *is* her job," Gert said. "I don't know what's wrong with the young ones today. No sense of responsibility. Look at your Judy. Tramped off to the mainland, dumping her youngster on you and Herb."

Nellie glared at her sister. "Don't you dare put Judy down," she said. "I'm proud of my daughter. At least she had the good sense to get away from here. Nothing for young people here on the island. I wishes I'd had the guts to leave."

Gert glanced up at her twin, a stunned look on her face. "Why'd you want to leave when you got Herb? He says you're the best thing that happened to him." She shook her head. "You'd never hear Jake say that about me. Jake don't appreciate me one bit. Always puttin' me down, he is. Sure, you're lucky to have a man like Herb."

You and Mom reminded me of that often enough, Nellie thought bitterly.

"Sure, Herb worships the ground you walks on," Gert continued. "I've heard him say more than once that he'd kill anyone who so much as harmed a hair on your head." She peered at her twin. "And I dare say he would too."

CHAPTER 21

❧

April 1963

I STUMBLED AROUND IN THE BLACKNESS TRYING TO FIND ZAKIA'S bassinet. Not a bassinet, really, just a wicker laundry basket Aunt Hattie had given Ma. Aunt Hattie had gone home now and Ma, tired out from the birth, was in bed. Da hadn't even bothered to come home. Probably still with Laverne.

It was so dark in the room, I couldn't see a thing. I felt my way around, bumping into the furniture. It took a while to find the basket where Zakia was sleeping. I reached inside and grasped her hand. It was icy cold, and as stiff as a piece of wood. "Poor baby," I crooned. Why didn't I have the good sense to take her into bed with me? As I bent to pick up her frail little body, a full moon shone through the window lighting up the room. I could see Zakia's pale face, her lips blue and still. Then a cloud passed over the moon, and the room was plunged back into darkness. Panic filled me. *Oh, no. Oh, dear God, no! Not again.* I felt a scream escape from deep inside me.

"Blanche?" Someone was shaking me. "Blanche, wake up!"

I opened my eyes to see Coop beside me, his eyes soft and filled with concern. I stared at him in confusion. I was stretched out on a bed, covered by a homemade quilt, a chenille bedspread beneath me. Puzzled, I took in my surroundings. The walls of the room were done in light panel. A bureau that stood against one wall held a brush, comb, water jug, and ceramic wash basin. There was a wardrobe with a mirror. Rays of sunshine poured through the sheer white curtains.

"You were having a bad dream," Coop said. "Christ, girl, you scared me half to death."

"I'm sorry," I said, feeling embarrassed. Everything came back to me then—the events of last night as well as this morning. Little Zakia had been born around two, but it was well past four before I got to bed. I got up at seven to go to work. Gert and Juney were in Corner Brook and wouldn't be back until Sunday. I had worked until noon—until the boarders had finished their tea. By that time, I was swaying on my feet from exhaustion. Coop had insisted I lie down for a rest. He led me upstairs to his bedroom. I had lain down on the soft mattress in the double bed. I recalled Coop getting a quilt from the closet and covering me as carefully as a mother covering her child. "Rest awhile," he told me, and closed the door softly. I had closed my eyes, intending only to rest for a few moments.

"You had a good long nap," Coop said.

I sat up and yawned. "What time is it?"

Coop looked at his watch. "'Tis nearly three."

"Oh my God," I said, getting to my feet. "I don't even have all the beds made yet." In my head, I ran through all the things I needed to do. "Your mother gave me a list of chores to do while she's away. I'm to clean out the cupboards in the pantry, dust the front room, and polish the top of the stove. Why didn't you wake me up?"

"Slow down, Blanche." Coop put a steadying hand on my arm. "I made all the beds, and the dishes is all done. The stove and the cupboards can wait."

"You didn't have to do that."

"Well, I did. I figured you must be exhausted. Don't know why you even bothered coming here today after last night."

"Thanks," I said. I felt better after the long sleep, but I couldn't help wondering what Gert would say if she found out about this.

"I even made a pound cake," Coop said.

I sniffed the air. "So that's what that delicious lemony smell is."

"Yup." Coop turned to leave. "Meet me downstairs. I'll make a pot of tea, and we can have some cake."

"I'll be down in a minute," I told him. I folded the quilt and straightened the bedspread. Coop's room was twice as large as the bedroom the four of us shared at home. I noticed a framed picture of Susan on the bureau. It was her graduation picture, and she was wearing a black cap and gown. A strip of photographs—the kind you take in the photo booth at Woolworths—was wedged into the frame of the mirror. I picked it up and studied it. Coop and Susan were smiling and making silly faces. Coop had his arm draped around her shoulder. On the wall, next to the bureau, was one of Kate's paintings. I was surprised that Coop had kept it all this time. Kate had drawn a picture of Riley with Coop at the reins. There were three kids on the sleigh, all smiling and happy. In the picture, it was snowing roses and daisies.

I ran my finger through my tousled hair as I studied myself in the mirror. Despite the long nap, there were bags under my eyes and my face was pale. The dream had left me feeling uneasy. I knew it had been about Hazel, not Zakia. I had found little Hazel dead in her crib one cold winter night when she was barely five months old. Tears welled in my eyes at the memory. Hazel cried a lot, and Da was always hollering for me to shut her up. Why hadn't I taken her into bed with me?

When I went downstairs, Coop had set the table. The dishes were blue china with little windmills painted on. It amazed me that Gert's plates, saucers, cups, and bowls all matched. Everything in the house matched, it seemed.

Coop pulled out a chair from around the table. "Have a seat, Blanche."

He poured me a cup of tea and cut me a slice of cake before taking a seat at the table across from me.

"The cake looks delicious," I said, digging my fork in.

"The proof is in the pudding," Coop said, "or in this case, the cake."

I took a bite, liking how its moist sweetness felt against my tongue. "It's as delicious as it looks and smells."

Coop regarded me keenly. "What was all that ruckus about? Do yeh always have such noisy dreams?"

I felt my face flush. "I dreamed Zakia had died," I said, "just the way Hazel did. It was me who found Hazel." I shrugged. "Zakia's birth must have triggered memories of that night."

Coop was silent for a long minute. "Poor little Hazel," he said after a while. "Heartbreaking that was. I remember helping the old man build her coffin. The smallest coffin I'd ever seen. I was heartsick when we finished." He looked at me. "I can only imagine what 'twas like for you. For your poor mother, and for the rest of the family. Nobody should have to go through that."

Coop's kindness made it harder to fight back the tears that threatened. "I wasn't feeling well the night it happened," I said. "I usually took her into bed with me."

Coop reached across the table and covered my hand with his. "Blanche, my love, 'tis not good to keep all that stuff bottled up inside you. You're not to blame for what happened. Babies… well, sometimes they just die. Sure, look at Aunt Dulcie and Uncle Austin. Lost two babies within three years."

"I know," I said in a small voice.

"Guilt will eat at you like acid if you lets it." He gave my hand a brief squeeze before letting go.

For a few moments, we ate in silence. "That's one of the best cakes I've ever tasted," I said. "Instead of carpentry, you should look into the cooking program at the vocational school."

"Nah, 'tis building stuff that makes me happy. Cooking's just a hobby."

I leaned toward him. "You're a real jack of all trades."

Coop grinned. "And a master of none, as the saying goes." He turned to look at me, and his voice became serious. "Blanche," he said, "have yeh heard any news from Gabe?"

"Nothing," I said. "Ma's worried sick."

Coop grew thoughtful. "Funny he should just up and leave."

Nothing strange about running from a brute who beats him up every chance he gets, I thought, but I merely nodded. "We think he boarded the *Northern Ranger*," I said. "He probably went off to the mainland."

"I imagine you'll hear from him before long," Coop said thoughtfully.

"I hope so." I gulped down the rest of my tea and stood up. "Well, I should get to work."

Coop stood up. "Help me peel some vegetables to go with the pot roast," he said. "Then go on home. Yeh mother probably needs you more than we do here."

"What about the dusting?" I glanced toward the small shelf where Gert kept her ornaments.

Coop followed my gaze, taking in the little glass elephants, giraffes, tigers, and other figurines on the side table.

"Frig the dusting," he said. "Ma spends too much time on those useless little trinkets as it is. You needs to go home. Sure, you hardly had any time to spend with your new baby sister." His eyes locked with mine. "And she's the cutest little thing. Aunt Hattie let me hold Zakia when I went to pick her up this morning." Coop shook his head in amazement. "That sweet little face and that full head of jet-black hair." He gave me one of his lopsided grins. "Sure, she reminds me of her big sister."

I left Gert's around three-thirty that afternoon. It was unusually warm for April. The sun was shining, the sky cloudless. By now, Ivy and Kate would be home from school. I wondered how Ma was coping with the new baby. I felt a swell of pride, recalling how Aunt Hattie had allowed me to assist with Zakia's birth. When she'd delivered Hazel, I was sent to Nellie Eastman's with the younger children. This time, I had watched Aunt Hattie cut the cord, and wrap the baby in the white flannel blanket she'd brought with her. *We're lucky to have Aunt Hattie*, I thought. She was going to drop by sometime that afternoon. Ma needed all the support she could get. Whenever I thought of Old AC with Laverne, I felt a twinge of bitterness. Useless as an udder on a bull, he was.

As I hurried along, I couldn't help thinking about Coop. How pleasant my life would be if he was in charge. I kept replaying his words in my mind. *That sweet little face and that full head of jet-black hair. Sure, she reminds me of her big sister.* Something stirred inside me. I had known Coop all my life and I had never known this side of him, so gentle. *Coop has a girlfriend*, I reminded myself sharply.

I recalled how they'd been huddled together last night. So close you couldn't fit a toothpick between them. And as for being kind— Coop was kind to everyone. I recalled the day he took off his coat and wrapped it around Danny Hunt, who was shivering from the cold. The Hunts had no father and were probably as poor as we were. When Coop was in school, all the little kids would hang around him. Coop played with them and gave them piggyback rides. It was just the kind of person he was. He was treating me no differently. I'm sure he saw me as a kid. Probably felt sorry for me. My cheeks burned at the thought.

As I approached the house, I saw that Ivy and Kate were playing outside with Eddie. There was a big puddle of water in front of the door that Eddie kept jumping into with both feet. Each time he made a splash, he laughed heartily. I winced as I saw mud splatter his trousers. It was going to be difficult getting the stains out. However, it was so rare that he laughed that I decided to let it go.

"You're home early," Ivy said as I neared her.

"It's good to see you all playing outside on a day like this," I said. "Eddie could use the fresh air."

"Da told us to stay outside and play," Kate said. "A Mountie came to see him and Ma."

"A Mountie?" I echoed.

Kate nodded. "He's still inside."

Ivy folded her arms. "I think he came with news about Gabe."

CHAPTER 22

❧

"SOMETHING SMELLS GOOD," MARTIN SAID WHEN HE WALKED INTO the cottage. It was nice having Linda and the kids visit. He'd missed coming home to a cooked meal, having someone to chat with while he ate.

"Supper's ready, Dad," Linda said. "Baked beans and corn bread."

Martin smiled affectionately at his daughter. She looked exactly like Emily at that age. In pictures, you couldn't tell them apart. "Linda, my love, you're spoiling me."

Linda stood on her toes and kissed her father's cheek.

At that moment, the boys came into the room, both talking at once. "Grandpa, come see what we made with our Lego."

"Later," Linda said firmly. "It's time for supper. Go wash up, you two."

As the children disappeared down the hallway, Linda turned to Martin. "Dad, you've had quite a day. I couldn't believe it when Sissy Foley called to tell me the news."

"I'm as baffled as you are," Martin admitted.

"Sissy told me that you believe Jake Pickford murdered the bishop."

"Right now he's a suspect."

"Do you think…It's hard to believe." Linda shuddered. "A murder was the last thing I expected. And Jake…"

The children came back into the room and the adults stopped talking. Linda went to the stove and began ladling up platters of beans.

"The nursing home called," Martin said after they were seated around the table. "Your mother has calmed down."

"Yes, I spoke with one of the staff this afternoon." Linda's eyes locked with Martin's. "Dad, I wish you'd consider moving back to the city. I know how much Mom loved it here, but…" She shrugged. "I don't think it matters to her now where she is. And I know you're anxious to get back to work."

"I've been giving it some thought," Martin said.

"If you move back to Corner Brook, Caroline, Marty, and the girls will be able to visit more often. They hardly get to see Mom."

"We'll stay for the summer," Martin said, "see how it works out."

Linda looked pleased, and for the rest of the meal they listened as the boys prattled on about their day.

After the main course, Linda brought out a bakeapple pie for her and Martin, and cookies and milk for the children.

"Can we eat dessert in the living room?" Timmy asked.

"Promise me you won't spill your milk."

"Promise," Timmy said. He looked at Myron, who nodded in agreement.

Linda put the children's dessert on a tray and carried it into the living room. When she returned, she cut a slice of pie for Martin and another for herself.

For a few moments, they ate in silence.

"I hate to think there's a murderer running loose," Linda said. "I kept the door locked while you were gone."

"Some of the people I spoke with are devastated." Martin broke off a piece of pie with his fork. He gave his daughter a searching look. "Linda, Skid Snooks says he saw you on the beach last night."

Linda gazed down at her plate before answering. "I went for a walk while you and the boys were watching television," she said. "I was gone no more than twenty minutes. I saw a number of young people, but I don't recall seeing Skid." She shook her head. "I don't recognize half the people around here anymore."

"Me neither," Martin admitted. "They grow up fast. But Linda, forensics will want to talk with you."

Nodding, Linda pushed away her plate. She got up from the table and busied herself making coffee. She was about to sit down again when the phone rang.

"Dad, it's for you," she said. "Bill Legge."

Martin raised an eyebrow.

Linda handed her father the phone and disappeared into the living room.

"What's up, Chief?" Martin asked.

"I have some bad news, Martin."

"Oh?"

"The ferry got damaged in the storm. She has to be brought to St. John's for repair. It will be late Sunday or even Monday before we can get anyone over there."

Martin sighed inwardly. "Not much we can do then but wait."

"I was able to dig up some information on Prospero, a.k.a. David Stevens," Bill continued.

"Oh?"

"Your hypnotist has quite a sordid past."

Martin lowered himself into a nearby chair. "How so?"

"He has a record; he's spent time in jail."

Martin wasn't expecting that. "On what charge?"

"Manslaughter."

From the living room, Martin could hear the children's chatter. The theme song to *Bewitched* was just coming on.

"We're still gathering facts," the chief said. "We do know he served three years of a five-year sentence."

Martin felt his mouth drop open. "What about Prospero's partner?"

"Debra Brown was a bit of a radical in her youth, but no criminal record."

"Well," Martin said, "that's all very interesting."

"Yes," Bill agreed. "I'll keep you updated."

"I'd appreciate that."

"Well, look...I know you've had a busy day. I won't keep you from your family."

Long after Bill said goodbye, Martin sat staring at the phone, sifting through what he'd learned. Manslaughter? Had Prospero killed someone in a fit of rage? After a while, he got up from the table. It was time to pay the good hypnotist a visit.

❧

WHEN MARTIN KNOCKED ON THE TRAILER DOOR, THERE WAS NO answer. The Chevy, he noticed, was gone. He was about to walk away when he saw a movement at the window. He knocked again, louder this time. Still, no one came to the door.

Martin was walking back to his truck when a van with Nova Scotia licence plates drove onto the beach. From the partially open window he could hear rock music blasting. Martin guessed they were the hippies Gert had talked so much about. He'd intended to have a chat with them, and now the opportunity had presented itself.

Martin approached the van and tapped lightly on the window. The driver, a young man with glasses, frowned. The man in the passenger seat was wearing a set of white love beads. Both men wore tie-dyed T-shirts, their hair down to their shoulders. A few moments went by before the driver rolled down the window. "What do you want?"

"I'm Detective Bursey," Martin said. "I'd like to ask you a few questions."

The driver turned off the music. "What about?"

"About the murder committed here on this beach Friday evening."

The driver stared at him a moment longer. "You want to climb aboard?"

Martin hesitated. Was it a good idea to get in a vehicle with strangers? He was not carrying a weapon.

The driver turned to the man in the passenger seat. "Give him your seat, Darren."

Nodding, Darren stepped out of the vehicle and gestured for Martin to get in. Martin climbed aboard and closed the door. Darren got back in the van through the side door.

The overpowering stink of stale smoke, beer, sweat, and dirty socks assaulted Martin's nostrils. Empty pop and beer bottles rolled around on the floor. Sleeping bags and blankets were piled high. Chips, cookies, and candy bars spilled from open bags.

Martin smiled at the driver, who gave him a quick once-over. "Where in Nova Scotia are you from?" he asked, taking the friendly approach.

"I'm from Amherst."

Martin reached for his notebook. "What are your names?"

"Steve Smith," said the driver.

"Darren Burns," the other man replied. He had taken a seat on the floor behind the driver's seat. "I'm from Truro."

"How many of you are staying here?"

"There are four of us," Steve said. "The others are Henry Lange and Rick Carey."

"Were you on the beach Friday evening?"

"I was with Rick and Henry," Steve said. "We drove around for a while."

"I went for a walk by myself," Darren said.

"Did any of you see the archbishop?"

"Yes," Darren answered. "He was walking that way." He pointed in the direction of Devil's Rock.

"And what time was that?"

"Between nine and nine-thirty."

"Was there anyone else around?"

"Lots of people," Darren said. "I saw two women walking this way."

Nellie and Gert, Martin thought.

"Have you checked with that guy who parks his station wagon just over there?" Darren pointed vaguely out the window. "His name's Ward something or other. His car's been here a few days now. He moved his vehicle this morning. Still, he has to be around somewhere."

"What did he look like?" Martin asked.

"A young guy," Steve said, "no more than sixteen or seventeen, if I had to guess. He comes around looking for pop bottles."

Must be the same guy Patsy saw, Martin thought. "Anyone else?"

"A couple of men," Steve said, "wearing jeans and jackets."
Could be almost anyone.

"There was a girl with long red hair," Steve broke in. "She was wearing a jacket with a pattern of dogs on it."

Martin tried not to show surprise. "What kind of dogs?" he asked. But even before Steve answered, he knew.

"Dalmatians."

CHAPTER 23

༺⚜༻

April 1963

I STARED AT THE HOUSE, ALMOST AFRAID TO GO INSIDE.

"Did the Mountie say what happened to Gabe?" I looked from Kate to Ivy.

Ivy shrugged. "They just got here."

"They?"

"There's a lady with him," Kate said. "She said she was a… um…a…"

"A social worker," Ivy said.

Kate nodded. "A social worker is what she is. D'ya think our Gabe's in trouble?"

"I don't think so," I said, even though I was not totally convinced. I looked around for Eddie and saw him wandering down toward the landwash. I caught up with him and grabbed his hand in mine. "Keep an eye on this guy," I told the girls. "The last thing we need is for him to go wandering off."

I took a deep breath and started toward the house.

A woman wearing a blue pleated skirt and matching sweater was sitting on one of the two chairs in the kitchen. She had taken off her coat and draped it over the back of her chair. A Mountie sat at the other end of the table. Da was sitting on one of the benches, a grim look on his face. "There's Blanche now," said Jimmy as if they'd been discussing me. Even though there was plenty of room at the table, he was perched on his apple crate in the corner of the room. I knew Jimmy was expected home today, but I didn't think it would be this early.

"Blanche, my love, you're early," Ma said.

"Gert's in Corner Brook, and Coop let me off early." I watched as Ma poured tea into mugs for her guests. The grey shift she wore was as baggy as a flour sack. She looked exhausted. The bags under her eyes were as dark as bruises.

I nodded at the visitors and tried to manage a smile. "Need any help?" I asked Ma.

Before she had a chance to answer, the baby began to cry. "I'll take care of the tea, Ma." I took off my jacket and hung it on the wooden peg.

"Thanks, Blanche, my love," Ma said as she hurried toward the bedroom.

The Mountie stood up. He was tall with dark hair that was just starting to go grey. "So this is Blanche," he said, smiling. "It's been years since I've seen you."

I stared at him, confused.

"I'm Martin Bursey," he said. "I've known you since you were this high." He placed his hand at waist level. "How have you been, my love?"

"Fine," I answered. "I'm sorry I didn't recognize you." Martin had grown up on the island. I remembered him coming summers with his wife and two children. It was probably why he'd been sent instead of another officer.

Martin gestured to the lady at the other end of the table. "This is Pamela Kelly," he said. "She's with Social Services."

Pamela stood, and stretched out her hand to me. "Nice to meet you, Blanche." She smiled, showing large straight teeth. Her auburn hair was a cap of tiny curls as if she'd just had a home perm. She wore cat's-eye glasses and pink lipstick.

"Pleased to meet you," I said, my throat thick with anxiety. Why were they here?

I went to the stove, picked up the teapot, and began pouring the tea into cups. Ma came out of the bedroom, carrying the baby. "I'm sorry we don't have milk for the tea," she said. She picked up the sugar bowl and brought it to the table.

Miss Kelly's eyes narrowed. "Do you have milk for the baby?"

"I've been nursing her," Ma said. She took a seat in the rocker and began patting Zakia's small back. I finished pouring the tea and took a seat on the bench across the table from Da.

"Nursing mothers need nutrition," Pamela said. "Are you eating well?"

"What do youse want?" Da asked bluntly. He looked at Martin. "You said it was about Gabe. What's he done?" I could tell he was starting to get angry. His eyes were narrowed and glassy. He didn't like outsiders coming around, poking in their noses and giving advice. A school inspector had come to the house once because Jimmy and Gabe had been missing so much school. He was a small man with a stutter. Da had grabbed him around the throat. "Mind yer own goddamn business," he snarled. I could still recall the look on the poor man's face, how he scrambled to get away. Over the years, I'd heard stories of him going to homes on the island. He never came back to our house.

"The news is not good," Martin said, bringing me out of my reverie.

Something cold closed around my heart. Glancing at Jimmy, I saw he was leaning forward, a worried frown on his face.

"Did something happen to Gabe?" Ma asked anxiously. "Is my boy okay?"

"Gabe stowed away on the *Northern Ranger*," Martin began.

"Sneaky little bastard," Da said. "I s'pose youse come to collect the money he owes for his fare. Well, I'll tell yeh this much—"

"No one's looking for money," Martin interrupted, "and I'm not here to press charges."

"Where's he to now?" Da asked.

"Gabe's in the hospital," Martin said. "He—"

"In the hospital?" Ma gasped. "Oh, my God!" She pressed her hand to her mouth. The baby started to cry.

Jimmy went to stand beside Ma. "Try not to get yourself worked up, Ma," he said. He turned to Martin. "What happened?"

"The crew didn't discover Gabe until they were going around the Bay of Islands," Martin continued. "They took him to the Western Memorial hospital in Corner Brook. They discovered he had two cracked ribs." He cast Da a reproachful look.

"Is Gabe going to be okay?" Ma asked. All the colour had drained from her face.

"Well," Martin said, and I could tell he was struggling with his words. "Gabe had been spitting up blood, something that concerned the crew. At the hospital, they not only X-rayed his ribs, but his lungs." He looked around the table, then back at Ma. "I'm sorry to have to tell you this, but Gabe has been diagnosed with tuberculosis."

Ma let out a cry. I got up from my seat and took the baby from her. Jimmy put a comforting hand on her shoulder. "How bad is it?" he asked.

"They didn't go into any detail at the hospital," Martin said. "They'll be sending you a report, I imagine. But TB is no longer the death sentence it was years ago. In fact, most people recover nowadays."

"That's true," Miss Kelly offered. "My niece came home from the san after ten months." She folded her hands on the table, and looked at Da. "However, that's not the only reason we're here, Mr. Ste Croix."

Da looked at her and frowned.

"You beat your son up pretty badly," the social worker said. "You could be charged with child abuse."

"Child abuse?" Da couldn't have looked more surprised if she'd said they had come to fly him to the moon.

"There was no need for what you did, Abe," Martin said.

"No need," Da sputtered. "What was I s'pose to do, take lip from a snot-nosed youngster?" He shook his head. "No siree. No way in hell."

"Mr. Ste Croix, your son is a minor," Miss Kelly said.

Da looked confused. "A minor what?"

"He's under the age of eighteen," Miss Kelly said.

"So?"

"No one deserves to be beaten and kicked like an animal," Ma said. She looked like she was about to cry.

"She's right," Martin said.

Da's mouth fell open, and his face turned red. "I'll do what I damn well likes with me own youngster," he said. "And nobody's gonna tell me any different." He banged his fist down hard on the table. "No goddamn way!"

"You could be charged," Martin said, "with assaulting a child."

"So, I'm s'pose to just stand by, keep me mouth shut while some saucy brat gives me lip? No youngster of mine is gonna talk to me that way." He shot a warning glance at Jimmy and then at me. "If I'd said half as much to me own fadder, he'd have me brains knocked out." He glared at Martin. "I don't care if yeh puts me in jail and fires away the key."

"Mr. Ste Croix, your son is very sick," Miss Kelly reminded him. "And we're concerned about the rest of your children."

"The rest of me children? Why is yeh worried about them?"

Miss Kelly looked down at a folder in front of her. "I see you have three other school-aged children besides Gabe. Are they attending school regularly?"

"Hardly," Jimmy answered.

"You shut the hell up and mind yer own business," Da roared.

"Blanche is in service with Gert Pickford," Jimmy said, ignoring Da's outburst.

Miss Kelly looked at me. "How long has that been going on?"

"Since November," I said, biting back a surge of resentment. "It wasn't my idea," I said, glancing at Da who was shaking with rage.

"And you're how old?" Miss Kelly asked. She picked up a page from her folder and turned it over.

"I'll turn fifteen in June," I said. The baby began to whimper, and I rubbed her back.

"The law requires that Blanche stay in school until she's fifteen and a half," Martin said. "I'm surprised Gert didn't know that."

I felt a wave of hope. Would I finally be able to go back to school?

Da's face darkened. "The school year's almost over."

He was right, I realized. There were only two months left. I had missed most of the year. I was kept so busy, I hadn't had time to keep up with my schoolwork.

"Miss Foster was going to help me prepare for the provincial exam," I said. I didn't know why I was telling them this. "She's helped a number of students get through school."

Da snorted. "Thinks she's Lady Alderdice, that one."

"Blanche appears to have a good head on her shoulders," Martin said. "She's capable of finishing high school, I'm sure. In any case, she's to return to school on Monday. It's the law." He glanced at the social worker, who gave a nod of confirmation.

I felt a surge of hope. No more slaving for Gert Pickford. Maybe I could make up for lost time. I could study over the summer holidays.

"There's lots around here that needs to be done," Da said. "What, with the new baby and the rest of the youngsters. Grace got her hands full, and she's not well. If Blanche is going off to school, she better make time to get things done around here."

I knew from his expression that Da was not going to make things easy.

CHAPTER 24

BLANCHE HEATED UP A CAN OF TOMATO SOUP AND ATE IT IN FRONT
of the television. The day's events had taken their toll, and she yawned
from exhaustion. *Why did I let Olive get under my skin?* she asked
herself. But she knew the answer. The past was still a raw wound.
Memories were never far from her mind. Her father's drunken rants,
her mother's bruised face, the threats and verbal abuse.

She finished her soup and reached for her cigarettes. On the
single channel, the news was just coming on. "All is not well at
24 Sussex Drive," the newscaster said. "It has been reported that
Prime Minster Trudeau is having marital problems. His young
wife, Margaret, hospitalized shortly after the election for a nervous
disorder, is having difficulty coping with being the wife of the
Prime Minister."

Blanched switched off the set. "That's old news," she said
aloud. She imagined people watching their television sets in St.
John's and Corner Brook, where the news was live. Bishop Malloy's
death would be the lead story, regional and national. She could only
imagine the horror of Catholics all over the province when they
learned their archbishop had been murdered.

Blanche sat quietly for a few moments, the events of the day
racing through her mind. She recalled the booze and pills she'd
found in Bishop Malloy's suitcase. *What kept you awake at night,*
Your Grace? What demons drove you to seek psychiatric counsel? Who

hated you enough to plunge a knife into your chest? It was then that
Blanche remembered the letters she'd hastily shoved into her pants
pocket that afternoon. She had changed since then, and hung the
pants in the closet of her room. She got up from the sofa, went
upstairs, and returned with the letters.

The first letter, dated June 1, was from Paul Lambert, a deacon
at St. Theresa's Parish. Blanche read with interest:

> *Please accept our apologies for not finding another home for your
> visit to Darby's Island for the July 18th weekend. We understand
> you are uncomfortable staying with Mrs. Gertrude Pickford
> whom you have described as "silly and intolerable." A couple
> of months ago, we contacted Mr. and Mrs. Gerald Thomas, a
> couple who lives on the north side of the island. They were more
> than willing to let you stay in their home. Unfortunately, Mr.
> Thomas's mother has taken ill, and they have gone to St. John's
> to be with her while she recovers. We express our deepest regret
> for this inconvenience and promise to rectify the situation as
> soon as we are able.*

Oh my, Blanche thought. What a slap in the face that would've
been to Gert. If this letter ever came to her attention, she'd be
devastated. She doubted Gert could ever recover from such an
insult. For the first time in her life, Blanche felt a wave of sympathy
for her mother-in-law.

The second letter, marked *Private and confidential,* was from
Father Michael Donovan. The same priest she had called about
the archbishop's death, Blanche realized. The return address was
a monastery on the southwest coast. Blanche reached inside the
envelope and found a single sheet of paper. It was dated January
7, 1975. Six months ago.

> *Dear Phillip,*
>
> *Thank you for your letter. I am sorry I could not take your call on
> Monday. As Brother Andrew explained, I was on a silent retreat.*
>
> *With regards to your letter, I think you are dealing with a very
> serious issue, and my advice would be to consult Alex Power in*

Public Relations. Ask him to tell this woman to stop harassing you. After all, it's been thirty years, and there is no proof that the allegations are true. The child in question would be an adult now.

I am on my way to Port Saunders, on the Northern Peninsula. I will speak with you when I return.

Yours in Christ,
Michael

Blanche reread the letter. *The child in question would be an adult now.* Had the archbishop fathered a child? The letter certainly seemed to suggest it. But would that be a motive for murder? *Not if it happened thirty years ago,* she reasoned. She went to the window and stared out at the storm. Although the wind had subsided, it was still raining, and water ran down the glass like tears. The island was quiet, every house in blackness except for the occasional porch light illuminating narrow pathways to its door.

Blanche recalled Nellie's words the evening they were standing outside the hall: "I'd say 'tis personal." Was Judy the archbishop's child? Blanche blew out her breath. It seemed logical when she thought about it. Nellie attended Bishop Malloy's parish. She'd been living in St. John's when she got pregnant. Blanche often wondered why Nellie never mentioned Judy's father. And it would explain her contempt for the church. Aunt Hattie once told Blanche that Nellie used to be a devout Catholic. Something must have happened to turn her against her faith. Bishop Malloy would have been a young priest at that time. She did a quick calculation—twenty-seven years old.

Blanche put the letter back in the envelope. Could Nellie have killed the archbishop? No, she thought. Despite her anger, Nellie was not a violent person. But what if the stabbing had been accidental? Blanche constructed a scenario in her mind that seemed plausible. Suppose Nellie had been walking on the beach when she found Herb's knife. Suppose she just *happened* to run into the archbishop. There could have been an altercation. Maybe Nellie hadn't intended to kill him. Blanche had seen it happen time and time again in domestic disputes. Men and women with no tendency for violence had harmed their spouses. She shook her head. *Don't let your imagination run wild*, she chided herself. *Talk with Nellie before jumping to conclusions.*

Blanche switched the television back on. An episode of *Happy Days* was playing. She had watched the episode so many times she knew it by heart. Switching off the set, she got up from the sofa and picked up the envelope of photographs Aunt Hattie had given her. She spread them out on the table, not sure she wanted to stir up the memories they held. There was a picture of her family, taken before Hazel and Zakia were born. Da was not in the picture, she noticed. Her mother was holding Eddie, who was an infant. Tears sprang in Blanche's eyes. She missed her family so much that at times her heart ached.

In another photograph, Kate and Ivy were standing near the old house. Blanche had to look closely to figure out who was who. Although they could pass for identical twins, they were very different: Ivy was an open book, whereas Kate was a mystery. Blanche often wondered what went on in Kate's head with the strange images she painted. She put down the photograph and picked up another. Kate, she realized—standing by a window. This photo was in colour, while most of the others were in black and white. It must have been taken after Kate got sent away. She looked to be about thirteen, but already had the hardness of an adult.

Blanche's throat tightened. The last time she'd seen Kate was a few months before her death. She had left Toronto and was working as a waitress at the Candlelight Restaurant in St. John's. Gabe and Blanche had met her after her shift. They went out to a movie, then dinner at a Chinese restaurant. Kate had been excited about an upcoming showing she had arranged at a small gallery on Water Street. She had already sold two of her paintings, and patrons were asking for more.

Kate had seemed happy that evening, and full of plans for the future. They had lingered at the restaurant, talking and drinking coffee long after everyone else had left. Gabe, who was closer to Kate than any of her other brothers and sisters, beamed with pride. "I knew you could do it, Katie," he kept telling her. "I always said—didn't I, Blanche?—that our Kate would be famous someday."

Blanche held back tears now, recalling how Kate had returned to Toronto shortly afterwards without a word to anyone. She didn't even stay around for her own art show. A couple of weeks later, Blanche got the phone call.

By ten o'clock, Blanche was exhausted. The day's drama had left her drained. She climbed into bed and fell into a deep, dreamless sleep. She was awoken some hours later by the sound of footsteps. Someone was in the cottage. Had she left the door open? Had some animal wandered in? Or had the intruder come to…No, she couldn't let her mind go there.

Cautiously, she got out of bed. Her gun was downstairs; she wished now that she'd kept it by her bedside. She never thought she'd need a gun while visiting Darby's Island. The archbishop's murder had changed everything.

Blanche heard the sound of a drawer being opened and closed. *Please, don't let him get my gun,* she prayed silently. She tiptoed to the landing, her heart pounding as she crept down the wooden steps. She had left a small light on. For years Blanche used to sleep with a light on in her bedroom. She had stopped doing that, but she still liked to leave a light on in the house.

She was near the bottom of the stairs when she saw him. A hooded man about six feet tall. She couldn't see his face in the feeble light, but she saw enough to know he was the man Patsy had described. She could just make out the peace symbol on the back of his sweater. He had his hand on the doorknob, ready to leave. Blanche's heart was pounding wildly. Was this the murderer running loose? In one quick motion, she leapt to the sideboard, opened the door, and grabbed her weapon. "Freeze," she called, but the intruder was already out the door. Blanche ran after him. "Freeze," she shouted again. Outside, all she could see was blackness. Moments later, she heard the sound of an engine and a car driving off into the night.

Blanche made herself a cup of tea, knowing sleep wouldn't come easily. What did the intruder want? Had he come to rob her? A quick check of the cottage revealed that nothing had been taken. None of it made sense.

It was nearly two-thirty before Blanche went back to bed. She was just dozing off when she heard a loud pounding on the door. *He's back.* Blanche reached for her gun and moved toward the door before common sense kicked in. What kind of an intruder pounds on doors in the middle of the night? Her next thought was of Reba. Had something happened to Reba? Panic grabbed at her stomach. *Surely someone would have telephoned,* she told herself as she went to the door.

From the outside light, she saw a woman standing on the doorstep clad in a white nightgown. With her long hair blowing in the wind and her nightgown swirling around her slender figure, she looked like a heroine from a gothic novel. Blanche opened the door, and the woman stumbled inside.

"Olive?" Blanche cried, taking in her bare feet. "What are you doing here at this hour?"

Olive's face was pale, her hair a tangled mess. The hem of her nightgown was wet and dirty. Was she sleepwalking? Blanche leaned in close and sniffed, a habit that came from years of living with an alcoholic father. Olive had been drinking, she realized. But it appeared to be more than that.

"Hope I didn't wake you," Olive said, her voice slurred. "I needed to talk with you."

Blanche looked at her watch. "It's past three. Is everything okay?"

Olive stared at her, eyes glazed and unfocused.

"I have to talk to you, Blanche," she repeated, her voice urgent.

Blanche led her to the sofa. "Have a seat," she said. "Can I get you some tea?"

Olive shook her head. "No thanks."

"Did you walk here?" Olive lived less than a mile from the cottage, but Blanche shuddered to think she'd driven in her condition.

"I drove," Olive said. "I couldn't sleep, not even after two sleeping pills."

Blanche stared at Olive. Sleeping pills and booze. No wonder Olive appeared disoriented. More and more doctors were prescribing barbiturates and other sleeping aids. She recalled a traffic accident on the Northern Peninsula a few months back. The driver had gone out after taking sleeping pills. The police found his car in the ditch, the driver asleep at the wheel.

Blanche reached for her cigarettes and held out the package. "Smoke?"

Nodding, Olive accepted the cigarette.

Blanche took a seat across from her. "What brings you here at this hour?"

"I didn't do it, you know."

"Didn't do what, Olive?"

"It wasn't me who'd been dipping into the funds at the nursing home."

She's guilty as hell, Blanche thought. "Why didn't you say so this afternoon?"

"My lawyer advised me not to speak to you without him present."

Blanche didn't bother to remind her there was no lawyer present now.

"I know you and Martin think I'm guilty," Olive continued.

Blanche folded her arms across her chest. "This has nothing to do with Martin. I'm conducting the investigation."

"Martin never liked me, that much is clear."

"Olive," Blanche said patiently. "There's thousands of dollars missing from the home. The residents are complaining about the quality of the food. Even if you didn't take the money, as the administrator, you're still accountable."

"And what about Lisa?" Olive asked, naming the accountant. "Maybe you should investigate her."

"We intend to speak with everyone involved," Blanche said. She didn't tell Olive it was Lisa Penny who'd blown the whistle.

"I hear you've been gambling," Blanche said.

Olive nodded. "I took a trip to Vegas last Christmas. I promised myself I'd only bet twenty dollars." Olive spread her hands helplessly. "Once I got started, I couldn't stop. I ended up losing a lot of money that evening. I kept trying to win it back, but got further and further behind." She shook her head. "I left the casino owing nearly ten thousand dollars."

Blanche stared at her in disbelief, stunned by her recklessness. She was even more amazed that Olive would reveal this, considering it would give her a motive. *Olive is under the influence,* she reminded herself. "Where did you get the money to pay the debt?" she asked.

"A number of places—banks, friends—I took out a second mortgage on the house." Olive yawned. "I should get going," she said, standing up. "It must be late."

"Why don't you stay here tonight?" Blanche suggested. "I can make up the spare bedroom. Otherwise, you'll have to walk home. As an officer of the law, I can't let you drive in the state you're in."

Olive looked at Blanche, and then toward the window with fat drops of rain rolling down. Blanche knew she was torn. The walk home in her nightgown would not be a pleasant. "I've imposed on you enough already," she said.

"It's no problem; I have an extra bed." Even as she spoke, Blanche realized this was probably not a good idea. She was an RCMP officer. She was investigating Olive for fraud.

Olive patted the sofa. "This is fine."

"At least let me get you a blanket." Blanche went upstairs and returned with a pillow and handmade quilt.

After Olive was settled, Blanche locked the door. In her room, she took out her case notebook and wrote down everything Olive had told her. If this case ever went to court, it would be good to have notes to back up Olive's claims. Blanche got into bed, but despite her weariness she was unable to sleep. She tossed and turned for most of the night, the strangeness of the last twenty-four hours sifting through her mind. The grey light of dawn was outside the window before she finally fell asleep.

She awoke a couple of hours later and got out of bed. She tiptoed into the living room careful not to disturb Olive. But Olive was gone, the quilt folded neatly on the davenport.

Blanche got dressed and wolfed down a bowl of cornflakes. It was still early. She would do some writing, she decided. She looked for her journal, the one with the kittens on the cover. It wasn't on the table where she'd left it. It had been there when she went to bed last evening. She knew she had not touched it since. Had Olive taken it?

First things first, Blanche thought. She needed to call Patsy, invite her for brunch. She would call Father Donovan as soon as she got to the hall. The most important thing on her agenda, however, was to find out who had broken into the cottage.

CHAPTER 25

June 1963

"You know your stuff, Blanche." Miss Foster smiled. "I see you've been studying."

"As much as I can," I told her.

Miss Foster started explaining how the provincial exams worked, but I was barely listening. I sneaked a glance at the clock on her desk. I couldn't help worrying about Ma and the little ones at home. Jimmy was away on another job—this time in Duck Cove. Kate was going to a friend's house down in the bottom of the harbour. I just hoped Ivy would have the good sense to go straight home after school. Yesterday when I got home, Ma was sleeping. Eddie had crawled into the cupboard. Zakia was crying in her crib. I thought after the baby came, Ma would get back to normal. However, she was still tired, still needed to sleep a lot.

"I know you can do this, Blanche," Miss Foster said.

At that moment, the door opened and Coop Pickford stood in the doorway holding a stack of papers. "Don't mean to interrupt," he said, looking at Miss Foster. "Just came by to drop off those exams you wanted."

"Come on in, Coop," Miss. Foster said. "We were just finishing up here."

Coop placed the papers on her desk. He looked handsome in his green windbreaker, his hair a bit longer than I remembered it.

"Thanks, Coop." Miss Foster turned to me. "I asked Coop to bring back the exam questions I gave him to study last year," she said. "Some of the questions are bound to be on this year's exam."

"There does seem to be a pattern," Coop said. "Learn the answers to all the questions, and you'll have a pretty good chance of passing." He grinned. "It worked for me."

I didn't know what to say, so I merely nodded.

"Blanche is doing really well," Miss Foster said.

"It's hard when the exams are made up by some bureaucrat in St. John's." Coop shook his head. "There were questions about the American Civil War, for God's sake."

"You managed to get through," Miss Foster said. "I'm proud of you, Coop. When do your classes at the vocational school begin?"

"September eighth. I have to be in Corner Brook by the sixth."

Miss Foster stood up. "You know, Coop. With your marks, you could easily get into university."

"University? Nah." Coop looked down at his hands. "I'm a builder," he said. "At vocational school, I'll be learning how to design and make cabinets. All kinds of interesting stuff. No need for me to go to university."

"Well, you're certainly talented at what you do."

Miss Foster turned to me. "Well, Blanche," she said, "that should do it for today. Tomorrow, we'll go over world geography."

I gathered up my books, and Coop and I walked outside together. It was cool for the first week of June, and a breeze blew in off the ocean. All the ice had left the harbour, but a single iceberg could be seen in the distance. "You're doing well, Blanche, my love," Coop said. "I'll help you over this summer, if you like."

"Thanks, Coop. I'll probably need all the help I can get. How's the new girl working out?"

"Ugh, Ma's got the poor thing rattled. I feels sorry for her."

We walked pass Jim Perry's stage, down over the hill pass the post office. I walked fast, and Coop trotted to keep up with me. "What's the big rush?" he asked.

"I'm concerned about Ma," I said. "She hasn't been feeling well since the baby's birth." I saw no reason to tell him that she was retreating more and more into herself. At times, she just sat and stared while the baby cried. Some days I made excuses to leave school so I could run home and check on her. To make sure Zakia and Eddie were okay.

"Liz found it hard after her second baby was born," Coop said, referring to his married sister in Corner Brook. "She felt tired and depressed. Ma spent a month with her to help out. How's little Zakia doing?"

"Zakia's fine. Growing like a weed. She's a happy baby. Barely cries."

We walked in companionable silence until we came to the lane that led to our house. "Take care, Blanche," Coop called. "Good luck with your exams, and with your study over the summer holidays."

"I'll see you later," I said as I hurried down the rutted path. As I neared the house, I saw the Jeep from the nursing station parked near the house. I broke into a run. Had something happened to Ma or the kids? As I approached the house, Nurse Little was getting out of the Jeep. She was a short woman with cropped greying hair. Winter and summer, she wore tall boots. She often dressed in men's trousers and shirts. "I've come to visit your mother," she said in her British accent. "Your father is very concerned about her."

"Concerned, is he?" I said, not bothering to hide my sarcasm. The nurse shot me a puzzled look.

I opened the door and she followed me inside. *Please God*, I prayed silently. *Please let everything be okay.*

Eddie had taken the pots and pans from the pantry and was playing with them in the middle of the floor. Zakia was crying in her crib. I picked her up. Her blanket was soaked through. "Where's Ma?" I asked Eddie.

Eddie pointed toward the bedroom. "Ma's sleeping." He put his fingers to his lips. "Shhh! Shhh!"

Nurse Little frowned as she scanned the room. I saw our house as she must have seen it: Diapers strung across a clothesline at the back of the stove, flies buzzing on the windows, a ceiling that bulged and sagged in places. The floor was rough and uneven, the linoleum worn so thin the boards peeked through.

ALICE WALSH

"Your little brother and sister should not be left unsuper-
vised," the nurse said.

I suddenly felt a surge of annoyance at Ivy for not coming
home after school.

Carrying Zakia in my arms, I walked to the bedroom at the
back of the house.

Ma lay under the sheets, curled into a tight ball. I approached
the bed and shook her shoulder. "Ma, get up," I said. "The nurse
is here to see you."

Ma sat up and rubbed her eyes. Her face was pale and gaunt,
her black hair matted and tangled. There were black circles under
her eyes.

"Nurse Little came to see you, Ma."

Ma glanced at Zakia in my arms. "Where's Eddie?"

"Eddie's in the kitchen. He's fine. But Ma, you must
try to stay awake when there's no one around to watch the
children."

Ma sank back against the pillows. "I don't know what's wrong
with me, Blanche. I feels so exhausted all the time. I just can't
keep my eyes open."

"I'll have her come to you," I said. I picked up Da's pants
and shirt from the floor and straightened the blankets on the bed.

When I went back to the kitchen, the nurse was kneeling
on the floor talking to Eddie. "My, what unusual eyes he has," she
said. "And such long eyelashes. He's going to be a heartthrob."

"Ma can see you now," I said.

She got up off the floor and I led her to Ma's bedroom.

The diapers hanging behind the stove were still damp. I
found an old towel, pinned it on Zakia, and put her back in her
crib. I glanced anxiously toward the bedroom where I could hear
murmuring voices.

Fifteen minutes later, the nurse came back to the kitchen.
"Your mother is suffering from extreme exhaustion," she told me.
She looked at Eddie and then toward the crib where Zakia was
kicking her feet and making little cooing noises. "She can't stay
alone with the children. Arrangements must be made for someone
to be here at all times."

"School's almost finished," I said. "I'll be home during the summer months."

The nurse gave me a stern look. "Your mother is not to be left alone with the children."

I swallowed. If someone needed to be with Ma, it would have to be me. I couldn't risk having the children taken away by Social Services.

"Dr. O'Connor will be on the island next week," the nurse continued. "I'll have him pop by and take a look at her." She took a brown bottle from her bag and placed it on the table. "In the meantime, see that she takes this tonic three times a day. It will help build up her strength."

Shortly after Nurse Little left, Da arrived home. He held a letter in his hand that he placed on the table. "I met the nurse," he said. "She thinks your mudder's mental." He snickered. "I've been sayin' that all along. She's no good around the house."

"Neither are you," I said under my breath. "Ma's worn out," I said aloud. "All she needs is a good rest. I'm going to quit school to stay home with her." I picked up the letter from the table. "News from Gabe?" My brother wrote from the san every couple of weeks.

Da shrugged, and I wondered why I'd even bothered to ask him. He couldn't read or write his own name. Whenever anyone asked how far he got in school, he would joke: "I got as far as Dick and Jane's dog, Spot. It barked at me so I didn't go back."

The sight of Gabe's small, cramped handwriting brightened my mood. I took the letter into the bedroom to read to Ma. News from my brother always cheered her. It was addressed to Mrs. Grace Ste Croix. Gabe never included Da's name on the envelope.

Ma was lying on the bed staring at the ceiling. I waved the envelope at her. "Our Gabe sent a letter," I said.

"God bless him." Ma struggled to a sitting position. I sat on the bed next to her and tore open the envelope.

Dear Ma,

How are you? I hope you all are well. I am doing fine. The doctor said my last x-ray was really good. It's hard to believe I been here for two months. I got a visit from Amy Pike. She was in Corner

Brook to visit her sister, and dropped by to see me. Always good to see people from home. Tell Kate I got the picture she sent me. I got it hanging over my bed. On Sundays people from some church group comes to visit. One of them is an art teacher. She said our Kate has a lot of talent. I guess she should know being an art teacher and all. Anyways, she was really taken with Kate's painting. She even asked me if Kate had training. I had a good chuckle at that. Darby's Island School of Fine Arts, I felt like telling her. (Ha Ha.) They have a teacher here who comes around three times a week. She is hoping I can finish grade seven while I'm stuck here. Say hi to all the family. I can't wait to see little Zakia. Tell Blanche I wish her well with her exams.

Love Gabe XOXOXOO

Tears rolled down Ma's cheek. "I miss my boy so much, Blanche," she said.

"We all do."

"So good that he got a chance to go to school," Ma said.

I nodded. Maybe someone in the family would have a chance to get an education.

CHAPTER 26

FATHER DONOVAN WAS ENJOYING A SECOND CUP OF COFFEE WHEN HIS housekeeper came into the dining room. "Father, I hate to disturb you," she said, "but there's an RCMP officer on the telephone; she says it's important."

The priest rose to his feet. "I'll take it in the library, Eliza."

What now, he wondered, as he walked down the wide hallway. News about Phillip, no doubt. Hopefully they had found the person responsible for his death. With a weary sigh, he picked up the telephone. "Father Donovan here."

"Good morning, Father. This is Constable Ste Croix. I spoke with you yesterday concerning the archbishop's death."

"Yes, officer. Are there any new developments?"

"No, I'm afraid not, Father. The reason I'm calling is because of a letter I found—a letter written by you to Bishop Malloy."

Sweet Virgin Mother. Father Donovan gripped the phone, his palms clammy. The objects in the room stood out with stark clarity. The statue of the Virgin Mary on a small pedestal had part of a toe missing. A picture of Pope Pius XXIV that hung on the far wall was slightly askew. "I've written Phil…er…Archbishop Malloy a number of letters," he said evasively. He had no doubt, however, which letter the constable was referring to. "Could you be more specific?"

"Of course, Father." Through the wires, Father Donovan heard the rustle of paper. "Okay, here's the gist of it," Constable Ste Croix said, reading aloud. *"I think you are dealing with a very serious issue, and my advice would be to consult Alex Power in Public Relations. Ask him to tell this woman to stop harassing you. After all, it's been more than thirty years, and there is no proof that the allegations are true. The child in question would be an adult now."*

Father Donovan felt his mouth go dry. He should never have written that letter. Back in January, he'd been at a silent retreat at the monastery when Phillip called. A monk had taken the call, informing the archbishop that Father Donovan was unable to come to the phone. A day later, the letter had arrived, hand-delivered by a parishioner on his way to St. John's. He had hastily written Phillip a reply. Well, at least he hadn't given everything away. The public relations people could put another spin on this if they needed to. He'd already spoken with Alex Power. He realized now that he should have referred the officer's call to him.

"Father?" The constable's voice stirred him back to the moment. "Was the archbishop having a problem with some woman?"

"Yes," Father Donovan admitted. "I thought the issue had been resolved. I doubt there's any truth to the allegations. You know how some women are. They will say anything."

"Right," she said, and Father Donovan thought he heard an edge to her voice. "Do you know the woman's name? It could be important to the investigation."

"No, I have no idea. The archbishop didn't reveal that."

"Was there a child?"

"I don't think so." Father Donovan felt the back of his neck grow hot. Sweat beaded his forehead. He hated telling lies, but he had to protect the church. He knew all the archbishop's secrets. Phillip had confided in him *inside* and *outside* the confessional. He knew his weakness for women, booze, and gambling. He could imagine the scandal—the dishonour to the church and to the archbishop's memory—if the things Phillip had told him got out. "What are you doing to find Bishop Malloy's killer?" he asked, deliberately steering the conversation away from an uncomfortable topic.

"We're doing everything we can under the circumstances," the constable said. "We will contact you if we have new information."

"I see."

"And if you recall anything you think might be pertinent to the case, please call me." She rattled off the number where she could be reached.

Father Donovan put down the receiver and wiped his brow. He walked to the window and looked through the rain-splattered glass. Despite the bad weather and early hour, traffic was heavy on West Street. The parking lot of Mill Brook Mall was filled with cars. He watched as shoppers carrying umbrellas hurried to their vehicles, boarded taxis and buses. "Damn," he muttered. He suddenly felt a surge of resentment toward the archbishop for putting him in this situation. Why in God's name would Phillip hang on to a letter like that?

Father Donovan moved away from the window and began pacing the floor. Phillip told him the young woman had tempted him in much the same way Eve had tempted Adam. He'd seen how women had shamelessly flocked around Phillip when he was a lad. He sighed. It was always women. And they were worse today than ever. Walking around in skirts up to their rear ends. Low-cut blouses that let everything hang out. Complaining because they were not treated like men. And now there was a pill that prevented them from getting pregnant. He'd seen the kind of immorality that led to. This was not the example set by the Virgin Mary. His own sainted mother had raised thirteen children without ever a complaint.

Still, he had to admit that Phillip had shown weakness in the face of temptation. He was as much to blame as the woman. And this was not the first time. Blessed Saviour. What would happen if other women came forward?

The old priest shook his head, trying to sort his conflicted feelings. "Phillip," he whispered, "this is one hell of a mess you got me into." He and the archbishop had been friends for a long time. Father Donovan recalled how the young Father Malloy had taken him under his wing when he came to Newfoundland from Ireland as a young priest. At first he'd been appalled by how much Phillip drank. He also loved to gamble and kept the other priests up half the night playing poker. They placed bets on everything from hockey games to wrestling matches. When Pope Leo XII died,

Phillip had set up a pool so they could bet on which cardinal would be chosen as pope. Father Donovan smiled now at the memory. He had put his money on Cardinal Angelo Giuseppe Roncalli who became Pope John XXIII, a choice that had won him close to fifty dollars that evening.

Father Donovan went back to the window and stood there for a long time. Phillip wasn't a perfect man, he told himself. But he'd been a loyal friend. Whatever his faults, he didn't deserve to be butchered on a beach. A single tear ran down the priest's wrinkled cheek and he made a silent vow. *Phillip, I will do everything I can to protect your honour.*

❧

Martin arrived at the hall shortly after Blanche got off the phone with Father Donovan. "Good morning," he greeted her cheerfully.

Blanche smiled. "You sound chipper."

Martin poured himself a cup of coffee and sat at the table across from her. "I'm sorry I can't say the same for you," he said. "You look exhausted."

"A lot has been happening," she told him.

Martin looked up at her.

"For starters, someone broke into the cottage last night," Blanche said. "Well, *walked* in, to be exact. I'd thought I'd locked the door." She told Martin about hearing a noise, going downstairs and seeing the strange man. "I probably could have shot him," she said. "But he was already leaving."

"You should have shot the son of a bitch," Martin said. He looked thoughtful. "Maybe it was Kate's paintings he was after. I hear they're going for a lot of money now."

"I don't know what he was after," Blanche said. "Gabe doesn't keep any of Kate's paintings at the cottage for that reason."

"Did you get a look at the intruder?"

"I didn't get to see much of him, but I'm sure he was the same guy Patsy described. He was tall and had on a hooded jacket with what looked like a peace sign on the back."

"Don't worry," Martin told her. "The young punk can't get off the island. As a matter of fact, I got a call from Bill last night. He told me the ferry got damaged in the storm. It will probably be tomorrow before it starts running again."

Just like Bill to call Martin instead of me, Blanche thought.

"Was anything taken?" Martin asked.

"Not that I could see. One of my journals is missing, but I can't imagine him wanting that." She sighed. "The intruder was not my only late-night visitor."

Martin raised an eyebrow. "Oh?"

"A couple of hours after I chased him away, Olive Beals showed up at my door in her nightgown. She'd obviously been drinking. She told me she was after taking sleeping pills. I suppose that could account for her strange behaviour. Anyway, she ended up staying the night."

"What did she want?"

"I'm not sure," Blanche said. "She rambled on about gambling debts. I thought she came to make a confession about dipping into the funds at the nursing home."

"I doubt that will happen," Martin said, "but how strange to show up at that hour."

"Not if you're an alcoholic," Blanche said. "They can engage in some very bizarre behaviour."

"Make sure to keep your doors locked, Blanche," Martin said. "At all times. You never know who you're dealing with."

"True enough," Blanche said.

Martin took a sip of coffee and put down the mug. "The main reason Bill called was to give me information he dug up on Prospero. It seems our hypnotist has an interesting past."

Blanche leaned forward. "What did he do?"

"Prospero was convicted of manslaughter," Martin said. "Bill is still trying to get all the details, but he learned that Prospero served three years of a five-year sentence. He has no other convictions, and he's been clean since." He shrugged. "Just one of those interesting tidbits that comes out in an investigation."

"I certainly didn't expect that."

"Me either," Martin said. "I went to his trailer last evening."

"What did he have to say for himself?"

"I didn't get to see him. He was home but wouldn't answer the door."

"What about Miranda?"

"From what Bill was able to dig up, she was a bit of a radical in her younger days. She's not allowed back in the United States because of her protesting. No criminal record, though. However, I'm sure we'll learn more before they leave here."

"For sure," Blanche said. "And they'll want to interview Patsy. In fact, I'm meeting her for brunch this morning at the cafeteria. Hopefully, I can get her to open up."

Martin was silent for a beat. "Blanche, last evening I talked with a couple of the guys from that van parked out on Gull's Head. One of them says he saw Patsy near Devil's Rock on Friday evening."

Blanche's lips parted in surprise. "Were they certain it was Patsy?"

"He described a young girl with long red hair wearing a jacket with Dalmatians," Martin said. "Not too many people on the island fitting that description."

Blanche bit her bottom lip. "I wonder why Patsy never mentioned it."

Martin shrugged.

"I'll ask her about it today," Blanche promised. "In the meantime, I think we should talk with Nellie again."

"Nellie?"

Blanche took a letter from her purse. "I found this in Bishop Malloy's suitcase while I was going through it yesterday. I'd forgotten about it until last night."

"Who is it from?"

"Father Michael Donovan, the priest who took my call after the archbishop was found murdered."

"I know Father Donovan," Martin said. "What does the letter say?"

Blanche removed it from the envelope and read aloud.

Martin frowned. "If I'm not mistaken, it suggests the archbishop fathered a child."

"It certainly sounds that way," Blanche agreed. "I called Father Donovan again this morning. He admitted that the archbishop had been having problems with some woman. He says he doesn't know anything about a child."

"Do you think the archbishop fathered Judy?"

Blanche sighed. "I'm not sure about anything anymore. But the timeline fits, and Nellie has always been very secretive about Judy's father."

"But murder?" Martin shook his head.

"She obviously had a grudge against the archbishop. She made that clear enough."

CHAPTER 27

❧

BLANCHE HAD NEVER SEEN NELLIE SO AGITATED. THERE WAS NO offer of tea or refreshments, barely a word of greeting. She ushered them into the kitchen and sat across from them at the table, a scowl on her face.

"Is Herb home?" Martin asked.

"He's helping Ben Parsons put down linoleum. Do you want me to call him?"

"No, that's okay," Blanche said. "Like I told you on the telephone, it's *you* we need to speak with. We want to know about your relationship with Bishop Malloy."

Nellie crossed her arms and glared at her. "I never had no relationship with the bishop."

"The evening we were standing outside the community hall, you indicated you had a personal vendetta against him," Blanche reminded her.

Nellie sighed. "What is it youse wants?"

Blanche took Father Donovan's letter from her pocket and read it aloud.

Nellie looked from Martin to Blanche, her eyes wide. "What's that got to do with me?"

Blanche cleared her throat. "Well, umm, while you were in St. John's you went to Bishop Malloy's church…and the date of Judy's birth, I mean…"

Nellie gave a short, bitter laugh. "You think Bishop Malloy is Judy's father?"

"I just thought…I mean, you never told anyone who her father was…and, well, I just assumed," Blanche finished sheepishly.

"Judy's father is nobody's business but mine." Nellie spat out the words. "If that horny old bastard knocked up some woman, it sure as hell wasn't me."

Blanche stared at Nellie, taken aback at her unusually strong language. "But why…?"

"Why did I hate the son of a bitch?"

Blanche had never seen this side of Nellie.

"Do you think 'twas me who killed him?" Nellie asked bluntly.

"We have to follow every lead," Martin said tactfully.

"You do seem to have had issues with the archbishop," Blanche reminded her.

Nellie leaned toward Blanche. "I never killed Bishop Malloy," she said. "But by Jesus, I would've liked nothing better than to plunge a knife through his black heart."

"Why?" Martin prompted.

Nellie folded her arms across her chest. "I knew Bishop Malloy—Father Malloy he was then—when he was a young priest in St. John's. We all thought he was the cat's meow." A look of disgust passed over her face. "The girls all swooned over the charming 'Father Phil,' as we called him back then. He'd show up at church dances, and we'd wait in line hoping to have a turn dancing with him."

"What happened?" Martin asked quietly.

Nellie twisted the gold band on her finger. "I got tangled up with a married man," she admitted. "Jim McCarthy was his name. Not something I'm proud of, but Jim said his marriage was on the rocks. He claimed his wife didn't love him. She was going to have their marriage annulled." Nellie's voice grew sad, the pain of memory etched on her face. "When I told him I was pregnant, he discarded me like an old shoe." She shook her head. "What a fool I was. I was that distraught, I wanted to make away with meself."

"You were taken advantage of," Blanche said gently.

"I knows that now, maid. But at the time I was foolish enough to believe Jim loved me."

Blanche nodded, wondering where the story was going, but more importantly what part the archbishop had played in it.

"Anyhow," Nellie continued. "Mrs. Burke, who owned the boarding house where I worked, told me I could stay as long as my condition didn't interfere with work. I was a good worker," she added with a touch of pride. "One of the best, according to Mrs. Burke. Both Mrs. Burke and Sharon, the girl I shared a room with, thought I should demand child support. They thought Jim should at least pay for a sitter while I worked."

Martin and Blanche exchanged looks.

Nellie folded her arms across her chest. "One evening after mass, I went to see Father Phil. After everybody left the church, we sat in a pew and talked. Didn't take me long to figure out Jim had already been to see him." Nellie caught her breath and continued. "Father Phil said Jim was a good family man. He said that I'd ruin all their lives if his wife found out about us." She balled her hands into fists. "Son of a bitch urged me to go into a home for unwed mothers. 'Give the baby to the Catholic orphanage,' he said. 'They'll find a good home for it.'"

"And you didn't want that," Blanche said.

Nellie shook her head. "I was determined to make Jim take responsibility for his child. And I was just as determined to stay on at the boarding house."

"What happened?" Martin asked.

"A few days later, Mrs. Burke told me I'd have to leave. I found out from Sharon that Father Malloy came to the boarding house." Nellie's eyes blazed at the memory. "He told Mrs. Burke I was a bad example for the other girls who worked there. And you knows how it is here in Newfoundland," she said bitterly. "The church got more power than the law." She shook her head helplessly. "What could I do…me four months gone? I couldn't get another job. Even if I did, Father Malloy would've probably ruined it for me."

"That wasn't right," Blanche said indignantly. "What you told him was confidential."

Nellie folded her hands on the table. "The hell that bastard cared about anything confidential."

For a moment no one spoke.

Martin reached out his hand and placed it on Nellie's arm. "I'm sorry," he said.

"All water under the bridge now," said Nellie. She turned to Blanche. "Patsy told me you invited her out for brunch this morning."

"We're meeting at the cafeteria," Blanche said. "It's important that we have a talk."

Nellie frowned. "I thought you questioned Patsy already."

"We feel there's something she's keeping from us," Martin said.

Nellie's eyes grew wide. "Why would you think that?"

"Well…for one thing, she was seen near Devil's Rock the night the archbishop was murdered," Martin said.

Nellie's face turned pale. "Our Patsy was at Devil's Rock?"

⁓⦇⦈⁓

"DID YOU SEE THE EXPRESSION ON NELLIE'S FACE?" BLANCHE SAID as she and Martin were walking to the car.

"She looked scared," Martin said.

"You don't think she's hiding anything."

"It's hard to say," Martin said.

"Martin, do you think we could pay a short visit to Olive? I want to see how she's making out after that episode last night."

"Why not?" Martin said. "Let's see if we can find out what she's up to."

However, Blanche had another reason for the visit. She wanted to see if Olive knew anything about the missing journal. As they approached her house, though, she wondered how she was going to broach the subject. She couldn't just come out and accuse Olive of stealing.

Despite everything, Blanche couldn't help but feel a tug of pity for Olive's predicament. Gambling was a disease every bit as destructive as alcoholism or drug addiction. Olive had paid dearly for her bad choices.

Martin opened the porch door, gesturing for Blanche to go ahead. The inside door was slightly ajar, and Blanche rapped lightly. When no one answered, she knocked louder. Still, there was no answer. "Olive must have stepped out," Martin said.

"She didn't take her car," Blanche said. She couldn't imagine Olive out walking in such bad weather.

Through the open door, they could hear the television. "Cyril Manning, come on down!" the host of some game show shouted as his audience cheered.

Something's not right, Blanche told herself. Pushing open the door, she called out: "Olive? It's Blanche and Martin." She stepped into the living room, Martin close behind. "Olive?" she called again. Blanche started down the hallway to the master bedroom. The bed was neatly made, the room tidy. Olive's robe lay at the foot of her bed.

The closet door was open and Blanche could see a fur coat and stole. There were silk evening gowns, some with price tags dangling from the sleeves. Expensive cashmere sweaters hung on padded hangers. A thin gold necklace and a silver charm bracelet lay on a night table.

"Olive?"

Blanche left the master bedroom and went into a bedroom across the hall. This room was smaller, with a single bed and chest of drawers. She was about to call Olive's name again when Martin called, "Blanche, out here. Quick!"

Alarmed by the urgency in Martin's tone, Blanche hurried down the hallway. She found him in a small area off the kitchen that was used as a laundry room. Martin was kneeling over Olive's crumpled form. "Oh, my God! What happened?" Blanche exclaimed, taking in the pool of blood on the tiled floor.

CHAPTER 28

⌒◦❧◦⌒

NELLIE STOOD BY THE WINDOW FOR A LONG TIME AFTER BLANCHE
and Martin left. She had no idea Patsy had gone to Devil's Rock
on Friday evening. Patsy never even mentioned it. Could she have
seen something? *God, help us,* Nellie prayed silently. She recalled
how oddly Patsy had been acting since the murder. There were
times when she barely came out of her room. Last night, Nellie
had heard her roaming around the house when she should've been
sleeping. And she was as jumpy as a cat.

Nellie got out her cleaning supplies. With a heavy heart, she
began scrubbing the spotless counter. Something had been weigh-
ing heavily on her mind since Saturday morning, and now she felt
as if the burden of it would crush her. Herb had lied to Blanche
and Martin. He told them he'd lost his knife on Friday morning.
Nellie knew that wasn't true. She'd seen the knife in his store late
Friday afternoon when she went looking for a screwdriver. Why
would Herb lie to the police? Nellie's mind rolled with possibilities,
none of them good. Did he run into Bishop Malloy on the beach
and stab him? Herb knew about the bad blood between Nellie
and the bishop. But that had happened years ago, and Herb was
not a violent man. Nellie had never even known him to raise his
voice. Still, there must have been a reason why he lied. Dear God
in heaven, was he protecting Patsy?

The ringing phone startled Nellie, causing her to jump.

"Nellie? It's Martin. I'm over at Olive's house. We're taking her in the ambulance."

"What happened?"

"I can't go into that now," Martin said. "Did Herb get home yet?"

"No, my son. He's still at Ben's, but I'll call and let him know. Is there anything I can do? Do you want me to come over there?"

"No, the ambulance is on its way," Martin said. "Maybe you and Herb can meet Olive at the hospital."

"Blessed Saviour in heaven," Nellie muttered as she broke the connection. "What now?"

With trembling hands, she dialled Ben's number. The line was busy.

Nellie replaced the receiver and went to the window, her heart pounding. She could hear the thin wail of the ambulance. Had Olive tried to make away with herself again? Nellie felt a wave of guilt. Olive had been her friend all through school. She never wanted Nellie to marry Herb. Not that Nellie blamed her. She tried to imagine her own father married to Olive, but it was just too bizarre.

I really messed things up, Nellie thought. What a sad state her life had become. At times she felt like a snared rabbit. She'd had big dreams when she worked at Burke's Boarding House. She was going to finish her education, apply to the nursing assistant program at St. Claire's Hospital. Having a baby at sixteen was not in her plans. Neither was marrying a man old enough to be her father. Yes, she'd grown fond of Herb over the years. He was kind and decent, and he'd accepted Judy as his own. But there had to be more to life than this.

Nellie moved away from the window. *Poor Judy suffered most for my mistakes*, she mused. She felt a twinge of guilt now as she recalled the resentment Nellie had felt toward her child. Judy must have sensed her mother's anger growing up. No surprise she'd left home at such a young age. No wonder they seldom heard from her. What kind of mother blames her child for her own unhappiness? Every time she changed a diaper, or got up at night with the baby, she'd felt resentment and bitterness. Judy was a constant reminder of everything that had gone wrong in her life. With Patsy it was different. She had welcomed her granddaughter with an open heart. Patsy had been a joy in her life from the moment she'd laid eyes on her.

Nellie tried the Parsonses' number again, but it was still busy. She reached for her sweater and went outside. She had intended to go for Herb, but found herself on Olive's doorstep. She entered without knocking, and followed the sound of voices to the laundry room.

Olive was stretched out on the floor. Someone had wrapped a blanket around her. Martin was checking her pulse. "How is she?" Blanche asked, anxiously.

"She has a rapid heartbeat," Martin said, "consistent with someone in shock."

"Thank God she's still alive." Blanche was holding a towel against Olive's shoulder and it was soaked with blood.

Nellie felt her stomach go queasy. "What happened?" she asked.

Both Martin and Blanche looked up at the same time.

"Nellie, you shouldn't be here," Martin said.

Nellie knelt down beside Olive. "What happened?" she repeated. She reached for Olive's hand and found it cold and clammy. She noticed her skin had a grey-blue tinge.

"Someone stabbed her," Blanche said, "just below her shoulder."

Nellie swallowed. "How bad is it?"

"It looks bad," Blanche said.

"Who could have done this?" Nellie asked.

"I wish the hell I knew," Martin said. "Two stabbings in two days."

At that moment they heard the ambulance drive up to the door. "Hang in there, Olive," Blanche whispered. "Help is on the way."

A short time later, Nurse Duncan came bustling into the kitchen, her heavy rubber boots tracking mud on the kitchen floor. She was a stout woman who wore her hair tied back in a ponytail. She was wearing a thick cable knit sweater that added to her bulk. With barely a nod, she knelt beside Olive and opened her black leather bag. "Good heavens, lass!" she exclaimed in her Scottish accent. "Who did this to you?"

Nellie exhaled, realizing she'd been holding her breath. She looked on as the nurse competently took Olive's vital signs. She looked for a vein to put an IV in her arm, all the while murmuring words of comfort.

Minutes later, Matt, followed by a man Nellie recognized as Victor Foley, brought a gurney into the house and lifted Olive onto it. An oxygen mask was placed over her face.

"Will she make it?" Nellie asked fearfully as Victor and Matt each took an end of the gurney and started toward the door.

"It's too early to speculate," the nurse replied. "The wound is deep, and she's lost a lot of blood. Her condition is critical, and we may have to fly her into St. John's by helicopter. The only thing we can do now is to stabilize her." She looked at Martin and then at Blanche. "It's a good thing you came by when you did."

"We should let Aunt Amy know," Blanche said. "She shouldn't find this out from someone else."

The nurse agreed. "I'll have the staff at the nursing home contact her."

Blanche looked around the kitchen. "I wonder what happened to the weapon."

"I can't believe this has happened," Nellie said.

"She's been assaulted in much the same way as the bishop," Blanche said. She turned to Martin. "Do you think the stabbings are related?"

"More than likely. It would be quite a coincidence if they weren't." Martin looked around the room. "We'll have to consider this place a crime scene," he said. He looked pointedly at Nellie. "We can't have people tramping in and out."

"I'll go find Herb," Nellie said. As she made her way to the door, she realized her hands were trembling.

CHAPTER 29

⁓⸎⁓

October 1963

It was a grey evening in early fall when they came to take our mother away. The nurse and Dr. O'Connor arrived at the house in the hospital Jeep. Dr. O'Connor was to accompany Ma on the ferry and make sure she got safely to the hospital. They gave her some kind of injection—"to relax her," the nurse said. Ma went willingly, her steps slow, like a prisoner in shackles. Kate screamed at Da, telling him he should be the one put in the Mental, not Ma. This earned her a slap across the face, and the rest of us a warning. In the end, Kate took hold of Ma's arm and walked her to the Jeep. Ivy followed, carrying a small plastic bag that held Ma's belongings. Old AC didn't even bother to see her off. "I'll stay here with the youngster," he said. I felt uneasy leaving him alone with Zakia, but I figured we wouldn't be gone long.

With Eddie in my arms, we walked the short distance to the government wharf. Kate and Ivy walked ahead of us. Fog blanketed the houses and fish stages; it crept onto the wharf, blurring the edges of barrels and freight sheds. The Jeep was already there when we arrived. I watched as Nurse Little helped Ma out of the vehicle. Dr. O'Connor took her arm and led her toward the ferry. She looked like she was in a stupor. As we approached her, I don't think she even knew who we were. When I hugged her, it was like hugging a wooden pole. Eddie reached out his small arms to her. Ma's expression was blank as he planted a kiss on her cheek. "Goodbye, Ma," I whispered. She looked so forlorn I thought my heart would break.

We stayed until the crew untied the ferry and it began backing away from the wharf. Ivy had tears rolling down her cheeks. Kate stood erect, arms folded, an angry look on her face. As I watched the ferry move out of the harbour, a bleak sense of loneliness swept through me. Eddie, who barely ever cried, put his head on my shoulder and sobbed. I bit my lip to keep from crying myself. Would the rest of Ma's life be spent inside the dreaded walls of the Mental? I wished Jimmy could've been here. He had finished his job in Duck Cove and was now working in Map Bay. He didn't even know that Ma was gone. I wondered how he'd react when he found out the news. He had been sending five-dollar money orders to help out.

Within days of Ma's departure, Da began bringing Laverne around. Sometimes her son, Freddy, came with her. He went around the house touching everything in sight. He would pull a chair over to the shelf and take down dishes. He asked so many questions I thought I'd go crazy: *Where did yeh get that? How much did that cost? Why don't yeh fix that hole in the window?* Da called him "an annoying little bastard." If Freddy wanted something, he would keep on until he got it, driving everyone crazy. One day he asked for a piece of lassy bread. I told him there was only enough bread for supper, and nothing to spare. "I wants a piece of lassy bread," he went on in his high-pitched, sing-song voice. "I wants a piece of lassy bread, I wants a piece of lassy bread, I wants a piece of lassy bread, I wants a piece of lassy bread..." He kept it up until Da swiped at the back of his head. "Will yeh shut the damn thing up," he yelled at Laverne.

Kate grew sullen and angry, often lashing out at Laverne and Freddy. There was so much tension in the house it felt as if we were all walking on eggshells. One evening, Kate and Laverne got into a nasty row. Kate told Laverne she should go home to her own husband.

"It's none of your business," Laverne said, looking to Da for support.

"Jesus Christ, can't youse all be civil?" Da glared at Kate. "Not one more goddamn word from the likes of you," he warned. "Keep that up, and I'll warm your arse with the belt. So help me Christ, I will."

"Why did you send Ma away?" Kate demanded.

"The crazy bitch belongs in the Mental." Da snickered. "And that's where I'll send you, if yeh keeps up that craziness."

"There's nothing wrong with Ma," Kate bellowed. "You got rid of her so you could bring that old bag around." She shot a reproachful look at Laverne. "She's already got a husband and you're not him."

Da jumped up so quickly his chair toppled over. He grabbed Kate by her ponytail, yanking it so hard her head snapped backward. "Goddamn you, Kate Ste Croix," he hollered. "You don't know when t' shut up, do yeh?"

"I'm not afraid of the likes of you," Kate said.

Da chased Kate into the bedroom, whipping off his belt as he went. I was holding the baby, and I put her back in her crib and followed. When I entered the bedroom, Kate was on the floor, rolled into a ball, her hands shielding her head as the belt cracked down on her.

I watched helplessly as the belt swung from Da's fist. He jumped up and down, a wild gleam in his eye as blows rained down on Kate's back. "That'll teach you," he said with each blow.

"Da, don't," I said, jumping between them.

He stopped beating Kate long enough to give me a push that sent me reeling.

"Please, Da," I begged. "No more." I was crying now. I went back into the kitchen.

"Laverne," I pleaded, "Da's really angry. I'm scared he'll hurt Kate. You got to make him stop."

"What can I do?" Laverne asked, but she got up and went into the bedroom. I don't know what she said to him, but Da stopped beating Kate.

Kate's back was black and blue with bruises. One of her eyes was swollen shut. "I didn't give Old AC the satisfaction of seeing me cry," she said. The coldness in her voice disturbed me as much as the beating itself.

That evening, Kate drew a snake with Da's face. The snake was carrying a pitchfork. She pinned it on the wall near the kitchen table.

"For the love of God, Kate," I told her. "Don't antagonize him. You're only hurting yourself. You know, as well as I do, the ugly moods he gets in." I was afraid Da would seriously hurt—even kill—Kate.

"I hates him," she said. "I'll always hate him for what he done to Ma." She peered at me. "Don't you hate him, Blanche?"

Yes, I wanted to say. *I hate the bastard as much as you do.* But what I said instead was, "He's our Da." I knew that despite everything, it was what Ma would want me to say. "Stay out of his way, Kate," I said. "I don't want you to get hurt."

She put her arms around my neck, and I could feel her thin body quivering. "I'm scared, Blanche," she said. "What's going to happen to us?"

I held her tight. "Nothing's going to happen," I tried to assure her. Still, I carried the same fears as she did. With Ma gone, I was in charge of the family. The responsibility was overwhelming. I tried to make sure Kate and Ivy attended school regularly. I made sure their clothes were clean. At times I looked in the pantry and became panicky at the lack of food. I made soups and stews, trying to stretch what little food we had as far as I could. Da, when he bothered to eat at home, complained. He wanted to know why in hell I'd put rice or barley in the stew. He didn't seem to understand what it took to feed six people with so little food. Sometimes I used everything I could find in the cupboard and it still wasn't enough.

Gabe learned about Ma's hospitalization before I had a chance to write him. A woman from the island who went to visit him in the san gave him the news. In his last letter, he sounded really concerned about the family. I wrote back, telling him what I told everyone: Ma was exhausted. She needed a rest. She would be home in no time. I tried to keep the letter positive. I told him

Zakia was growing into a beautiful baby. She smiled a lot and was just starting to crawl. Kate was pleased that an art teacher liked her drawings. I saw no reason to tell him about how chaotic our home had become. How increasingly worried I was becoming about Kate. That I feared Da might seriously harm her. And I certainly didn't tell him how trapped and overwhelmed I felt.

To keep the fire going, we often collected driftwood from the beach. One fall day, I bundled up Zakia and Eddie. I got a couple of brim bags from the pantry and handed them to Ivy and Kate. "We need to start collecting as much driftwood as we can for winter," I told them.

"Let's walk out toward Devil's Rock," Kate said eagerly. "Maybe we'll find some treasures."

"Sure, you never knows what kind of stuff might drift ashore," Ivy said.

I recalled the beautiful plate and butter dish Gabe had found on the beach last spring. They were still in the cupboard. Ivy once found a doll that was in almost perfect condition. We found dishes, plastic containers, toys, perfume bottles, and other things washed ashore by the tide. "Do you remember the time Jimmy found the crate of oranges?" I asked.

"That was a good find." Ivy licked her lips. "I can still taste them."

"I remembers Ma making orange juice," Kate said. "She saved the peels to make marmalade jam." She smiled at the memory.

It was a bright, sunny day, and as we walked along the shore I felt my spirits lift.

"What's that boat doing here?" Ivy said, pointing to a cabin cruiser that had anchored in the cove.

"It has to be tourists," I said. "No one around here owns anything that fancy."

We had not gone far when we met Gert and Nellie, who were also gathering wood. Nellie was holding Patsy by one hand while dragging a full bag with the other. As they neared, Eddie let go of Kate's hand and began running toward them. "Passy!" he called all excited.

I couldn't help but smile. Eddie loved Patsy.

"My Passy," he said, reaching for her hand. Patsy put both her arms around him, hugging him hard.

"My goodness!" Nellie said. "Be careful you don't knock Eddie over." She turned to me then, her eyes lighting up when she saw Zakia. "Oh, the beautiful little thing," she said, taking her from my arms. "She's just like a living doll. And look at all that hair. Look, Gert. Isn't she gorgeous? She's the face and eyes of Blanche when she was that age."

"Sure, she's not bad looking," Gert said.

Nellie handed back the baby. "Heard any news from your mother, Blanche, my love?"

"Not yet. The nurse said all she needs is a good rest. I expect her home soon." I picked up a piece of driftwood and handed it to Ivy. "Don't know why she had to be sent away in the first place."

"Sure, I said the same thing to Herb," Nellie said. "Your poor mother was runned right down. A good rest and she'll be home as good as new."

"I don't know," Gert said, shaking her head. "Not many people gets out of that place. And when they does, they're never the same. Look at poor old Howard Gould from across the bay. Kept him in there for nearly fifteen years. Worse now than he ever was."

I glanced at Ivy and Kate who were walking ahead of us with Patsy and Eddie. I hoped they hadn't heard what Gert had said.

"Howard's case was different than Grace's," Nellie said. She looked from Gert to me. "I hear Gabe's doing really well," she said in an obvious attempt to steer the conversation away from Gert's negativity.

"The doctors gave him a good report," I said, eager to change the subject.

"Lucky they caught the TB early," Nellie said. "I hear they got new drugs now that's supposed to work wonders." She touched my elbow. "Don't worry, my love. Gabe is going to be just fine."

"I don't know," Gert said. "Once the lungs is weakened, a person's never the same." She pressed her lips together. "Poor old Marion White came back in a box. And then there's Jack Foley." She shook her head. "Sure, they couldn't even get Jack's body home. It being the middle of winter."

Before anyone had a chance to respond, Ivy pointed toward the boat in the harbour. "They're coming ashore, looks like."

We watched as a lifeboat was lowered into the water. A man started down a rope ladder. The boat rocked, and for a moment I was afraid it might overturn. Moments later, a second man began climbing down the ladder.

Nellie shielded her eyes with both hands. "What are they doing here?"

Gert pressed her lips together. "Hope 'tis not that Pentecostal crowd from over in the bay. Got us drove crazy with their foolishness. I tells them I'm Catholic, but they won't give up."

"I don't think 'tis that bunch," Nellie said. "They comes here by ferry. I sees them getting off the boat with their Bibles."

The small boat was heading toward shore. We watched as it got closer and closer. After a while we were able to get a look at the two men. One was very tall, the other short. Both were wearing black overcoats. The taller man stepped out of the lifeboat and pulled it up on the shore. The other man got out and began walking toward us. I saw he was wearing horn-rimmed glasses. Beneath his unbuttoned overcoat, he wore a blue shirt and a little black bow tie. "Well, for heaven's sake," Gert said, as he neared us. "Sure, 'tis the Barrelman."

Joey Smallwood? I tried not to stare as he approached us. It was the first time I'd seen our premier in person. He waved as he approached us. "Joseph R. Smallwood," he said, holding out his hand to Gert. He pointed to the man who was securing the lifeboat. "And that's Mr. Peddle."

"Sure, everybody knows who you is," Gert said, taking his outstretched hand. "I used to listen to you years ago when you was the Barrelman."

Smallwood smiled. "I've been premier for nearly fifteen years now, but folks still think of me as the Barrelman."

"Poor Pop never missed that show," Gert said.

Mr. Smallwood shook hands with the rest of us, even Eddie and Patsy. By this time, Zakia was asleep in my arms.

"What brings you to this neck of the woods, Mr. Smallwood?" Nellie asked.

"I'm here to offer a better and brighter future," he said.

I heard Kate smother a giggle.

The premier looked at the bags of driftwood we'd collected. "With electric heat, you wouldn't have to gather wood," he said. "It's much cleaner too."

"You've come to offer us electricity?" Kate said. She looked at Ivy, and I was afraid they were going to start giggling. I shot them a warning look.

Mr. Smallwood looked at each of us in turn. "I've come to offer not only electricity, but better health care, cars and trucks, better working conditions, and better schools for your children."

Nellie stared at him. "Where's we going to get all that stuff from, my love?"

"My dear good woman, there's no end to the things you can have now that I've brought us into Confederation."

"We've been waiting for almost fifteen years," Gert said.

Mr. Smallwood took off his glasses and wiped them on a handkerchief. "I don't know if you've heard of my resettlement program," he said. "My plan is to move folks out of settlements like this one and into bigger growth centres."

I stared at him. So all the rumours were true then.

"You wants us to move?" Nellie said. "Where to?"

"Any place you like," he told her. "Well, any big town or city. Deer Lake, Corner Brook, St. John's, even Gander or Eagles Nest. He looked across the harbour at the fishing boats bobbing at their moorings. "You can tell your husbands they can burn their boats. Lots of good-paying factory jobs in the cities. And, of course, there are the paper mills in Grand Falls and Corner Brook." By this time, Mr. Peddle had come to stand beside him, but Smallwood didn't seem to notice. "Each family will get a sum of money," he continued, "enough for a decent home. Enough to get your family resettled."

Gert folded her arms. "I got a decent home," she said, "and I'm not going nowheres. Poor Mom and Pop is buried here. As well as a brother who died while he was still a youngster. Jake loves fishing. You couldn't pay him enough money to move away from Darby's Island."

"But he could do so much better," Smallwood assured her. "How much does he make a year fishing?"

"That's neither here nor there," Gert said. "Like I said, we're not going nowheres."

Smallwood seemed taken aback that she would refuse such an offer. He glanced at Zakia, who was asleep in my arms. "How old is your baby, missus?"

"Oh. She's my baby sister. She's nearly five months old."

"Your parents live nearby?"

"We lives in that house over there," Ivy said, pointing. "Our Ma's in the…the hospital."

"And your father? Is he home today?"

Kate tipped an imaginary bottle to her lips. "Da's probably out getting drunk."

"Ah, the drink." Smallwood shook his head. "My own father was obsessed with the bottle. He would go on binges for weeks at a time. A terrible thing, the drink."

Mr. Peddle put a hand on Smallwood's arm. "We should be going, Joe," he said. "We have a lot of houses to visit."

Smallwood shook hands with us all once again. "Give what I said some thought," he said.

Gert shook her head. "No, my son. No amount of money will take me away from this place. This is where I was born and 'tis where I'll die."

Although Smallwood nodded, he seemed perplexed. It was as if he thought everyone would jump at the chance to leave the island. "Well," he said, "make sure you vote in the next election. Mark your X for Smallwood even if you have to crawl on your hands and knees in the worst kind of weather to do so."

We watched as they walked away, Mr. Peddle leading the way.

"I can't see meself moving to Corner Brook when I can't even stand to visit," Gert said. "Sure, the smell of the mill alone is enough to poison a dog."

"It would be nice to live in bigger place," Nellie said. "Somewheres like St. John's or Corner Brook. Even Gander is so much bigger than the island. They even got an airport." She shook her head. "But I can't imagine Herb working in a factory."

"I hopes to God people don't take Joey up on his offer," Gert said. "Once people starts moving away, they'll have no need for the ferry. And what would we do then?"

Nellie turned to me. "You think Abe might move? You could all be closer to your mother if you moves to St. John's. Or in Corner Brook, you'll be able to visit Gabe anytime."

A cold fear clutched my stomach. I hugged the baby tighter against my chest. I could see it now. Da would never turn down money. Once he had it, he'd blow through it like candy. We'd be stuck in some strange place without money or a place to live.

CHAPTER 30

❦

It was nearly eleven-thirty by the time Blanche got to the cafeteria. Staff from the clinic and nursing home were filing in for their lunch break. She found Patsy sitting alone by the window, her fingers tapping impatiently on the table. Blanche realized she had kept her waiting for nearly twenty minutes.

"Patsy?"

The girl jumped nervously. "Blanche?" she said, putting her hand to her heart.

"Sorry I'm late, Patsy. I'm didn't mean to keep you waiting so long."

"It's okay."

"Ready to order?" Blanche sniffed the air. "Something smells good."

"I *am* kind of hungry," Patsy admitted.

"Well, c'mon. Let's go order."

They joined a queue of people holding plastic orange trays. Servers in white coats, their heads covered with hairnets, served scrambled eggs, toast, muffins, and pancakes from chafing bowls behind a glass counter.

Patsy ordered a grilled cheese sandwich and French fries, Blanche pancakes and coffee. Blanche paid for the meal, and they took their trays of food back to the table. For a few minutes they busied themselves opening packages of sugar, catsup, syrup, and little containers of milk.

Blanche stirred her coffee and turned to Patsy. "What grade are you going into this year?"

"Grade ten. Only four of us this year. Me, Joey Ryan, Millie Coles, and Bob Batten."

Blanche nodded. "It was a one-room schoolhouse when I was a girl. Primary through grade eleven all together in one classroom."

"Only one grade nine student this year," Patsy said. "My friend Iris failed her math test by six points."

"And she has to repeat the whole grade?"

Patsy shrugged. "I s'pose. We only got our exams back on Thursday."

"Such a shame."

"At least we don't have provincial exams anymore."

"Ah, provincial exams." Blanche pursed her lips. "They had those back when I was in school. What a curse they were. So many students dropped out because of it. It was difficult to pass an exam made up by someone in St. John's who had no idea what outport students were being taught."

"Enough students dropping out as it is," Patsy said. "Some leaves as soon as they're old enough. Some even before that time."

"I hope you'll stay in school until you graduate, Patsy."

"Nan says I have to stay even if it takes me until I'm twenty-five."

Blanche smiled. That sounded like Nellie. "What are your plans after graduation?"

"Mom wants me to apply to a university in Halifax. That way, I can stay with her."

"You must be looking forward to spending time with your mother."

Patsy dipped a French fry in catsup. "Yes, but I'll miss Nan and Grandpa."

"I'm sure they'll miss you too." Blanche paused a moment. "Patsy," she said. "Tell me again about the hooded man you saw on Friday evening."

Patsy glanced up at her, a puzzled look on her face. "You mean that guy who was searching the beach for pop bottles?"

"Did he tell you his name?"

"No, but I saw him again yesterday. He was coming out of Aunt Olive's house. I waved to him but I don't think he saw me."

Blanche sat up straighter. "What time was that?"

"It was after supper. Six-thirty, maybe seven."

"What was he doing there?"

Patsy shrugged. "I don't know. Maybe he was looking for more pop bottles."

Blanche was silent a beat. She glanced at Patsy's finger. "I see you've changed the stone in your ring."

Patsy looked down at her hand.

Blanche stirred milk in her coffee. "Do you still have the red stone?"

"It fell out," Patsy said, giving Blanche a curious look.

"Any idea where you might have lost it?"

Patsy shook her head and lowered her eyes.

"When did you lose the stone?"

Patsy shrugged. "It must've been last evening…I guess."

"Patsy," Blanche said, leaning forward until her eyes were fixed firmly on hers. "Martin found a stone identical to the one in the ring you were wearing on Friday evening."

Patsy stared at her, a baffled look on her face.

"He found it on the archbishop's body, just under his collar."

Patsy's head jerked up. She gave Blanche a startled look. "He did?"

Blanche nodded. "We both thought it was strange."

Patsy shrugged. "Lots of people have rings like mine."

Blanche leaned in closer. "Patsy, were you on the beach the evening Bishop Malloy was murdered?"

Patsy pushed French fries around on her plate. She avoided looking at Blanche.

"Patsy," Blanche said quietly, "if you know anything, now's the time to speak up."

"I was on the beach Friday evening," Patsy admitted, still not able meet Blanche's eye. "I saw someone…fighting, it looked like, with the archbishop."

Although Blanche expected something was up, she drew back in surprise. "Did you see who it was?"

Patsy shook her head. "They were too far away."

"Was it a man or a woman?"

"I…I'm not sure," Patsy said. "All I know is that it wasn't Uncle Jake."

Blanche studied her carefully. "How do you know that? You said you were too far away to see the person."

"Uncle Jake walked by later. He looked like he was in a daze. I called out to him, but he kept walking."

"Did you go to the archbishop? Offer help?"

"I didn't realize he was hurt," Patsy said, her eyes on her untouched food.

"How come you never mentioned this when you spoke to us yesterday?" Blanche's tone made it clear she wasn't buying Patsy's story.

Patsy put down her fork. "I didn't think anyone would believe me."

"It does sound far-fetched."

"I know," Patsy said. "That's why I didn't say anything."

Blanche continued to stare at her. What had Patsy gotten herself mixed up in?

Patsy met Blanche's gaze. "Will I have to testify?"

"First, you'll need to give a formal statement to the forensics team. After that, I'm not sure what will happen."

"When will they get here?"

"They've been delayed, but they will be here eventually. And Patsy," she added, her voice firm. Patsy looked up at her. "It's a crime to give false information to a law officer. You could be charged with obstructing justice."

CHAPTER 31

⁓⁓⁓

WARD HELD OUT HIS CUP. "COULD I HAVE SOME MORE HOT WATER?" he asked the elderly grey-haired woman who worked at the cafeteria. Her name tag said *Hi I'm Beatrice, Volunteer.*

"My love, that tea bag must be getting kind of weak," she said. "You sure I can't get you a fresh one?"

Not for twenty cents, Ward thought. He was running out of money and needed every cent. He had splurged seventy-five cents on a plate of chips. "Nah, I likes it weak," he told the server. "No need to be wasteful."

Ward took his tea back to a table by the window. He liked it here at the nursing home where it was warm. He had slept in the station wagon last night, and woke up stiff and shivering from the cold. Until Friday, he'd been sleeping at a cottage, but he'd returned that evening to see a police cruiser parked outside the door. At first, he thought someone had called to report him. He had been careful to avoid suspicion, and only went to the cottage after dark. He had kept his station wagon on the beach, and even set up a small tent there.

Ward stared out the window at the rain. He'd had a close call last night. *Stupid of me to go back to the cottage with a cop staying there,* he chided himself. *She could have shot me.* He had intended to get in and out as quickly as he could. He knew he was taking a risk, but he needed his wallet. He'd waited until he'd seen the cop car leave on Friday and went back to collect his things. Later he'd discovered that he'd left his wallet with his money and ID behind. He wondered now if she had gotten a good look at him when she chased him out the door. He didn't want to go back in daylight. Not now, when everyone was being questioned by the police. Everyone was on high alert. He was a stranger here, and he knew strangers were regarded with more suspicion than the local people. Especially now that a murder had been committed.

For sure the police would want to question him. It would only be a matter of time. His station wagon had been parked on the beach in plain sight the night the bishop was murdered. This morning he had moved it to a secluded spot not far from the nursing home. He would hole up there until the storm was over, he decided. He couldn't wait to get the hell away from this place. He knew he was in trouble whichever way he turned. He had a story ready for when the police questioned him. He would tell them he went to sleep around nine that evening, and didn't wake up until six the next morning. No one could prove anything different. He wasn't going to tell them what he knew. He wouldn't even tell them that he knew the bishop. Lots of people knew Bishop Malloy, he reasoned. No, he would only answer the questions they asked. No need to tell them he'd seen the bishop leaving Olive Beals's office on Friday afternoon either. He wasn't going to get dragged into this any more than he had to. He was in enough trouble as it was.

Ward finished his tea and left the cafeteria. He was driving back to his secluded spot in the woods when he noticed a car in the ditch. He pulled over to the side of the road and got out. The car was a blue Chevy, and he knew at once that it belonged to the hypnotist. It had hit a telephone pole, and the windshield was smashed. As Ward approached the car, a woman—Miranda, he realized—got out.

"Miranda," he called, rushing toward her. "What happened? Are you okay?"

"The roads here are so narrow," she said. "With the bad weather it was difficult to see. I'm not used to driving on unpaved roads."

"Are you hurt?" Ward noticed she walked with a limp.

Miranda's hand went to her head. "I banged my noggin," she said, "and my leg got cut from the flying glass." She surveyed the damage to her car. "It could have been a lot worse."

"Yes," Ward agreed, taking in the car's smashed bumper. There was glass all over the ground. "As long as you're okay—that's the main thing."

Miranda looked at Ward as if seeing him for the first time. "You're our neighbour," she said, "the guy who collects pop bottles. What is your name again?"

He smiled. "It's still Ward—Ward Thompson. Can I give you a lift back to your trailer?"

"Oh, bless you. That would be wonderful."

It wasn't until Miranda was seated next to him in the passenger seat that Ward realized she'd been drinking. He could smell it on her breath. Also she had the beginning of a nasty bruise on her forehead.

"Some bad weather we're having," Ward said in an attempt to make conversation.

Miranda smiled. "You're an angel, Ward Thompson, and I just adore your accent."

A few minutes later, Ward manoeuvred the wagon down the steep incline to the beach. He parked a few feet away from the trailer. Miranda thanked him and got out. He watched as she limped up the steps to the trailer door.

Ward was driving away when he noticed Miranda's purse on the floor of the car. He stopped, picked up the purse, and got out. He was about to knock on the trailer door when he heard raised voices. Great, he thought. They were having an argument. Ward thought of leaving the purse on the doorstep. He could hear Prospero's voice through the thin walls. "How could you get behind the wheel of a car after drinking? What the hell were you thinking?"

Ward knocked on the door. A few moments went by before Prospero opened it. "We don't have any bottles today," he said curtly.

He was about to close the door when Ward held up the purse. "Miranda left this in my car."

"Oh." Prospero looked sheepish. "Thank you," he said, taking the purse. As Ward was walking away, he could hear Prospero through the closed door. "You'll be in big trouble if that kid tells the RCMP you were driving impaired."

"I didn't have that much to drink," Miranda said.

"Your judgement was impaired enough that you wrecked our car."

"It was the bad weather..."

As Ward got back into his car, he realized there was something different about Prospero—something he couldn't put his finger on. It was only after he was driving away that he realized the hypnotist had lost his British accent.

Back at his secluded spot, Ward stretched out his legs, trying to get comfortable. The car's seat was back as far as it would go, but he still felt squished. He turned back to the journal he'd been reading.

December 22,

My heart is breaking for our Kate. She is very unhappy at the orphanage. She says the nuns are not treating her well. I feel so helpless not being able to do anything about it. Jimmy and Da are always at each other's throats. Jimmy's had it in for Da ever since he signed forms to have Ma committed to the Mental. He was just as upset when Kate got sent away. Jimmy says Kate belongs at home with the family. I couldn't agree more. Laverne and Freddy stopped coming around. Laverne got mad after Da hit Freddy so hard his nose bled. Da hardly comes home at all, and most of the time we are left to fend for ourselves. To make matters worse, Da is thinking about moving. He's been bragging about how much money he can get from the resettlement program.

The good news is that our Gabe is out of the hospital. He's spending Christmas with Dr. Harris and his family. They've kind of adopted him. They want him to go to university. As much as I miss Gabe, I know he's better off where he is. We got a Christmas card from Ma, but I could tell it was signed by someone else. It makes me sad to think she might be in that place forever.

Not exactly *The Waltons*, Ward thought, shaking his head. He closed the journal and briefly considered the envelope he'd taken, filled with photographs and newspaper clippings. On second thought, he reached for the single sheet of paper he'd stolen from the typewriter.

December 24, 1963

Even now, I have nightmares of that horrible Christmas Eve. I have come to think of it as the night that changed our lives forever. We were all feeling bad that some of our family members could not be with us at Christmastime. That afternoon I found Ivy crying in our room. She said she missed Ma, Kate, and Gabe. Jimmy kept pacing the floor like he had something on his mind.

The evening started out well enough. Aunt Hattie came by in the afternoon with a Christmas box. Along with the mitts, scarves, and vamps she brought every year, there was a box of chocolates for the children. I let each of them have one after supper. I baked a pot of beans and made brown bread to serve with it. Jimmy had cut down a scrawny Christmas tree, and Eddie and Ivy had decorated it with paper chains. Eddie was all excited, and kept running to the window hoping to see Santa.

Around ten o'clock, Jimmy and Da got into a heated argument. Ivy was really nervous—I could tell by the way she kept chewing her fingernails. She stayed out of Da's way as much as she could. I was glad Eddie and Zakia were in bed, and hoped the shouting wouldn't wake them. After a while, Da got up from his chair and stood in the middle of the floor, his fists clenched. "You wanna fight," he kept challenging Jimmy. "I'm game."

"Go to bed, old man, you're making a fool of yourself," Jimmy told him.

Still Da kept it up. "What are you afraid of, you little bastard?" He pushed Jimmy into the stove.

Jimmy was putting on his coat when Da punched him in the side of the head. Jimmy turned around and punched him in the face. Da ran into the bedroom. He came out carrying the rifle he kept mounted on the wall. To my horror, he pointed it at Jimmy.

Ivy screamed, "No! Don't hurt him, Da."

Although it was late and dark outside, I asked Ivy to go for Martin Bursey. He was visiting his family on the island with his wife and kids. Ivy ran out in the freezing cold without even bothering to put her coat on.

The next part is fuzzy. Maybe because it happened so fast. Or perhaps because it was too horrible to remember. I recall trying to get Da to put the gun away. He wouldn't listen and kept pushing me out of the way. Then the thing I feared most happened. Da pulled the trigger. I think I might have screamed when the shot rang out. I didn't see Jimmy fall, but the next thing I remember was that he lay stretched out on the floor. For a long moment, I stood paralyzed with horror. Da flopped down on the daybed, still holding the gun. I crept closer to Jimmy, and saw blood pooling on the floor. He didn't seem to be breathing. I checked his pulse, my own hand trembling on his wrist. "What have you done?" I screamed at Da.

Da looked at me, his eyes glassy and unfocused. He put the gun to his own head

A knocking on the window startled Ward. He turned to see a man staring in at him. He gestured for Ward to roll down the window. Ward knew the man was Martin Bursey, the same man he had been reading about in the journal. He was the officer investigating the archbishop's murder. Now what? Should he gun the engine? But where could he go on a small island?

Ward rolled down the window. "Yeah?"

"I'm Martin Bursey with the RCMP," he said, eyeing Ward critically. He didn't show his badge like they usually do. Probably because he didn't have it with him. Ward knew the Mountie was here on vacation.

"You don't look like an RCMP officer."

Bursey ignored the remark. "Can I see your driver's licence, insurance, and registration?"

Ward found his licence. He pretended to look for the registration and insurance he didn't have. "I'm sorry, officer," he said.

"I must have dropped the documents on the beach. I had my car parked down there before the storm."

Bursey eyed the journal Ward had placed on the seat beside him. "Where did you get that?"

"Ah...I...was just writing to pass the time." Ward shoved the journal in his knapsack, along with the typewritten page he had stolen.

"Could you step out of the car?"

Christ, what now? Is he going to read me my rights? Ward thought as he opened the door and got out.

"Where are you from?" Bursey asked.

"Oh, here, there, and everywhere."

Bursey glared at him. "Were you anywhere near Gabe Ste Croix's cabin last night?"

The question was so unexpected that Ward's mouth gaped open. "No...no..." he managed to stammer.

"You were seen leaving Olive Beals's house last evening."

Ward was speechless. Christ, they'd been checking up on him. "So?" he managed to say.

"Olive is in the hospital. Someone stabbed her."

Stabbed her? Someone had stabbed Olive Beals?

Bursey took a step toward him. Fear grabbed at Ward's insides. Not knowing what else to do, he found himself running toward the woods.

CHAPTER 32

❧

May 1966

"You should get changed, my love," Ellen, my co-worker, told me. "Don't you have a class this evening?" She was a tall, elderly woman with salt-and-pepper hair. Ellen had taken me under her wing since I came to work at the Glynmill Inn.

"Shirley's dad is picking me up," I told her. I glanced at the clock on the wall and saw it was nearly ten to six. "He said he'd be here around six."

In the locker room, I stepped out of my uniform and pulled on jeans and a blue pullover. I ran my hands through my newly cut hair before grabbing my purse and heading to the lobby.

"Have a good evening, Miss Ste Croix," Charlie, the man at the desk, said.

"You too, Charlie," I said. The phone rang and he picked it up.

I was walking toward the door when I saw a tall man get up from one of the chairs grouped around a polished table. His white-blond hair came down to his shoulders. He was dressed in bell-bottom jeans and a brown wool sweater with a zipper up the front. I could only stare in disbelief as he walked toward me.

"Blanche?"

"Coop?" I said, taken aback. Except for his longish hair, he looked the same.

We stared at each other for a moment longer before he enveloped me in a hug. "Good to see yeh, my love." He held me at arm's length. "You cut your hair."

"Well, yes," I said, feeling self-conscious.

"It suits you."

"What are you doing here?" I said. "Juney told me you were living in Grand Falls."

"I'll be here 'til Sunday," Coop said. "I'm doing a job over at City Hall. Let's sit over there." He put his hand on the small of my back and steered me toward a group of chairs. I took a seat on a small sofa, and Coop sat in an easy chair across from me.

"How you been, Blanche?"

"Busy," I said. "I work full-time and go to school."

Coop looked at me, concern etched on his face. "I heard about what happened."

I looked down at my hands. "You and everyone else in Newfoundland," I said. The story had been on the news and in all the newspapers. Reporters had even come to the foster home where I was living.

"I was shocked when I heard," Coop said. "How's the rest of the family?"

"As well as can be expected, considering we're all living in different places."

Coop nodded slowly. "I heard Gabe got adopted."

"Yes," I confirmed. "After he was well enough to leave the san, they sent him to live with the Carters, a family in Gander." I didn't add that they were afraid to send him home—afraid he wouldn't get the right nutrition and would relapse. "After the... the incident, his foster family decided to adopt him. He's in his second year at MUN. He calls me from time to time. We plan to get together for Christmas."

"Are the others close by?"

"Eddie and Ivy are in foster care in Deer Lake. Zakia was adopted by a family on the mainland."

"And Kate? Is she still at the orphanage?"

"I don't know where Kate is right now." I looked down at my hands. "She ran away from the orphanage. It's the third time this month. The police are looking for her. She's very unhappy there, and complains about being mistreated."

Coop frowned. "Is there anything anyone can do about it?"

"I tried, believe me." I forced a smile. "And you…how are you doing?" I asked, eager to change the subject. "Are you staying here at the hotel?"

"I'm staying at the Holiday Inn up the street." Seeing my questioning look, he added, "I came here to see you. I tried calling. Didn't you get my message?"

"No," I said, feeling a surge of outrage. I lived in a rooming house owned by an elderly Chinese couple who didn't speak English. Marjorie, the housekeeper, took all the phone calls. This was not the first time she hadn't given me my messages.

"I was hoping to take you out to dinner," Coop said.

"Dinner?" I echoed, pleased that he'd thought about me.

"I thought we could go for Chinese food at the Seven Seas."

"I can't this evening," I said. "I have a class. Someone's coming to pick me up any minute now." I glanced toward the window.

"Juney told me you were working toward your high school diploma." Coop smiled at me. "Good for you. But surely you can find time between now and Sunday to have dinner with me."

"I don't know," I said. "I'm working a double shift tomorrow. And on Sunday I have to catch the bus to Deer Lake. I haven't seen Ivy or Eddie in nearly a month. I was planning to go a couple of weeks ago, but we had that freak snowstorm. Poor little Eddie probably thinks I've abandoned him."

"Sure, I can drive you to Deer Lake on Sunday," Coop said. "I'll take you and the kids out for dinner. We can go to that new place near the airport. The Apple Cellar, I think it's called."

"Coop, you don't have to—"

He held up a hand. "I want to," he said. "My sister Liz told me they have a great kid's menu. She takes her youngsters there all the time."

"Thanks, Coop," I said. "It'll save me the hassle of having to take the bus there and back."

A car pulled up outside the hotel. "There's my ride," I said. "I have to go." I scribbled down my address on a napkin. "I'll see you on Sunday, then."

I could barely keep my mind on my lessons that evening. Coop had made a special trip to the hotel to see me—to take me out. Did that mean he was interested in me? Or was he just being kind? Juney had told me he was no longer seeing Susan.

I had been surprised to get a phone call from Juney. She was studying nursing at the vocational school. At first, I wasn't keen on the idea. But Juney had changed. Aunt Hattie said she'd matured in the last couple of years. And she seemed genuinely concerned about me. I could tell she was really shaken up by what had happened to my family. Although I was always happy to see people from the island, their visits took me back to a time in my life that I would rather forget. That horrible night was never far from my mind. Because the ferry had stopped running for the season, detectives had to be flown in by helicopter. At the foster home in St. John's, I walked around in a daze for weeks. I left shortly after my sixteenth birthday, moved to Corner Brook, found a job, and registered for night school. I threw myself into my work and studies. It helped stop the panic and fear from taking over. At night I was so tired I fell into a sound, dreamless sleep.

Sometimes I wondered if I'd ever get over that night, and all that I'd lost. At times, the ache in my chest was almost more than I could bear. I didn't sleep well, and I was jumpy and nervous. I'd be at work, making beds or scrubbing toilets, when out of the blue it would all come back to me. My mind would play out the horror like scenes from a movie. I would stop working and find something to focus on. I'd read the hotel's policy or the instructions about what to do in case of an emergency. I'd read it over and over until I felt calm. One day when a car backfired outside the hotel, I panicked and ran. Ellen found me crouched in the linen closet, clutching a pillow to my chest.

On Saturday, I stopped at Woolworths and bought gifts for Ivy and Eddie. Ivy liked doing crosswords and putting together jigsaw puzzles. Eddie loved crayons and colouring. I left the store with a five-hundred-piece puzzle for Ivy, crayons and a colouring book for Eddie. I picked up chocolate bars and other small treats. The only thing that kept me going on those hopeless days filled with emptiness was my brothers and sisters. My goal was for all of us to be together someday.

I rose early on Sunday morning and put on my one good blouse and tan pants. I carefully applied mascara and eyeliner. I waited for Coop on the front porch of my rooming house. He showed up in a blue van with *Pickford's Renovations & Restoration* written on the sides. He parked on the street and got out. He was wearing white jeans and a blue pullover. I felt a rush of happiness as I went to meet him.

Coop smiled when he saw me. "Sorry I'm late," he said. "It took me a while to put the back seat back in. Something I should have dealt with last night."

"It's a beautiful day for a drive," I said. The sun was already high in the sky. Robins were singing in the backyard.

"We couldn't order a better day than this," Coop agreed. "Spring's finally arrived." He opened the van door and I got in.

I leaned back against the soft upholstery, feeling contented. Coop got in the driver's side and closed the door. "I'm looking forward to my visit with Ivy and Eddie," I said. "It's been a while."

"Do you get to see much of your family?" Coop asked as he started the engine.

"I visit Eddie and Ivy about once every two weeks," I said. "And I try to get to St. John's to see Ma once a month. And Kate when she hasn't run off."

"How's your mother?"

"Not well. She doesn't know me anymore. It's the shock treatments, I imagine. I get depressed whenever I go to see her. I hate seeing her in such a state. And Kate is...well, she's always angry."

Coop looked at me, his hazel eyes soft.

"But I'm pleased Eddie's doing so well. For a while he wasn't talking, but he's coming out of his shell. He started school back in September. He's struggling, but slowly making progress. Ivy lives close by, and she visits him whenever she can."

Coop stopped for a light. "How old is Eddie now?"

"He turned six back in November."

"And what about you, Blanche? How are you handling all of this?"

"I get by," I told him. "I stay busy and do what needs to be done."

Coop continued up West Valley Road, passing one- and two-storey houses with neatly mowed lawns. The warm weather had brought people out of their homes. They were doing yardwork or sitting on their decks. Children played outside with balls and skipping ropes. Little kids rode tricycles up and down the driveways. At the top of the street, a sign with an arrow pointing right said *Deer Lake, 32.8 miles*. Coop waited until the coast was clear before turning onto the Trans-Canada.

"It's beautiful here," I said, gazing out the window.

Coop nodded. "Corner Brook is one of the prettiest cities in Newfoundland."

After some time, we came to the Humber River. Mountains towered on both sides of the narrow, twisting road. The scenery never failed to awe. It felt good to be sitting next to Coop, on my way to see Ivy and Eddie. I had not felt this good in a long time.

The trip took about forty minutes. It was quarter past ten when we pulled into the driveway at 34 Carson Lane. The house was a split-level in a subdivision of similar homes. The yard had a swing set, slide, sandbox, and playhouse.

I glanced toward the large bay window overlooking the yard. "I don't see Eddie," I said. "He's usually waiting for me by the window. Sometimes he waits for hours." I noticed that the family station wagon was not in the driveway. "I wonder if they've gone out."

"Are they expecting you?"

"I called a couple of weeks ago to tell Janice—that's Eddie's foster mother—I'd be coming today." I glanced at my watch again. "I usually don't get here until after eleven. Maybe I should've called ahead to tell them I'd be early."

"Well, if they're out, I'm sure they'll be back soon," Coop said. "We can go get Ivy, and come back later if you like."

"First let's check to see if there's anyone home."

We walked up a narrow path to the front door and rang the doorbell. A few minutes went by before Janice's mother, Charlotte, opened the door. She looked from me to Coop, a surprised look on her face. "Blanche?"

"This is Coop Pickford from home," I told her. I tried to see around the door. "Is Eddie here? We've come to take him out."

"Oh, my love, didn't you get the message?"

"Message?"

"Come in, my love," Charlotte stepped aside so we could enter. I walked down the hallway to the kitchen, Coop trailing behind me. I had a feeling something was wrong. "Is Eddie, okay?" I asked, trying to keep my voice steady.

"Have a seat, Blanche." Charlotte gestured to a wooden table with six chairs.

Coop pulled out a chair for me and one for himself.

"Can I get you a cup of tea?" Charlotte asked, after we were seated.

"No...no, thanks, I'm fine. Where's Eddie? Is he gone out with Janice and Dave?"

Charlotte sat down wearily in a chair across the table from us. "My love," she began, "I don't know how to tell you this..." She paused, taking a deep breath.

"Is Eddie okay?" I looked at Coop who had a worried frown on his face. I braced myself for the bad news I knew was coming.

"Janice left a message at your boarding house," Charlotte continued. "She thought you would want to come see your brother before he left."

"Left?" I felt panic rising in me. "Eddie's gone?"

I felt Coop's hand on my arm.

"Children's Aid came and took him." Charlotte could barely look at me as she spoke. "He's going to be adopted by a family in St. John's."

For a moment, I was too stunned to speak.

"When did that happen?" I heard Coop ask.

"Nearly a week ago, now." Charlotte shook her head. "We wondered if you got the message."

"Do you know where they took him?" I asked. "Do you have a phone number?"

"No, my love, I don't, and I don't think Janice and Dave do either." She looked at me, her face sad. "You might try calling Children's Aid."

I felt my whole body go numb. They had taken away my brother. I didn't even get a chance to say goodbye.

The phone rang at that moment. "I should get that," Charlotte said.

"We'll see ourselves out," Coop said. He reached for my arm, pulled me to my feet, and steered me toward the door. Numbly, I let him lead me to the van. He opened the door and I got in, my heart breaking.

Coop closed the door and went around to the driver's side. "Are you going to be okay?"

I stared out the window. Eddie was gone. How could I ever be okay? The tears that I had been holding back came in a flood.

Coop put his arms around me, pulling me tight. I could hear his heart beat, smell the spiciness of his cologne. I sobbed against his chest, tears soaking his shirt while he rubbed my arms and patted my back. We stayed that way for a long time, grief ripping through me like streaks of lightning. If Eddie was adopted, chances were I would never see him again. Another brother lost.

CHAPTER 33

❦

NO SENSE GOING AFTER HIM, MARTIN THOUGHT AS HE WATCHED Ward Thompson disappear into the woods. He looked at the driver's licence and saw the date of birth was 1959. The face staring out looked younger and more clean-cut than the scruffy young man who had just run into the woods. *I have his car keys,* Martin thought. *If he doesn't have a spare, he won't get far.* He opened the door of the wagon and looked inside. There was a sleeping bag and pillow in the back seat. Beside them were a couple of paperback mysteries and a book of crossword puzzles. There was also a manila envelope. A quick look inside revealed a number of letters and newspaper clippings.

In the glove compartment, Martin found the registration and insurance policy. The car was registered to a Richard Collins from Glovertown. *Jesus Christ, a stolen car. No wonder he took off when I tried to question him.* No doubt it was Thompson who had broken into Gabe's cottage the night before. About half an hour ago, Blanche had called Martin to tell him Thompson had been seen coming out of Olive's house last evening. He could have gone back again this morning. For all Martin knew, he could have murdered the archbishop and tried to kill Olive.

Martin got in his truck and headed back to the hall. He and Blanche had planned to pay a visit to Prospero that afternoon. At least now, Blanche would know what had happened to her journal.

When Martin arrived at the hall, Blanche was not there. He dumped the contents of the envelope on the table. The newspaper clippings were at least a decade old. *Double Murder on Darby's Island* ran a headline from the *Telegram*. A headline from the *Globe* read *Father and Son Dead in Murder Suicide*. There were various other clippings, all dealing with the Ste Croix Massacre, as the incident had come to be known. There were articles written about Kate too. *Kate Ste Croix's Painting "The Island at Dusk" auctioned off for $25,000.*

Martin picked up a letter from Kate to Gabe. It had a St. John's postmark. Martin scanned it quickly. *Please get me out of this place,* she wrote. *They beat me here, and they cut off my hair. They say I am full of pride. They won't let me paint here.* Martin shook his head. He'd heard bad things about that orphanage. No wonder Kate had kept running away. Such a beautiful, talented girl. It tore Martin up knowing what she must have endured.

Martin was sorting through the items when Blanche came in. "I've found your intruder," he said. "Name's Ward Thompson, barely sixteen years old."

"How did you find him?"

"He was hiding in the woods in a stolen station wagon," Martin said. "Took off when I confronted him." He gestured to the items on the table. "He took all this from the cottage. My guess is that he was staying there before you came."

"Why would he take this stuff?"

Martin shrugged. "Maybe he came here hoping to get his hands on one of Kate's paintings. Why else would he have those clippings?"

Blanche looked at the letters and clippings spread out on the table. Martin saw her wince as she read the headline *Bloor Street Prostitute Posthumously Nominated for Governor General's Award.*

"I'm sorry," Martin said.

Blanche picked up the article. "Bloor Street prostitute," she said. "Kate was more than that. She was my sister. She had a family who loved her."

It was late morning by the time Blanche and Martin got around to visiting Prospero and Miranda.

Prospero met them at the door. "Well," he said, "this is a pleasant surprise."

Blanche could tell his smile was forced.

"We would like a word with you," Martin said.

Prospero folded his arms in front of him. "I already told Constable Ste Croix everything I know."

"There's been...new developments," Martin said.

"Well, in that case, come in." Prospero made a sweeping gesture with his arms.

The trailer seemed small and even more claustrophobic with four people crammed inside.

"Have a seat." Prospero began pulling out chairs from around the small table.

"So, you're Debra Brown," Martin said, turning to the woman standing near the window with her arms folded. He frowned. "What happened to your face?"

"Just a little accident," she said evasively.

"Have you had it looked at?" Blanche asked.

"It's just a bruise."

Martin kept his eyes fixed on her, a curious expression on his face. "Where are you from, Debra Brown?"

"Call me Miranda," she said, an edge to her voice. "Prospero and I are in the process of changing our names."

"Okay," Martin said. "Where are you from, Miranda?"

"I'm from Mississauga," she said.

"Is that where you were born?"

"My parents moved there from Montreal."

"And they're still there?"

"They're both dead."

"I'm sorry," Martin said.

Prospero chuckled. "So much small talk." He turned to Martin. "I admire the skilful way you have of extracting the information you need."

"Ah, you're onto me," Martin said lightly.

Prospero folded his hands on the table. "Is there anything we can do for you today, Detective?"

"I spoke with the Chief of Police last evening," Martin said. "He called with some information he's dug up on you."

Blanche saw Miranda and Prospero exchange panicked looks.

"He told me about your record," Martin continued.

"Ah, yes, my record." Blanche could tell Prospero was trying to make light of the situation. However, his face had gone pale. He stood and began pacing the small trailer. "What does my record have to do with the archbishop's murder?"

"We are looking into people's backgrounds," Martin said.

"Prospero has paid dearly for his mistakes," Miranda said.

"Yes, I'm sure he has," Blanche said.

"Well then, why don't you leave him alone?"

"We are not here to judge," Blanche said.

Martin put a hand on Prospero's shoulder. "Could you please sit down, Mr....umm, Prospero?"

Prospero sat in one of the chairs, his feet tapping the floor.

"I understand you spent three years in prison on charges of manslaughter," Martin said.

Still tapping, Prospero looked at Martin. Moments passed before he spoke. "Yes, I've spent time in jail," he said.

"Tell us what happened," Blanche urged.

"You don't have to tell those people anything," Miranda said. "They probably know everything anyway."

Prospero seemed to consider this. "No," he agreed, "I don't have to tell them anything. Still, I think it would be better if they knew the full story." Sighing, he looked from Blanche to Martin. "It's a long story."

"Take all the time you need," Blanche said.

"I was stupid and careless," Prospero began. "At the time, I was heavy into drugs. Cocaine, LSD, marijuana. I tried to convince myself they actually improved my dentistry work." He paused, taking a deep breath. "I left one of my patients, a sixteen-year-old girl, alone after I had performed a procedure. She died in my clinic." He covered his face with his hands. "I will live with the consequences of that for the rest of my life."

"You have paid dearly for your mistakes," Blanche said, feeling a wave of sympathy. "Your licence was revoked, you spent time in prison."

Prospero nodded, as if grateful for her understanding. "The girl's name was Ruby Jennings," he continued. "Not a day goes by that I don't think of her. She would have been twenty-four years old now. She was a beautiful girl, a gifted ballerina who won a scholarship to the National Ballet School. Now, because of my poor judgment, Ruby Jennings will never dance again."

"Prospero has started a scholarship in her name," Miranda said.

"Little comfort that is to her parents, and those who loved her," he said.

"Has anything like this ever happened before?" Martin asked.

Prospero stared at him. "What do you mean?"

"Have any of your subjects been harmed?"

"Of course not," Prospero said with a trace of indignation. "Not only is hypnosis good stage entertainment, but it can be quite beneficial. Right now, I am working with a psychologist. We are making a tape to help patients with insomnia." He let out an exasperated breath. "What is it that you want from me, Detective?"

Miranda glared at Martin. "This could ruin Prospero's reputation if the press finds out."

"Chances are the press will not hear about it," Martin said.

"The important thing is that I didn't kill the archbishop," Prospero said. "How could I, when I was in bed and asleep by nine-fifteen that evening?"

"I'm willing to swear to that," Miranda said.

Martin gave her a small smile. "Of course," he said.

"How long do we have to stay here?" she asked.

Martin reached across the table, touching her sleeve in a reassuring gesture. "Don't worry," he said. "Everything's going to work out just fine."

CHAPTER 34

⌒~✦~⌒

On her way home, Blanche decided to stop at her in-laws' house. Maybe Gert or Jake had noticed something this morning. They were Olive's closest neighbours, after all. No sooner had she parked the car when Gert came to stand in the doorway. "What happened to Olive?" she called. "The ambulance came for her this morning."

Blanche wondered how much she should reveal. "Olive was stabbed," she said, after a pause.

"Stabbed? Somebody stabbed poor Olive?" Gert put her hand over her chest. "What in heaven's name is going on? You never knows what's gonna happen now from one day to the next. There's strangers coming and going all the time." She looked at Blanche, her eyes filled with fear. "Is Olive gonna be okay?"

"I'm not sure," Blanche answered honestly.

"Come in," Gert said, and Blanche followed her into the kitchen. She took a seat in a rocking chair by the window. Gert stood by the table, her arms folded in front of her. "There's tea on the back of the stove."

"No thanks, Gert. I only have a moment. I just need to ask you a few questions."

Gert eyed her warily.

"Did you see anyone coming or going from Olive's house this morning?"

"Young Joey Ryan delivered her groceries, oh…about two hours ago now."

"He delivers groceries on Sunday?"

"Joey couldn't get to all the houses yesterday on account of the storm," Gert explained.

"Did you notice what time he left?"

"No, but he'll be able to tell you that his own self. I expects him here any minute now. He forgot me Javex. I phoned, and he said he'd bring it right over."

"Well," Blanche said, "in that case, I'll wait for him."

"When I seen the ambulance this morning, I thought Olive tried to make away with herself again."

"Make away with herself?" Blanche repeated. "Olive tried to kill herself?"

"Tried more than once," Gert said. "The first time she took a whole bottle of sleeping pills. They had to fly her to St. John's. She almost died that time." Gert shook her head. "Must've been in a bad way to do the likes of that."

"When did it happen?"

"Oh…must be about four months ago now."

Was it because she was so far in debt? Did Olive feel she was in over her head?

"Coop called here," Gert said. "He's some worried about you. He's been trying to reach you at the cottage."

Blanche smiled. Despite his easygoing nature, Coop was a worrier. Still, she was pleased to hear he was concerned about her.

"He put Reba on the phone," Gert said. "She sung me a song she'd heard on television. Something about a little bunny. My, don't she talk some good for a youngster her age." Blanche noted the pride in Gert's voice. "Smart as a whip that one."

"Yes, she's very bright."

The phone in the front room rang and Gert went to answer it.

Blanche looked around the room. There were pictures of Gert's children and grandchildren, including Reba. In one photograph, Coop was holding a newborn Reba, a wide smile on his face. In another, Reba was dressed as a black cat at Halloween. There was a picture of Blanche standing next to Coop. It was taken at high school gymnasium during Blanche's graduation from the adult education program. She was proudly clutching her high school diploma. Coop was standing beside her, his arm draped over her shoulder. Blanche was surprised Gert had included that one.

That night had been the beginning of a relationship that was more than that of friends. They had left the dance at the gym and had gone to a restaurant. Blanche smiled now, remembering how Coop had kissed her for the first time. They had stayed at the restaurant until closing time. Blanche had told him about her anxiety: she still couldn't go to sleep without a light on. She told him about applying for a job in the crime lab at the police department. Now that she had her high school diploma, she had a chance of being accepted.

She recalled how shy Coop had been when he kissed her that evening. "I was scared you would reject me," he told her later. "Don't know what I would have done if that happened." They had made plans to go to a movie the following weekend.

The sound of a vehicle pulling into the yard brought Blanche back to the present. Through the window, she saw a young man get out of a truck.

Gert came back into the kitchen. "There's young Joey now," she said

A minute later, they heard footsteps on the stoop. "Aunt Gert," Joey called, "I'll leave your Javex in the porch, okay?"

"Come in, Joey, my son," Gert said. "Blanche is here, and she wants to talk to you."

Joey came to stand in the doorway, a puzzled expression on his face. He looked to be about Patsy's age. He wore faded jeans and a red windbreaker. With his haircut, granny glasses, and long straight nose, he looked like a younger version of John Lennon.

"I understand you delivered groceries to Olive this morning," Blanche said.

"Yeah."

"Was she okay when you left?"

Joey pushed his glasses up on his nose. "I s'pose. I sung out to her, and when she didn't answer I put the groceries on top of the deep freeze in her porch like I always do."

"So you didn't see Olive then?" Blanche asked.

"Nope."

"Did you see anyone else around her place?"

Joey looked from Blanche to Gert. "What's going on?"

"My son, somebody tried to kill poor Olive," Gert said. "Carved her up with a knife—just like they done with the archbishop." She shook her head. "Probably them hippies that got their van parked out on Gull's Head. I've been wary of that bunch ever since they got here."

Joey's face went pale. "Olive gonna be okay?"

"We hope so," Blanche said.

Joey pulled a chair away from the kitchen table and sat down. "Who did it?" he asked, his brown eyes wide.

"That's what we're trying to find out," Blanche said. "Did you see anyone around when you delivered groceries this morning?"

"Well, not then."

Blanche glanced up at him.

"I went back to look for me watch," Joey explained. "It must have slipped off when I was delivering the groceries." He looked down at his arm. "I was about to go back to Olive's when I found it on the ground. I was walking to the truck when I seen Linda come out of the house. I called out to her, but I don't think she heard me. She ran and got in her car."

"Linda Pearce was at Olive's house this morning?" Blanche asked. "Are you sure?"

Joey nodded.

Blanche felt as if the bottom was about to fall out of her stomach. Linda had been on the beach the night the archbishop was murdered. Was she involved in his death? Could she have harmed Olive? Blanche couldn't imagine it. Still, she needed to find out what was going on. Another thought struck her. Was it Linda Patsy was protecting? Patsy loved Linda like a second mother. But what possible motive could she have to harm Olive or the archbishop? It made no sense.

"Sure I can't get you a cup of tea?" Gert asked.

"No thanks," Blanche said, rising to her feet. "I need to go back to the cottage."

As soon as I have a chance to call Reba, I'll pay Linda a visit, Blanche decided. She should at least be able to explain why she was at Olive's this morning.

The rain had let up some by the time Blanche reached the cottage. She was about to insert the key in the lock when she saw that the door was already ajar. How could that be? After last night's intrusion, she'd made a point of locking the door this morning. Pulling her gun from her holster, she cautiously entered the cottage.

A man sat in the rocker holding her journal. He glanced up at Blanche as she entered. In a split second, Blanche took in his scraggly hair and red hooded sweater. There was no doubt this was Ward Thompson, intruder, car thief, and possible killer.

"What the hell are you doing here?" Blanche demanded.

The intruder looked at Blanche, a smirk on his face. "Good reading," he said, holding up a single typed page.

Blanche pointed her gun directly at him. "I'm giving you ten seconds. Ten seconds to get your ass out of here."

He made no attempt to move. Instead he began to read. *"I recall trying to get Da to put the gun away...Da pulled the trigger. I didn't see Jimmy fall, but the next thing I remember was that he lay stretched out on the floor...Da flopped down on the daybed, still holding the gun...Da looked at me, his eyes glassy and unfocused. He put the gun to his own head."*

Blanche felt anger rise in her.

"That's not how I remembers it," the intruder said.

Blanche was too stunned to speak. "Who are you?" she asked, taking in the long hair and dirty clothes. She moved toward him. He had long dark eyelashes. And his eyes were most unusual. One of the irises was bigger than the other and darker in colour.

Blanche stared at him in disbelief. "Eddie?"

CHAPTER 35

"Careful you don't break me ribs," Ward said after Blanche had hugged him for the third time. She was laughing and crying.

"Am I dreaming?" Blanche asked. "Is any of this real?" She took his face in her hands. "My little brother has returned all grown up. I never thought I'd see you again. I can't wait to tell Gabe and Ivy."

"Never thought I'd see you either," Ward said.

Blanche took his hand. "Come sit at the table. You're probably hungry."

Ward took a seat while Blanche put the kettle on. She got out tea biscuits, cheese, and cookies and arranged it on plates.

"Why didn't you tell me who you were from the beginning?" Blanche asked after she'd had a chance to sit down.

"I wasn't sure you'd want to see me." Ward shrugged. "I didn't know what to expect."

Blanche felt tears prick her eyes. "Oh, Ed—Ward. Not a day went by that I didn't think of you. The day I learned you were going to be adopted was the saddest of my life."

Ward reached for a cookie. "When they told me I was going to get a new mom and dad, I asked if you'd know where to find me. Someone...a social worker, I guess, told me I had a new family. She said it would be best to forget you."

Blanche looked at him tenderly. "But you didn't forget."

"No, I didn't."

"How did you find me?"

"My mother helped…after I started bugging her to."

The kettle began to whistle, and Blanche got up from the table to take it off the burner. She poured water into the teapot and brought it to the table.

"It's amazing what you remember," Blanche said. "You were barely four years old when…"

"That night is burned in my mind," Ward said. "For years I had nightmares."

Blanche squeezed his shoulder before sitting down.

"I was scared to death of Old AC."

Old AC. Blanche smiled sadly. "You remember his nickname."

"I thought it was his real name," Ward said. "It took me years to figure out he was my father. To me, he was just some mean, angry drunk who came to visit." He reached for another cookie. "I was scared he was going to send me away like he did with Gabe and Ma and Kate." Ward looked up at her. "And it happened."

Blanche touched his hand. "I can only imagine how confusing everything must have seemed to you then."

"I was that scared, I used to hide under the bed," Ward admitted.

Blanche poured herself a cup of tea and stirred in milk. Memories of that night were hazy. Da had kicked a chair across the room. He pulled the tablecloth from the table, causing dishes to clatter to the floor. He yelled at Jimmy, calling him every name he could think of. Blanche turned to Eddie now. "I'm sorry for all you had to endure," she said. "I'm just glad we finally found each other again."

"The scariest part was wondering if you'd accept me."

"Oh, Ward. Having you here means the world to me. I know Gabe and Ivy will be just as happy. We love you…Ward. We never stopped loving you. Sure, Ivy spoke about you just a couple of weeks ago while I was visiting her."

"I'm looking forward to seeing them again."

"What else do you remember about that night?" Blanche asked.

Ward's face went pale.

"You don't have to tell me if you don't want to."

Ward looked down at his plate, and then at Blanche. "It was you who shot Old AC, wasn't it?" he said. "You killed him."

There was a brief silence.

Whenever she thought of her secret getting out, Blanche imagined it would have the explosiveness of a bomb. But her brother was so matter-of-fact he could have been talking about the weather.

"Yes," she admitted. "I killed him."

Ward nodded, ever so slightly.

"I was scared he'd kill me," Blanche said. "I should've told the truth from the beginning. Martin didn't want me to go through the trauma of a trial."

"I didn't realize Old AC was dead," Ward said. "When I saw him lying on the floor, blood coming out of his mouth, I thought he was only hurt."

Blanche winced.

"I never told nobody what I saw," Ward said. "And I don't plan to."

"Still, this might be a good time for me to come clean," Blanche said.

Ward shrugged. "That cop, Bursey, thinks I stabbed Olive Beals."

"Well, surely, you can understand how it looks." Blanche ran a finger around the edge of her mug. "You were seen coming out of her house yesterday evening."

"But I didn't hurt her, I swear."

"You came here in a stolen car," Blanche pointed out. "You ran off when Martin confronted you."

"It looks bad," Ward admitted. "I got scared."

"Why did you go to Olive's house last evening?"

"I found out that she was involved with our family. I just wanted to talk with her, is all."

"And did you?"

"She was just getting up when I arrived. She asked me to come to her office on Monday."

"And what about that car you stole?"

"It belongs to Rick," Ward said, "my stepfather. He'll get it back."

"Are your parents divorced?"

"Dad died when I was ten," Ward said. "Then Mom married Rick."

Blanche peered at her younger brother. "Did you have a happy childhood, Ward?"

He shrugged. "I s'pose. It was great when Dad was alive. I wasn't too thrilled when Mom married Rick."

"What does Rick do?"

"He works for Parks Canada. We're living in Glovertown now, but the year he and Mom got married, they dragged me off to River of Ponds."

Blanche looked at her watch. "Ward," she said. "I have to go out. Will you be okay here by yourself?"

Ward grinned. "I was staying here alone up until Friday afternoon."

Blanche gave him a playful swat. "While I'm gone, why don't you call your mother? She's probably worried sick, not knowing where you are. And maybe you can persuade her to convince your stepfather not to press charges."

⤜⤐⤑⤛

"It's so nice to finally meet you," Linda said, ushering Blanche inside the cottage. "Dad talks about you so much, I feel like I know you."

"He talks about you too," Blanche said. "You and the boys." She looked around the cozy room with its comfortable furniture and large brick fireplace. "Nice place you've got here."

"The family all helped build it." Linda led Blanche into a combined kitchen and dining room with rows of tall windows overlooking a pond. Outside the window she could hear birds chirping in the trees. Squirrels ran along the wide branches.

"Looks like someone was baking," Blanche commented, taking in the measuring spoons, flour, oil, and other ingredients spread out on the counter. Two little boys were sitting at the kitchen table licking batter from spoons.

"We made muffins," the oldest child said.

"Have a seat," Linda said, pulling out a chair.

Blanche sat down.

Linda smiled. "These are my boys, Timmy and Myron."

The children eyed her with interest. "This is Blanche," Linda said. "She's a Mountie like Grandpa."

"But she's a girl," said Timmy.

Both boys had blond hair and emerald eyes like their mother. Blanche smiled at them. "Now, how old are you two?"

"I'm six," said Timmy. "I'm the oldest."

Myron regarded Blanche warily, his eyes wide.

"He's shy," Timmy said, "and he's only four."

Linda threw Blanche an amused look.

The little boys were beautiful, but it was Linda who captured Blanche's attention.

She was as lovely as she was gracious. Her blond hair was cut in a shag style that reminded Blanche of the mother on *The Brady Bunch*. She had the same perky personality. "Linda," she said, "that's a lovely haircut."

Linda raked her fingers through her short mane. "I had it cut before I left St. John's." She nodded toward the boys. "It's easier to take care of now that I have these two."

"It's very fashionable," Blanche said.

"Thank you, Blanche." Linda picked up a carton of milk and took it to the fridge. "Dad called just before you arrived. Should be here any minute now." She closed the fridge door and turned to look at Blanche. "He told me what happened to Olive—" Linda broke off, looking sheepish. "Maybe he shouldn't have."

"It's okay," Blanche said. "It won't remain a secret much longer." She met Linda's gaze. "How well do you know Olive?"

Linda spooned the last of the batter into a muffin tin. "I met Olive on a couple of occasions. The first time was when Mom was admitted to the nursing home."

"We gonna go see Grandma today?" Timmy cut in.

"Later this afternoon, darling." Linda opened the oven door and put the muffins inside.

"After the muffins gets cooked."

"Yes, sometime after that."

"I hope Grandma remembers who I am," Timmy said. He looked at Blanche and then back at his mother. "Last time we visited, she thought I was Uncle Marty."

Linda rubbed her son's back, her eyes sad. "Sometimes Grandma gets confused, sweetheart."

"I saw your mom while I was at the nursing home this morning," Blanche said.

Linda sighed. "Dad says they have her sedated; I hate seeing her like that."

Blanche realized how difficult it must be for Linda to see her beautiful, articulate mother reduced to a shell. Emily had always taken pride in her appearance. She dressed in the latest fashions, and her hair was always styled.

"I haven't been to see her since Friday morning. I had hoped to go yesterday, but with the storm and Dad gone…" Linda shrugged. "Mom was very upset. We found out this morning that she ran out of the nursing home on Friday evening."

"Yes, Aunt Hattie told me."

"She was gone a good twenty minutes." Linda's beautiful eyes were troubled. "I don't know why they didn't call us. Anything could have happened to her during that time."

"Your dad said she was dredging up memories of her father's death."

"It was like she was obsessed with it," Linda said. "They said she was running around the nursing home shouting, 'Father fell.' We thought Mom had gotten over Grampy Crocker's death years ago." She shrugged. "God only knows what goes on in her mind now."

Blanche stared at Linda, her thoughts working overtime. "Oh," she said after a moment.

"What is it?" Linda asked.

Blanche didn't answer, but a realization had begun to stir. Like pieces slotting into a jigsaw puzzle, everything was falling into place—making an alarming kind of sense. *Dear God, could it be possible?* She knew now who had killed the archbishop. Martin knew too, she realized, and he'd been prepared to let the killer go free.

Linda took a cloth, wiped down the counter, and began putting things away. "I heard the ferry won't be arriving until tomorrow," she said. "You're probably eager to be going home."

"Huh?"

Linda laughed. "Blanche, you're miles away."

At that moment, a vehicle drove past the window.

"There's Dad now," Linda said.

"Grandpa," Myron said, climbing down from his chair.

Both boys ran to the window. As soon as Martin appeared in the doorway, they ran to him. Myron wrapped his arms around Martin's leg. Timmy pulled on his arms, and they clung to him like monkeys.

Moments went by before Martin noticed Blanche. He raised an eyebrow in surprise.

"You asked me to drop by," she said, "and here I am. I was just having a chat with your delightful daughter."

Martin smiled, but his eyes told her he knew there was another reason for her visit.

"We made muffins," Timmy said.

"I just put them in the oven," said Linda.

"Carrot?" Martin asked.

Linda nodded. "With nuts and raisins just the way you like them." She turned to Blanche. "I hope you can stay and have some."

"Thanks, Linda, but right now I was hoping to have a word with your dad, alone."

"Let's go to my study," Martin said.

Blanche followed Martin into the living room and down a short hallway. The door to his study was open, and he motioned Blanche inside. The room had a desk with an electric typewriter on it. There were two shelves filled with books. Martin gestured to an office chair. "Have a seat."

A black cat was asleep in the only other chair, and he shooed it away before sitting down.

"The young punk in the stolen car is nowhere to be found," he said.

Blanche took a deep breath. "That young punk is my brother."

Martin stared at her. "Your brother?"

Blanche nodded. "Eddie."

Martin continued to stare at her, a look of disbelief on his face. "How…"

"He was adopted," Blanche explained. "He came to Darby's Island to learn about his family. That's why he went to see Olive."

Martin ran a hand through his hair. "Edward Joseph Thompson. On his driver's licence. Of course, it meant nothing to me then. Where is he?"

"He's at the cottage." Blanche folded her hands. "I'm sure he had no part in Olive's or the archbishop's murder. The car he stole belongs to his stepfather. Martin, I don't want to make excuses for him, but he came here to search for his family."

"Christ," Martin said.

"That's not all," Blanche said. "He remembers everything about…about that night."

"Jesus. How old was he?"

"He was just four at the time." Blanche sighed. "Maybe it's time the truth came out. However, I don't want to get into that right now. I came here about another matter."

Martin looked up at her.

"I know who killed the archbishop."

CHAPTER 36

NELLIE'S HEART WAS RACING AS SHE SAT WITH HERB IN THE WAITING room at the clinic. They'd been waiting for over an hour now with no news about Olive's condition. Nellie could see the worry etched on Herb's face. Martin had come by briefly to talk with them. It wasn't a robbery, he told them; nothing was taken from the house. He'd asked if they knew of anyone who'd want to harm Olive.

"Poor Olive," Herb said, his voice breaking.

"We have to believe she's going to be okay," Nellie said.

"I know," he agreed, "but I can't stop worrying."

"Herb," Nellie said, "I hates to bring this up at a time like this, but there's something I needs to know."

"What is it, Nellie?"

She leaned back in her chair. "Why did you lie to the police?"

Herb stared at her for a long moment. "Lie?"

"You told Martin and Blanche your knife went missing on Friday morning." Nellie's eyes locked with Herb's. "Now, we both knows that's not true."

Herb shifted uncomfortably in his chair.

"Why would you lie?"

Herb looked down at the floor as if he could find the answer there. A few moments passed before he spoke. "I thought I was protecting Olive," he said. "She took the knife on Friday afternoon, said she needed it to fillet a salmon."

"You think Olive killed Bishop Malloy?"

"It did cross my mind," Herb admitted. "But Olive returned the knife hours later."

"How do you know that?"

"I found out this morning that Sid Batten borrowed the knife. He came by the store just as Olive was leaving." Herb shook his head. "Everybody knows what a scatterbrain Sid is. He probably dropped the knife on the beach. Anyhow, Martin thinks whoever stabbed Olive was the same person who stabbed the bishop."

"But why would you even *think* Olive might've killed Bishop Malloy?"

"I don't know, maid." Herb leaned back in his chair. "Olive's always getting herself into one scrape or another. She's been stealing from the nursing home. That's why Blanche is here—to investigate. Olive's in big trouble if she pulls out of this."

"Why would Olive steal money when she's got a good job?"

"She started gambling again," Herb said. "Owes thousands of dollars."

Nellie shook her head. "Heavenly Father! And here I was nearly out of me mind with worry. I thought perhaps you had something to do with it."

Herb gaped at her. "Me? What made you think I'd kill the archbishop?"

"What was I s'pose to think when you lied to the police?"

"For heaven's sake, woman! I had no reason to kill Bishop Malloy."

"Blanche and Martin wants to question Patsy again."

"What for?"

"She was out near Devil's Rock the evening of the murder. Blanche thinks she might've seen something." Nellie sighed. "Maybe they thinks Patsy had something to do with the murder."

Herb stared at Nellie in disbelief. "Our Patsy?"

Nellie shrugged. "All I knows is that Patsy's been acting odd since this whole mess started."

Before Herb could respond, the nurse came into the waiting room. "Mr. and Mrs. Eastman?"

Herb and Nellie stood up. "How's Olive?" Herb asked anxiously.

"There's been no change in her condition," the nurse said.

"Can we see her?" Herb asked.

The nurse looked at Nellie then turned to Herb. "I'm sorry, but she can have only one person at a time in the room with her."

"You go, Herb," Nellie said. "I'll go to the cafeteria and wait."

⌦⌫

PATSY ORDERED A CUP OF COCOA AND TOOK IT TO A TABLE BY THE window. For a long time, she stared out at the rain, Blanche's words ringing in her ears. "It's a crime to give false information to a law officer." *Why didn't I just tell the truth?* Patsy asked herself as she shifted her weight on the hard cafeteria chair. She was getting in deeper and deeper. It would only be a matter of time now before it all came out. She couldn't let Uncle Jake get blamed for Bishop Malloy's murder. What she had told Blanche about Uncle Jake walking by in a daze and picking up the knife was true at least. What she couldn't tell her was who had killed the bishop. Patsy shuddered. Blanche said Martin had found the stone from her ring on the archbishop's body. After the killer left, she had come out of her hiding place. She had felt the bishop's neck like they taught her in her first aid class. The stone must have fallen out then.

After leaving the house on Friday evening, Patsy had walked around the island, wondering how she was going to explain to Nan why she had left the bishop in the house alone. She had stopped at Ryan's, bought a Popsicle, and used her last dime to call Nan at the hall.

The woman who answered the phone told her that everyone had left the building. Rodney Batten came into the store then. He told her that Uncle Jake had run out of the hall after being hypnotized. Patsy went down to the beach to look for him. She was walking along the shore when she saw the archbishop by the water's edge, his purple robes fluttering in the breeze. Not wanting to be seen, she had hidden behind a piling under Frank Murphy's wharf. She couldn't remember how long she stayed there before the killer—

"Patsy?" A voice snapped her out of her thoughts. She looked up to see her grandmother standing by the table.

"Nan? What are you doing here?"

Nellie slid into the chair across from Patsy. "Somebody tried to kill your aunt Olive. Blanche and Martin found her this morning."

Patsy's mouth dropped open. "Is she okay?"

"They're taking her into St. John's by helicopter. Your grandfather's with her now. All we knows is that she's in critical condition."

"Blanche never mentioned nothing about it."

"I s'pose they wanted to notify her sons first."

"Do they know who tried to kill her?" Patsy asked.

"Blanche and Martin thinks it was the same person who killed the archbishop."

Patsy's head jerked up. "No, it can't be."

"Patsy, you've gone as white as a sheet." Nellie touched her arm. "Don't worry, Olive's gonna be okay. They're doing all they can, sure."

"I don't understand," Patsy said. "First the bishop and now Aunt Olive."

Nellie leaned across the table. "Patsy, if you knows anything, you better tell Blanche or Martin. This has gone on long enough."

Patsy looked down at her hands.

"Your grandfather already lied to the police."

"Why would Grandpa lie?"

"He thought Olive was involved. He wanted to protect her." Nellie shook her head. "Anyway, that's not important. But Patsy," she pleaded, her voice urgent, "if you knows anything, don't keep it to yourself."

Tears filled Patsy's eyes. She took a deep breath and let it out. Nan was right, but how could this turn out right? How could she turn in the killer?

"It'll all come to light in the end," Nellie said. "Mark my words."

Patsy's voice dropped to a whisper. "I was on the beach last evening and—"

At that moment, a man and woman approached them. "Can we borrow one of these chairs?" the man asked, indicating the two empty chairs at their table.

"Go ahead, my son," Nellie said. "Sure, we won't need them."

"Thank you," the man said. "I didn't think it would get this crowded."

The woman smiled and nodded at Nellie and Patsy.

Patsy gaped at them as they walked to a nearby table. "Nan," she asked, "who are those people?"

"That's the great Prospero and his partner, Miranda," she said. "Now, what is it you wants to tell me?"

CHAPTER 37

❧

MARTIN STARED AT THE FAR WALL, A BLANK EXPRESSION ON HIS FACE.

"I know who killed the archbishop," Blanche repeated.

Martin raised an eyebrow, but said nothing.

"I think you know too," Blanche continued.

He looked at her sharply.

"Martin, please. Let's be honest here."

He let out his breath slowly.

"I recalled something Nellie said about the archbishop while we were at her house earlier," Blanche said. "It has new meaning now."

Martin remained silent.

"When the bishop was a young priest, they called him Father Phil," Blanche pressed on.

Martin shrugged. "So?"

"What Emily was shouting yesterday wasn't Father *fell* like everyone assumed, but Father *Phil*. Apparently, she was upset by the archbishop's visit."

Martin leaned back in his chair looking defeated. "I always said you were observant, Blanche. You have what it takes to make a great detective. But tell me then," he challenged, "*who* killed Bishop Malloy?"

"I didn't figure that out until today," Blanche said. "Not until I met Linda." She looked at Martin. "When did *you* figure it out? Was it while we were at Miranda and Prospero's trailer this afternoon?"

"What are you talking about?"

"Linda and Miranda could pass for identical twins." Blanche's eyes locked with Martin's. "Miranda is Emily's daughter, isn't she?"

Martin exhaled heavily. "Yes," he admitted.

"No wonder Joey mistook Miranda for Linda this morning. And most likely it was Miranda who Skid saw on the beach." Blanche shook her head. "No doubt, Patsy thinks she's protecting Linda. Even Aunt Hattie got them mixed up." Blanche recalled her aunt referring to Linda's long blond hair. Blanche knew now what had been nagging her about Emily—it was her resemblance to Miranda.

"I had no idea," Martin said.

Blanche nodded. "I saw the way you were looking at Miranda when we visited her and Prospero this morning. It must have been quite a shock."

"It was like seeing Emily as a young girl." Martin's eyes brimmed with tears. "I wish I'd become involved with Emily sooner. I would have taken that little girl in, raised her as my own."

"But Martin, surely Emily must have told you about her."

"Emily told me she gave a baby up for adoption. All I knew was that the child was the result of an inappropriate relationship with someone in the church."

"Not Bishop Malloy?"

Martin rubbed his chin. "I only learned about that today. Emily never wanted to discuss the issue." He peered at Blanche. "You probably heard that Emily had a nervous breakdown."

"Yes. I heard it was because of her father's death."

"That's what everyone believed at the time," Martin said. "It was about the baby she gave away. There was a lot of shame around Emily's pregnancy. And, of course, Lucille didn't make it easier. She sent Emily to live with her sister and brother-in-law on Eagle Cliff. Do you know it? It's a tiny island, off the Avalon Peninsula. They were the lighthouse keepers. Only Aunt Amy knew about the pregnancy."

"Emily never discussed the matter with you?"

"When we were first married, I tried to get Emily to open up, but it was too upsetting. She never told me who the baby's father was."

For a brief moment, Martin seemed lost in the past. "Lucille was adamant that I not pursue it. She told me some things are best left alone."

Blanche shook her head. "Sweep it under the rug."

"Lucille would go to any length to protect the Church. I should've pressed for more details." Martin looked at Blanche as if pleading for her understanding. "Emily was so happy after we married and, well…I didn't want to dredge up unpleasant memories."

"You had no idea who the baby's father was?"

"I assumed it was Brother Nathaniel," Martin said. "You probably heard of him, accused of having affairs with young women, most of them underage."

Blanche nodded. For years it had been a much-talked-about case in Newfoundland. "Had Emily ever mentioned her baby during all the years you were together?"

"Only once," Martin said. "It was shortly after we brought Linda home. One morning I found Emily staring into her crib, crying. 'She looks exactly like Cassandra,'" she said.

"That's so sad."

"Emily told me her child had the option to contact her once she turned twenty-one." Martin shifted in his chair. "You know, Blanche, I had my suspicions about the archbishop when I visited Emily on Saturday. I figured something must have happened for her to get that upset. The only thing I could think of was Bishop Malloy's visit."

Blanche pursed her lips. "That man was reckless."

"There are still many unanswered questions," Martin said. "I assume it's no coincidence that Miranda was on the island the same time as the bishop."

Blanche leaned forward. "Martin," she said, "I'm sorry, but we have to do the right thing."

"Yes," Martin agreed. "It's time to bring Miranda in for questioning."

CHAPTER 38

❦

PROSPERO MADE NO ATTEMPT TO HIDE HIS ANNOYANCE WHEN Blanche and Martin showed up again at his trailer. "What now?" he asked.

"We need to talk with Miranda," Blanche said.

"Deb?" Prospero looked taken aback.

"May we come in?" Martin asked.

Prospero stared at them a long moment. "This is getting to be a nuisance," he said. However, he stepped aside and waved them in.

Miranda stood by the tiny window, her arms folded.

"Miss Brown," Blanche said, "can we have a word with you?"

Miranda eyed them suspiciously. "What do you want?"

"You are a suspect in the murder of Archbishop Malloy," Blanche said.

"And the attempted murder of Olive Beals," Martin added. "We have an eye witness who saw you at her house this morning."

Miranda's eyes widened in alarm.

"What?" Prospero laughed.

"Am I under arrest?" Miranda asked.

"At this point we simply want a statement," Blanche said. "You can come with us now, or you can wait for forensics. Once they get here, you won't have a say in the matter."

"Deb didn't even know those people," Prospero said, outraged.

Miranda took a step back. "Why would *I* murder the archbishop?"

"Probably because you learned he was your father," Martin said.

"What?" Prospero gave a short laugh. "Have you gone mad?"

"Bishop Malloy was Miranda's father," Martin stated. "My wife, Emily, is her mother."

"Is this some kind of joke?"

"Sadly, it's no joke." Martin turned to Miranda. "Miss Brown, will you come with us?"

"Call me Miranda," she said.

"Okay. *Miranda*. Will you come with us?"

"They're crazy," Prospero said. "Tell them, Deb. Tell them you had nothing to do with it."

"I should go with them," Miranda said, her voice subdued.

"You don't have to go anywhere," Prospero protested.

"Yes, I probably should."

Blanche realized Miranda was having difficulty looking Prospero in the eye.

Prospero stared at her in disbelief. "What the hell is going on?"

Miranda turned to Martin. "Is it okay if Dave...umm... Prospero comes with me?"

Martin shrugged. "Sure."

Prospero reached for his jacket. "Okay, let's get this charade over with."

In silence, they walked to the police cruiser. Prospero got in the back with Miranda; Blanche and Martin got in front. No one spoke as they drove down the narrow dirt road to the hall.

After everyone was seated around the small table, Blanche got out her pen and notebook. "Miss Brown...Miranda," she began. "Were you on the beach the evening of Friday, July 18, between nine and ten o'clock?"

"She was with me," Prospero said.

Martin frowned. "Mr. Stevens, if you wish to remain here with Miranda, you can't interrupt. Is that clear?"

"I'm only trying to protect her." Prospero touched Miranda's arm. "Maybe you shouldn't talk without an attorney present."

"It's okay," Miranda said. She turned her attention back to Blanche. "Yes, I was on the beach Friday evening from about nine-fifteen until just after ten."

"Did you stab the archbishop?" Blanche asked.

Miranda nodded, ever so slightly.

Prospero looked dumbstruck.

"I didn't come here to kill him," Miranda said. "That was not my intention."

"Why exactly *did* you come here?" Blanche asked.

"I've been trying to find my birth mother for some time now," Miranda said. "The social worker involved in the case is dead. Someone said Olive Beals might be able to help."

"Why wait until now?" Martin asked. "Emily gave you the option to contact her once you turned twenty-one, a condition your adoptive parents agreed to."

"My mother didn't give me the letter until she was on her deathbed," Miranda said with a trace of resentment. "Emily wrote that my father was a priest at Holy Redeemer Parish. She didn't say who he was. Olive Beals found out it was Archbishop Malloy."

Martin leaned toward her. "How would Olive know that?"

"It wouldn't be *too* difficult," Blanche said, "once she had the name of the parish. Or, maybe she found out from Aunt Amy. She would have been the midwife at the time."

"Who the hell is Olive—" Prospero began, but Martin raised a hand to silence him.

"Olive told me about Emily's illness," Miranda continued. "She said it wasn't a good time for me to come here. She said it would only upset the family."

Martin crossed his arms. "Who the hell gave her the right to make that call?"

"Why didn't you tell me any of this, Deb?" Prospero said, forgetting Martin's warning to be quiet. "When we discussed coming to Newfoundland, you never said a word about finding your mother."

"You don't like confrontation," Miranda said. "I was afraid you wouldn't go along with my plan."

Prospero flattened his lips. "You tricked me."

Blanche looked at Prospero. "I take it you knew nothing of this."

"No," he said, crossing his arms over his chest. "I feel like a fool. We were in Corner Brook when Deb showed me a brochure for Darby's Island that she had picked up at the tourist bureau. She knew I wouldn't be able to resist a place like this." He paused. "She manipulated me, and I played right into her hands."

"How did you get in touch with the bishop?" Blanche asked, turning her attention back to Miranda.

"I wrote Bishop Malloy," she explained. "I told him I thought he might be my father. When I didn't hear back from him, I called the glebe in Corner Brook. He wouldn't take my calls. I kept calling until finally I got through to him. He said I had no proof that I was his daughter. He asked me not to call again."

"How did you know he'd be on Darby's Island this weekend?" Martin asked.

"When we arrived in Corner Brook on Tuesday, I called the glebe, and asked the secretary if the bishop would be at Sunday's mass." Miranda folded her hands. "I thought of standing up in church and embarrassing him in front of the congregation."

Prospero stared hard at Miranda. "What else does my darling have up her sleeve?"

Miranda lowered her eyes.

"For God's sake, Deb," Prospero almost shouted. "What kind of trouble have you gotten yourself into?"

"The secretary told me the bishop was in St. John's," Miranda continued. "She also said he would be on Darby's Island this weekend for the blessing of the fleet. It worked out better than I had imagined—both parents in the same place."

"When did you go to see Emily?" Blanche asked.

"Shortly after we arrived, I told Prospero I needed to buy pantyhose. I went to the nursing home." She glanced at Martin. "I didn't intend to upset Emily; I was just curious."

Martin nodded without comment.

"I was nervous," Miranda admitted. "I didn't know what I was going to say to Emily. But I didn't have to say anything. As soon as I walked into the room, she got up from her chair and touched my cheek. She called me Cassandra."

"Cassandra?" Blanche repeated, incredulously.

"After her mind started to wander, Emily sometimes called Linda Cassandra," Martin said, his voice sad.

"I was in her room less than five minutes when I heard someone outside the door," Miranda said. "I ducked into the bathroom, thinking it might be a family member." She looked at Martin. "I didn't want to have to explain myself."

Martin nodded his understanding.

"The door was slightly ajar. I heard a male voice. I peeked through the crack in the door—and that's when I saw him."

"Who?" Prospero asked.

Blanche shot him a warning look.

"The archbishop," Miranda replied. "All decked out in purple. I'd seen him drive on the ferry when we crossed over. For the entire trip, he sat in his car reading."

Martin's face turned red. "That son of a bitch was in Emily's room?"

Blanche laid a quieting hand on his arm.

"When I found out I was adopted, I used to imagine my parents young and in love," Miranda said. "I imagined them forced apart like Romeo and Juliet." For a moment, she seemed to have lost sight of her small audience, and was wrapped up in her own memories. "When I saw them together Friday afternoon, I knew there'd never been any love between them. Emily looked scared. She actually backed away from him."

Blanche glanced at Martin, and saw his jaw clench.

"I was about to come out of the bathroom and confront the bishop," Miranda pressed on. "But a nurse came into the room. I heard Bishop Malloy say, 'It seems poor Emily is upset.'"

"What happened then?" Martin asked.

"'Emily sometimes misses her family,' I heard the nurse say. The bishop left shortly afterwards, and the nurse took Emily to the TV room."

Blanche scribbled in her notebook. "When did you see the archbishop again?"

"David went to bed just before nine-thirty, and I went for a walk on the beach." Miranda bit her lip. "I hadn't walked far when I saw him again. I could have spotted him a mile away in his ridiculous purple getup. I hurried to catch up to him. I didn't want to harm him, only talk with him. Just before I reached him, he bent down and picked up something off the beach. I saw it was a knife."

Prospero had a look of disbelief on his face.

"The bishop and I had words," Miranda said. "I threatened to let everyone know I was his daughter. 'The church will not pay you a cent,' he told me. He must have thought it was money I was after. All I wanted was the truth."

Martin and Blanche were looking at her curiously.

"What happened then?" Martin asked.

"I got angry," Miranda said. "There were more words, more accusations. I remember yelling, cursing at him."

Prospero dropped his head into his hands.

"I kicked the bishop in the knee, he dropped the knife, and I picked it up," Miranda went on. "I didn't mean to stab him, but…I …it just…happened."

Prospero's face was a mask of horror.

"What did you do with the knife?" Martin asked.

"I…I don't recall," Miranda said. "I had it in my hand. I must have dropped it when I left. I don't even remember walking back to the trailer."

"Did you also stab Olive Beals?" Martin asked.

Miranda closed her eyes momentarily. "I was at the cafeteria on Saturday morning when Olive came up to me. 'You must be Debra Brown,' she said. She must have noticed the family resemblance. A couple of people had already mistaken me for Linda." Miranda sighed. "Olive wasted no time telling me she suspected me of killing the archbishop. I denied it, of course. But she said the police were going to be very interested to know I was the archbishop's daughter." Miranda looked around the table, her eyes resting on Martin. "She told me she would keep my secret safe if I gave her twenty thousand dollars. I told her I didn't have that kind of money and I walked away."

"But you went back to her house this morning," Blanche said.

"To try to reason with her," Miranda said. "I thought we could work something out. Olive said if I wanted to stay out of jail,

I'd better cough up the money." Miranda covered her face with her hands. "We had a nasty argument."

"Tell me about it," Martin prompted.

Miranda rolled up the leg of her pants. There was a bandage on her leg, blood seeping through. "Olive grabbed a knife from the kitchen counter and stabbed me. It was like…like she went crazy. I tried to get away from her, but she blocked the doorway. I ran into a room off the kitchen, and she followed me. We fought for the knife. Finally, I was able to wrestle it from her hand, and…and I stabbed her." She looked pleadingly at Blanche. "I didn't mean for it to happen…I was afraid for my life."

Prospero's mouth hung open. "You told me you cut your leg in the accident. Jesus Christ, Deb," he exploded. "What have you gotten yourself into?"

CHAPTER 39

꧁

"IT'S GOOD TO BE FINALLY GOING HOME," BLANCHE TOLD MARTIN AS they stood at the ferry terminal watching passengers disembark.

"How's Eddie doing?"

Blanche glanced toward the station wagon where Eddie sat waiting. "He's eager to see the rest of the family. I invited him to visit us next weekend. Ivy and Gabe are really excited to meet him again."

"I imagine he's been in touch with his adopted family."

"His stepfather is not going to press charges," Blanche said.

"The past few days have been crazy," Martin said. "More than I could have imagined."

"I'm sorry about Miranda."

Martin shrugged. "It's out of my hands now."

Blanche nodded. The police had taken Miranda into custody. When she got off the ferry, she would be escorted to Corner Brook. Martin had recommended Paul Hamlyn, one of the best defence lawyers in the province. Hamlyn had already filed a motion for bail.

"Things don't look good for Miranda," Martin said. "Linda is very upset. She had hoped to meet her sister someday, but not like this."

"Miranda may be able to convince a jury that she was acting in self-defence when she stabbed Olive. The murder of Bishop Malloy is going to be a more difficult defence."

"I got a report on Olive a few hours ago," Martin said. "She's off the critical list."

"She's going to need a good lawyer too," Blanche said.

"Yes," Martin agreed, his expression grim. He looked away for a few moments. "Blanche, I've talked with Bill," he said after a while.

Blanche waited.

"I let him know how you cracked the case. I told him that you showed great leadership, that you handled the case like a pro."

"And?"

"He agreed. Well, reluctantly."

"I'm not sure that will make a difference as far as Bill is concerned."

"I'll remind him every day." Martin smiled. "I'll remind him when you're up for promotions. You deserve a lot of credit, Blanche, and I'm going to see that you get it."

"Thank you, Martin," Blanche said. "I appreciate having you in my corner."

"I also told Bill the truth about what happened. With your father."

"What did he say?"

"He thinks it would be better to let sleeping dogs lie."

Blanche considered this. She had been a minor at the time. It would be Martin they would come down hard on. And Martin had given so much to the force. If this came out, it could destroy his reputation. She also realized that there would be a hearing. Did she really want to face that? What purpose would it serve?

"The detectives at the scene have always known what happened," Martin said. "Or, at least, knew things were not as we described them."

"Blanche?"

At the sound of her name, Blanche looked around. She spotted Patsy waving at her from the edge of the wharf. Smiling, she waved back. "Poor kid's been through a lot," she said.

"She's been carrying a heavy burden the last couple of days," Martin agreed. "I hope having to testify won't be too traumatic for her."

"Jake has been cleared of all charges," Blanche said. "He still doesn't remember picking up the knife. But according to Patsy, that's what happened."

An announcement came over the loudspeaker: "All passengers are to return to their vehicles. The ferry will be loading in a few minutes."

There were only a handful of cars in the lot, but walk-on passengers began making their way toward the ferry.

"Well, I better go," Blanche said. She held out her hand to Martin. "Take care of yourself, and give my love to your family."

"I'll see you at the end of the summer when I return to work," Martin told her.

"I'm glad you decided to come back," Blanche said.

⁂

WARD AND BLANCHE STOOD ON DECK OF THE FERRY AS IT NEARED the Crow's Nest terminal. The rain had cleared, and the sun was struggling to break through the clouds. They could see a cluster of buildings in the distance. "We will be docking in a few minutes," a voice over a loudspeaker announced. "Passengers may now return to their cars."

Blanche and Ward stood by the railing for another moment. "We should be going," she told Ward. Just as she was about to turn away, she saw a blue Pontiac turn in to the ferry terminal. *Coop has a car like that,* she thought. She watched as the car pulled into the lot and the driver got out. "It *is* Coop," she said aloud.

"Huh?" Ward said, a confused expression on his face.

Blanche watched as Coop, holding Reba's hand, walked toward the ferry terminal. "Let's go," she told Ward. "My family has come to meet me."